# CRAVING LILY

### THE ACES' SONS

## BY NICOLE JACQUELYN

*Craving Lily*
Copyright © 2017 by Nicole Jacquelyn
Print Edition
All Rights Reserved

No part of this book may be reproduced or transmitted in any form or by any means, electronic or mechanical, including photocopying, recording, or by any information storage and retrieval system without the written permission of the author, except for the use of brief quotations in a book review.

This is a work of fiction. Names, characters, businesses, places, events, and incidents are either the products of the author's imagination or used in a fictitious manner. Any resemblance to actual persons, living or dead, or actual events is purely coincidental. The author acknowledges the trademarked status and trademark owners of various products referenced in this work of fiction, which have been used without permission. The publication/use of these trademarks is not authorized, associated with, or sponsored by the trademark owners.

## Dedication

*For the human I'm growing.*

*Without you, this book would have been finished two months earlier.*

*I love you already.*

# PROLOGUE

# LILY

I USED TO be blind. That's not a metaphorical statement. I was literally and legally blind for six years. There was no real explanation. The doctors called it conversion disorder. My parents called it hysterical blindness. All I know is that one day during a family party, I was shoved to the ground and covered by both of my grandmas, their perfume mixing with the scent of the grass beneath me as they shielded me from a spray of bullets. I'd squeezed my eyes shut as they whispered that everything was going to be okay even as their bodies jerked and went still.

When it was over and my dad pulled their dead bodies off me, I opened my eyes and I couldn't see him. I couldn't see anything.

Over time, my other senses sharpened to make up for the missing sight, and life went on. It was different, sure. For a long time, I'd been afraid to walk, or be left alone, or even eat. What if there was a bug in my food and I had no idea? What if I tripped and lost what little sense of direction I had? What if something happened when I was all alone and I wasn't able to react because I couldn't see the threat? I'd even refused to sleep if I couldn't hear my dad snoring down the hall. Eventually, though, it became my new normal. Kids are resilient, and I was no different.

My sight came back in increments so small that they were barely noticeable. The night my sister packed her bags and headed to Southern California, begging me to wait until morning to tell my parents she was gone, I remember wondering why she hadn't turned the light off after she tucked me into her bed and left. I knew the bedroom was bright, but I didn't really comprehend that until later, when my cousin Rose questioned why I began automatically turning on the light when I walked into a room.

For months, I only saw light and shadows, like I was trying to see through a white sheet, and then suddenly, as if it had never gone away, my sight was back. Just like that.

I thought about those sightless years as the man in front of me paced slowly back and forth, his hair standing straight up from the many times he'd run his fingers through it. He was well dressed. Russian. Younger than I'd first believed, but more powerful, too. His partner was less intimidating. Larger, but warmer. The two of them had been discussing something in Russian for the past twenty minutes, and I had no idea what they were saying.

I also had no idea how they'd gotten onto the property. Cam and Trix's property was gated, fenced, and within walking distance of the Aces Motorcycle Club's compound. Once upon a time, the house had belonged to my grandparents, and had been built to withstand an attack. My grandpa had been the president of the club, so he'd even built a panic room in the home office. Unfortunately, I hadn't had time to get there after the men pushed their way into the house. I had, however, been able to gesture to my nephews, who were out of view. God, I hoped they'd understood what I'd wanted them to do.

"Your name?" the younger one asked me for the tenth time.

I didn't answer. I had no idea what they were planning, but if they had any information on the club all the men in my family belonged to, my name would put a bulls-eye in the middle of my forehead, for sure.

"What's *your* name?" I replied, crossing my arms over my chest. I was getting cocky, and I knew it, but I couldn't seem to curb the impulse. After shoving me into a chair when they'd pushed their way into the house, neither man had touched me. I got the impression that they'd stop me if I tried to leave, but otherwise, they seemed unwilling to harm me. I just needed to keep their attention focused on me so they didn't go poking around the house.

The bigger guy glanced toward the front door and mumbled something ominously, causing the young one to become even more twitchy. They were waiting for something, but I couldn't figure out what it was.

"You know, you should probably get out of here," I said, watching the guy fidget. "If someone realizes you're here, you're dead."

"Shut up, bitch," the bigger one said in words so accented it took me a minute to translate. "Just shut up."

"I'm not kidding. You guys are fucked," I continued as I watched the young one pace. "Just leave and I don't even have to tell—"

The big one must have been pissed that I'd ignored his warning, because a meaty fist hit the side of my head and everything went black.

When I woke up sometime later, I thought for a moment that the blindness had come back. I couldn't see anything, not a single shape or light. It wasn't until my eyes started to sting that I realized I wasn't blind. Then I began to cough as the smoke surrounded me.

# Part 1

## Chapter 1

# LEO

"YOU WANNA GO to that party up at the culvert tonight?" Cecilia asked as I dropped down beside her on the couch. I was tired as fuck, but I'd promised her that I'd stop by, so I'd dragged my ass to her parents' house. It was weird as shit being there. I hated it.

It had only been a little over a year since the party where I'd been shot in the fucking face in their backyard, but I'd never let anyone know how uneasy it made me to step inside that house. I'd never hear the end of it.

"Nah, not tonight," I groaned, dropping my head back against the couch. "I'm wiped."

"Hi, Leo," a sweet voice called out, and I watched as Cecilia's little sister Lily came into the room, followed by their cousin Rose. She wasn't moving fast, but there also wasn't any hesitation in her steps as she came forward and knelt on the carpet in front of us.

"Can't you do that somewhere else, Lil?" Cecilia bitched as Lily set a book down on the coffee table.

"No," Lilly muttered. "Mom said to do it down here. It's not like I can see you, so do whatever you want."

"Uh, no. Don't," Rose grumbled. "*I* can still see you."

"Just ignore them," Lily replied easily. "I do."

"Aw, Dandelion," I teased, grinning at her smart mouth. "You know you can't ignore me."

"I do my best," she shot back, waving her hand in a shooing motion. She opened up her book and I leaned forward a little to catch a glimpse of a really simple children's story written in braille and text.

"Ready?" Rose asked, turning a little so she faced away from me and Cecilia.

"I guess." Lily's face grew serious as her finger touched the first page and slid along the edge until she found the little bumps. Her lips moved as she slowly ran the pad of her finger over the braille. "There," she sounded out slowly, "was…"

"Oh, shit. You haven't seen this yet," Cecilia whispered, grabbing a pen off the sidetable. "Watch."

Before I could stop her, she threw the pen straight at Lily.

Anger rose so quickly that before she'd even dropped her arm, I had her wrist gripped tightly in my fist.

My mouth fell open in surprise as Lily fucking dodged the pen, smacking it out of the air like she'd seen it coming.

"What the fuck, Cecilia?" she said, her face turning red.

"Watch your mouth," Cecilia snapped back, yanking her arm away from my hand. "You know you're not supposed to talk like that."

"Fuck you!" Lily seethed. She slammed her fists against the coffee table, making the entire thing rattle.

"You're such assholes," Rose hissed, glaring at us.

"I knew you'd catch it," Cecilia argued, glancing at me before looking at her sister again. "You always catch them."

"Not if I'm doing something else!" Lily screamed back, obviously embarrassed. "What the fuck is wrong with you? Why would you do that?" She climbed to her feet and almost tipped sideways as her foot slid on the pen.

My heart pounded and my stomach churned as tears filled Lily's eyes. Jesus Christ. I hadn't been in on Cecilia's little demonstration, and I still felt guilty as fuck.

"What the hell is going on in here?" Farrah asked as she came jogging into the room.

Lily lifted her chin and didn't say a word as her mom took a few steps forward.

"Well?" Farrah glanced around at our faces, finally stopping on Rose's. "What happened?"

When Rose refused to answer, Farrah looked at Lily. "You wanna tell me why I could hear you yelling obscenities all the way upstairs?"

"Snitches get stitches," Lily mumbled back, her face dark. Then she lifted her fist in Rose's direction and waited for her to tap it with her knuckles.

"Christ, you've been spending too much time at the club," Farrah scoffed. "You have, too." She pointed at Rose, then glanced down at where Lily was trying to hide the pen with her foot.

"Cecilia," Farrah said flatly, her eyes rising to us. "Tell me you didn't throw a fucking pen at your sister."

"She always catches it!" Ceecee replied, shrugging her shoulders. "It's not like I thought it would hit her."

Farrah glanced at me and then back at Lily before she spoke again. "They've been spending too much time at the club," she waved at Rose and Lily. "But you've clearly not been spending enough. Learn some fucking loyalty, Cecilia. Your sister isn't a goddamn circus act."

Ceecee's chin trembled and she glanced at me before jumping to her feet and running out of the room.

"Seems like you'd know better," Farrah said derisively in my direction before Rose cut her off.

"He tried to stop her, Aunt Farrah," Rose said quietly. "Actually, you might want to let Uncle Casper know so he doesn't kill Leo tomorrow when he sees the bruise on Ceecee's wrist."

"I didn't know what she was doing," I said, directing my words to Lily, who was standing there awkwardly silent. "When I realized she was going to throw it, I just tried to grab her arm before she let it go."

"I'm sure Cecilia's fine," Farrah said with a wave of her hand. "Rose, it's time to take you home, kiddo. Go get your stuff."

"Can I stay the night at her house?" Lily asked quickly, giving her mom a cheesy grin.

"Nope," Farrah replied. "You guys have been together for two weeks straight. You can handle being apart for one night."

"Aw, man," Rose complained, sulking as she left the room.

"You riding with us, Lilypad?" Farrah asked as she picked up her purse and slid her feet into shoes.

"No."

"Stop pouting. Your face is going to stay like that."

"Fine with me, it's not like I can see it."

"Well, at least have a little compassion for your mother and don't make her look at it," Farrah said dryly. "Let's go, Rose!"

I watched it all play out, but I didn't move from the couch as Farrah ushered Rose outside and closed the door behind them. I wanted to leave, but I knew if I did, Cecilia would blow up my phone once she came downstairs and realized I was gone. I wasn't even sure why I put up with her shit anymore. I guessed it was just easier to let her play her games than to deal with the bullshit I'd land in if I dropped her ass.

"You can go upstairs, you know," Lily muttered as she reached down and picked up her book. "No one's here to stop you."

"I'm good," I replied.

She took two steps to the side and reached out toward the recliner in the corner of the room, running her hand down the arm until she was sure of her positioning. Then she dropped into it with a sigh.

"She loves me, you know," Lily said after a few minutes of quiet. "She was just showing off."

"It was an asshole move."

"It wasn't a big deal," she argued, shaking her head. "Shit like that happens all the time at school."

"People been giving you trouble?" I asked darkly, leaning forward in my seat. The idea of anyone messing with the little girl in front of me made me want to go kick middle school asses.

"Oh, knock it off," she chirped, throwing her hands in the air. "I can take care of myself, and anyone I can't handle, Rose takes care of."

"That's fucked. Nobody should be messing with you at all."

"It's fine. If I was a boy, you'd tell me to handle it myself. I don't need anyone's help."

"No, I wouldn't. If one of the boys had a problem, I'd take care of it."

"You mean, if one of the boys was *blind* and had a problem," she replied knowingly, shaking her head. "School is fine. I just meant that you shouldn't think Cecilia is some horrible person. She's not. She was just trying to show off."

"Known Ceecee since we were babies, Dandelion. I think I've got her measure by now." It was the truth. Also the truth? Most of the time, Cecilia acted like a spoiled brat. I wasn't about to say that to her baby sister, though. "Now, tell me what the kids at school've been doin'."

"God! Nothing," she replied. "Did kids at school fuck with you when you got your face messed up?"

"Damn, Dandelion." I grimaced. Most people didn't mention my face. They tiptoed around it or acted like they didn't notice, which was stupid as hell. Of course they could see the scar running along my cheek from my jaw to the corner of my eye. Not like I was trying to hide it. "Nah, no one messed with me. They know better."

"Is it bad?" she asked, turning her face in my direction. "Your scar?"

"Not great," I mumbled reaching up to run my finger along the skin I couldn't feel anymore.

"Can I feel it?"

"What?"

"Can I feel your scar? Nobody wants to describe it, even when I ask."

I stared at her wide eyes for almost a full minute. Lily was a sweet kid. Pretty in a way that you knew she'd be a knockout when she was grown, but still so innocent looking that it made your teeth ache. She had her mom's bone structure and her dad's dark hair and tan skin. The best of both parents, though I'd never tell Cecilia that, with her blonde hair and fair skin. Lily didn't have a mean bone in her body, and no way would she say something about my scar unless she'd been thinking on it for a while.

"Uh, sure," I finally answered, clearing my throat.

She hopped off the chair before I could move from the couch and carefully came around the coffee table, making sure not to bump into anything. As soon as I'd leaned forward in my seat, she was in front of me, her hands raised in front of her chest.

"Which side?" she asked, tilting her head. "Show me where it is."

My heart thumped hard and I took a deep breath as I grabbed one of her hands and brought it to my face. No one had touched the scar except me and the doctor who'd sewn me up. Even Cecilia was banned from putting her hands on my face. It felt too fucking weird when the numb skin was touched. That shit made me nauseous.

It was also ugly as fuck. I was still coming to terms with that, no joke. Before I'd been shot, I'd been swimming in pussy, even though I'd rarely partaken. After? Only the freaks with fetishes and daddy issues came calling.

And Cecilia. But I swear to Christ, the bitch always sat on the opposite side of my scar so she didn't have to look at it.

"It's…" Lily paused as she lifted her other hand and ran her fingers down both sides of my face. Then she ran just one down the jagged line of the still slightly raised skin. "It's barely anything!" she said in annoyance. "You act like you're the Hunchback of Notre Dame, and this is all there is?"

I opened my mouth, then snapped it shut in surprise as she lightly slapped my scarred cheek. "Don't be such a pussy, Leo."

I barked out a surprised laugh just as footsteps came thumping down the stairs.

"What are you guys doing?" Cecilia asked suspiciously.

"Say what?" I said ominously. She'd better not be implying what it sounded like.

"N-Nothing," Lily stammered, dropping her hands and sidestepping the coffee table. Her cheeks went beet red as she carefully scooted away.

Her awkwardly measured steps moved her into the kitchen and I looked at Cecilia in disgust when I found her laughing.

"*Someone's got a crush,*" she sang, pointing her thumb at where Lily had just gone. Her little sweetheart of a sister that could sure as shit still hear her, and was probably dying of embarrassment.

I ground my teeth together as I got to my feet.

"Sometimes, you're a fuckin' bitch, you know that?" I shook my head as I walked past her and out the front door.

I had no fucking clue why Cecilia treated her baby sister the way she did. I'd done plenty of shit to bother my older sister, Trix, when I was a kid, but I'd fucking cut my arm off before I hurt her on purpose. It made no sense to me that Cecilia couldn't stop herself from the little digs against Lily that she made constantly.

I was livid as I climbed on my motorcycle, but couldn't help but chuckle at the little shit's last words to me. Damn, I hoped she wasn't upset about Cecilia being an asshole.

Just to make sure she was fine, I jogged back up the porch stairs and stuck my head in the front door.

"Girls aren't supposed to have such dirty mouths, Dandelion!" I yelled through the opening.

I didn't have to wait long for her reply.

"Bullshit! Have you met my mother?"

I grinned as I closed the door again and headed to my bike. Lily would be fine. The kid had a thick skin.

# Chapter 2
# LILY

*Four years later*

"What about Molly and Will's?" Rose asked, rushing around the room and stuffing things into a backpack.

"Nah." I shook my head. "Charlie's over playing with Reb. They'd be all up in our shit. Plus, Will's probably home. I thought the whole idea was to have our dates pick us up somewhere that they *wouldn't* get the crap scared out of them."

"Good point. I'd like to actually date during high school, and you know Jayden would spread it around if one of the guys threatened him. Pussy."

"Why'd you even say yes to him?" I asked, flopping backward on her bed.

"No one else asked," she answered pragmatically. "I wasn't about to go to prom without a date."

"Yeah," I mumbled. "Same."

"You were dreaming of going with Leo, huh? You kind of hit the jackpot with Brent, though," she replied, dropping down next to me on the bed.

"Yeah? He seems nice. Good hands." I ignored her comment about Leo. That was a conversation that I didn't want to have again.

"Jesus." Rose laughed. "Brent looks like a model. I'll take a picture for you. That way, if your sight doesn't come back until after he's old and fat, you can see what he looks like now. Total jackpot."

"A model?" I tried to picture what that could mean, but drew a blank. The men I knew were rough around the edges. I really only remembered clearly how the men in my family looked. They were more mugshot than model material.

"Yeah, he's *pretty*," Rose replied, dragging out the last word.

I turned that over in my head for a minute, then grinned. "Then it's probably a good thing our dads aren't going to see him. Can you imagine the shit they'd stir up?"

"Why do you think I pushed to get picked up somewhere other than our houses?" she joked. "It sure as shit wasn't for my date. Jayden might be a pussy, but he's still built like a tank and has the face of a bulldog."

My giggle turned into a full-on belly laugh. "We're fuckin' pathetic," I wheezed out.

"Truth. Now where the hell are we going to get ready?"

"Trix and Cam's?"

"*Beep*! Wrong."

"Poet and Amy's?"

"You're kidding, right?"

"What about Tommy's place? Isn't he out with Leo tonight?" I asked, rolling to my side. "Hawk would be cool about it."

"Keeping tabs on Leo, huh?"

"My *sister* was talking about it on the phone earlier." I pushed myself to my feet and reached down to center myself in the room. I was right between the left side of Rose's dresser and the wall, which meant I was two medium sized steps from the end of the bed.

"You're such an eavesdropper," Rose replied as she climbed off the bed.

"Kind of hard to ignore her when she's in the same room," I shot back.

"Fair enough," she agreed. "I'll call Hawk and see what's up."

★ ★ ★

AN HOUR LATER, we were hauling our dresses and backpacks full of beauty supplies into Tommy and Hawk's house. I had to be careful. They'd been remodeling the place for a few years, and since things were never in the same place twice and there were power tools lying around all the time, it had never been safe for me to hang out there. I got around pretty good without my sight, but Tommy's place was a fucking crucible for me.

"Oh, your dress is gorgeous, Lil," Hawk said as she took it out of my hand. "Not my style, but it's going to look hot as hell on you. I'll hang it up so it doesn't get wrinkled as shit, yeah?"

"Thanks, Hawk." I smiled in her general direction and tried to slow down my racing heart. I liked going to Tommy and Hawk's house. It always smelled good, and Hawk was awesome. But after the time that I'd stepped on a nail so hard that it had come through the top of my foot, I'd never been able to relax there. I'd thought Tommy was going to fucking cry when that happened. He'd tried so hard to make sure there was nothing left out that could hurt me.

"What about my dress?" Rose asked, taking my hand and setting it on her shoulder as she started walking. I followed her easily, trusting that she wouldn't run me into anything. I'd been following my cousin around for five years, letting her be my eyes when I needed them, and she'd never let me down. Not once.

"I've already seen yours," Hawk reminded her. "You guys can get ready in the downstairs guest room. We set it up for when one of the guys crashes here and they're too drunk to make it up the stairs. Works out well with the connected bathroom."

"Thanks," Rose said, slowing down. "Walking through a doorway, Lil."

I reached out and slid my hand against the doorframe as we walked inside the room.

"Want me to help with your makeup?" Hawk asked as she sat down on the bed, making it squeak.

My eyes widened in horror right before Rose's laughter-filled voice answered.

"Goth isn't really our style."

"Hey, now," Hawk replied. "I've mellowed!"

"Not enough," Rose said as she reached up and patted my hand. "No dresser in here, Lil. Straight ahead and to your left are walls. Bed is a queen, about three steps forward and one step to your right. Bathroom door is about a foot to the right of the door we just came in. No lamps and the bed doesn't have a headboard or footboard. Shit, this room is depressing."

"It houses drunk men. It doesn't need to be cheery," Hawk cut in.

"Oh, and the comforter on the bed is a lovely shade of puke green, in case you were wondering."

"I wasn't wondering," I said dryly. "But thanks for the info."

Moving gingerly into the room, I followed Rose's directions until I'd reached the foot of the bed and dropped my bag on top. I didn't have much in the way of beauty supplies, but I'd carried over a ton of Rose's stuff. She did my makeup whenever we had something going on that warranted it, but for the most part I just went without. My skin was pretty clear most of the time, and I'd never really been self-conscious about my looks. It probably had something to do with the fact that I hadn't even seen my reflection in years. I was slender and strong, and even though I didn't have big boobs or an ass like Rose—yes, when she'd grown hips she'd let me feel them, and anytime she thought her ass was getting bigger she'd ask me to check, because I always remembered her size—but I was happy with what I had. My parents weren't very big people, so I'd never really imagined myself as anything different.

"Should we get dressed first, or—"

"No," Rose answered me quickly. "We need to do makeup and hair first. That way if I drop something, I won't get anything on our dresses."

"I'm helping," Hawk said firmly, smacking the bed. "I was never into the prom thing, but you guys are fucking adorable and I want in."

"Not with makeup, though," I answered, my lips twitching. I hadn't seen Hawk's face in years, but I remembered the Mohawk and thick black eyeliner she'd worn back when she used to hang out with Rose's brother Mick. They were best friends until Micky died on the day I'd lost my sight. She'd shown back up a couple years later and started hooking up with Rose's other brother Tommy, and they'd been together ever since.

"I can do hair," Hawk replied. "What's the plan on that?"

"I just want mine in a loose French braid," I said quickly before Rose could go off on one of her rants.

"That's so boring. Why don't you put it up?" Rose argued.

"Because I *like* French braids. They're classic. Plus, I don't have to worry about it falling down and not being able to fix it."

"It's not like I'd let you walk around with fucked up hair," Rose grumbled.

"I don't want you to babysit me all night."

"Oh, what the fuck ever. If you think I'm leaving you with Brent, you're outta your mind."

"What's your date going to think of that?"

"I'm pretty sure when he asked me to go with him, he thought he was getting two for the price of one!" Rose yelled in frustration.

We both went silent for a long moment, then burst out laughing.

"Nuh-uh," I argued.

"Oh, yeah. He asked if you were coming with us. I think he was going to get you a corsage or some shit." Rose snorted.

"That would have went over well with your brothers," Hawk said.

"Probably a good thing I got my own date," I replied.

"And he's pretty," Rose added.

"Oh, yeah? How pretty?" Hawk asked.

"Like a model from one of those stores in the mall that smell like a broken cologne bottle."

"Eh, not my type," Hawk said. "I like them a bit more manly."

"Oh, whatever," Rose replied. "You got with *Tommy*. Not sure you're that picky."

We turned on some music that Hawk complained about and spent the next two hours gossiping as we got ready for the dance. My dress was actually two pieces. The skirt was black and sat high on my waist, just barely poofy, and went all the way to the floor to cover up the flats I was planning on wearing. High heels just weren't an option for me, unless I wanted to land flat on my face. The crop top was a white lacy thing, high necked with bare shoulders. I'd tried on a bunch of dresses, but it was hard not seeing the colors I was trying on. I was glad I'd chosen black and white. They were classic, and the pieces were so simple that I could easily picture them in my head.

Rose was just finishing my lips when someone started knocking on the front door.

"Oh, shit," Hawk said in surprise. "What time did you tell the guys to pick you up?"

"I told Jayden seven," Rose muttered. "Dammit."

"That's what I texted Brent, too. He never answered, though," I said.

"I'll go see which one it is. You guys ready?"

"As I'll ever be," Rose answered. "You're all done, Lil. Stay right there, I'm going to take a picture of us looking all hot."

"Cheese," I called out cheekily as I felt Rose press her face close to mine.

"You're such a pain in the ass," she complained, kissing my cheek. "But I love you anyway."

"Back atcha, cousin."

"Rose, Jayden's here!" Hawk called from the living room.

I followed Rose out of our beauty salon and smiled huge as I heard Jayden's intake of breath when he saw us.

"Holy shit. You look gorgeous, Rose," he said quietly.

"Thanks, dude," Rose replied, making Hawk snicker.

"You too, Lily," Jayden said.

"Thanks!" I nervously reached down to fiddle with the bangles on my wrist. I hated when I knew people were looking right at me. It was probably a pretty common occurrence, but most of the time I had no idea for sure. It was much harder knowing that someone was checking you out and you couldn't see the look on their face.

"Back to me," Rose said, becoming the center of attention again. "You got me a *corsage*?"

I tried hard to stifle the laugh I could feel building in my throat. She'd totally called that one.

"Yeah. I wasn't sure what shade of purple you were wearing, so my mom said to just get white roses," Jayden chattered nervously.

"I think he's going to pee himself," Hawk whispered so low that I knew she was talking to only me. "And he got her *roses?*"

"It's sweet."

"Yeah, if you like leading a guy around by the short and curlies. It'll never last. Rose'll walk all over him." She paused, then said even quieter, "Plus, he kind of looks like a bulldog."

I coughed to cover up my laugh. I wished I could see him.

"Where the heck is Brent?" Rose asked a few minutes later. "He's late."

"Only like fifteen minutes," I replied.

"More like twenty-five," Jayden said kindly. "I was ten minutes late."

"Oh." I laughed awkwardly, reaching for my phone. "Maybe I should call him?"

"I'll text him," Rose said, taking the phone out of my hand.

"Don't be an asshole. Maybe he got lost."

"Then he should have called," she said irritably.

Ten minutes later, Brent still hadn't shown up.

Twenty minutes later, I could feel a blush creeping up my neck. Thankfully, I didn't really think anyone could see it. Rose wasn't helping the situation, though. She was practically ranting as she paced the floor. I could hear her high heels clicking on the hardwood with every pass around the room.

"You guys should go," I said finally, cutting off her diatribe.

"Oh, shut the fuck up," she replied. "I'm not leaving without you."

She came to a stop in front of me and grabbed my hand, lifting it to her shoulder. "We go together."

"Rose," I replied softly, squeezing her shoulder. "This is embarrassing. Jayden's been waiting almost an hour. Just go."

"Nope."

"Please," I whispered, almost inaudibly. "Go. Don't make this worse."

"Not happening."

"Rose," I gritted through my teeth, loving her loyalty but cursing her stubbornness. "If you don't leave with your fucking date so I can go change out of this bullshit dress, I'm going to have you killed."

She was silent for a long time, but she must have seen something in my face because she finally mumbled, "I knew I should have told Jayden to bring two corsages. I'm going to punch Brent in the ballsack when I see him."

"Good. I'm not sure how tall he is, so I'd probably miss if I tried."

"You sure?" she asked, reaching up to put her hand on mine.

"I'm sure." I swallowed hard. "Go."

Ten minutes later, I was still standing in the exact same spot, my heart thumping hard in my chest, when Tommy and Leo came noisily through the front door.

"Man, you need to work on that fucking exhaust," Leo said. "It sounds like shit."

"Fuck yo—" Tommy's reply cut off. "Hey, Lil, I thought you guys would be gone already."

I laughed humorlessly and reached for the bangles on my wrist, sliding them around and around. "It's just me. Rose left already."

"Weren't you supposed to leave like an hour ago? Dude get lost?" Tommy joked.

"Tommy," Hawk snapped, coming out of the kitchen, where she'd gone to give me a little bit of privacy. "Shut up."

"What?" he asked in confusion? "What'd I say?"

"He never showed?" Leo asked gently.

"Maybe he fell in a sinkhole?" I replied around the lump forming in my throat.

"That motherfucker," Tommy growled. "What's his name?"

"On what planet do you fight my battles, Thomas Hawthorne?" I asked in irritation.

"This one," he snapped back.

"Wrong."

"Fine, I'll ask Rose."

"She won't tell you shit and you know it."

"She fuckin' better!"

"Knock it off, you two," Hawk butted in. "Tommy, leave her alone."

My cousin didn't say another word, but jabbed me in the side as he and Hawk passed me. His girlfriend must have been dragging him away. He wouldn't have let it go otherwise.

"You're beautiful," Leo said after they'd gone. "Let's see the whole thing."

Smiling, I lifted my arms out to the sides and did a slow twirl.

"You better be glad your dad didn't see you in this, Dandelion," Leo said with a whistle. "He never woulda let you outta the house."

"Which would have worked out fine, since my date never fucking showed," I replied, dropping my arms to my sides.

"His loss, sweetheart."

"Yeah, well, I better change. I need to call and see if my mom will come pick me up."

"You want me to give you a ride?" His footsteps clunked on the floor until his voice was much closer than it was before.

I opened my mouth to answer and then shut it again. When I was a kid, I loved riding on the back of my dad's bike. Saturday mornings, he'd wake me up before my brother and sister and we'd sneak out of the house to take a long ride before everyone got up. It was something just for us. After I'd gone blind, though, that had changed. Being on the bike was disorienting. The wind felt heavier and my balance felt off. It didn't matter how hard I held on to my dad's waist, it had never again felt like it had before. Like flying. Like freedom.

"I don't know," I said quietly, trying to work up my courage. Years ago, I'd ridden with my brother and uncle, but since I'd lost my sight, I'd only been able to ride with my dad. I just hadn't been able to make myself ride with anyone else.

But I really wanted to be on the back of Leo's bike. More than I should have, considering his on again, off again relationship with my older sister, even if they were mostly off lately.

"I'll take it easy," he said, laughing. "Go get your stuff and change outta that skirt."

"I—" I stuttered, then cleared my throat uncomfortably. "I don't know where the bedroom is."

"Oh, shit. Right." Leo's hand met my waist as he wrapped an arm around my back and turned us in the right direction. "Sometimes I completely fuckin' forget," he mumbled in my ear.

"How?"

"Don't know. Guess it's just not one of the things I notice about ya."

"Uh, how can you ignore the lack of eye contact?"

"Usually staring at your tits," he joked, grunting as I elbowed him in the stomach.

"I'm kiddin'. Mostly."

We shuffled into the bedroom and Leo awkwardly left after making sure that I knew where everything was. He even handed me the jeans I'd been wearing earlier, like I wouldn't have been able to find them folded neatly on top of my backpack. I wasn't sure how he'd known the difference between mine and Rose's, but he had.

I shook my head as I set my skirt on the end of the bed and shimmied into my jeans. Of all the things that could have happened, having my date stand me up was quite possibly the last thing I would have imagined. It wasn't like I'd asked him. He'd come to me. It was his fucking idea.

I hoped Rose was having a good time, but I was pretty sure she was spending the evening in a snit, telling everyone at school that she was going to nut-punch Brent. It wouldn't even occur to her to keep the fact that I'd been stood up to herself. She didn't get embarrassed by things like that, and wouldn't expect me to either.

I *was* embarrassed, though. I was so embarrassed, I was already dreading school on Monday. Everyone was going to know. Even if Rose hadn't said anything, people would know. Our school wasn't that big, and when the blind chick and the model planned on going to prom together and then never showed up, they would notice. It was the nature of high school.

After my coat and backpack were secure on my shoulders, I moved forward until I found the door, opening it slowly. I could hear voices in the living room, and was pretty sure I could find my way there without any mishaps, but I still paused in the open doorway.

Leo… well, he was everything. He was the guy who made sure that there wasn't anything that I would trip on in the forecourt of the clubhouse. The one who made sure that everyone started pushing their chairs in so I wouldn't run into them. The guy who sat through *Titanic* with me even though I couldn't actually see it, but fast-forwarded through all of the heavy breathing parts like *he* was embarrassed. I was pretty sure he was the first non-family member who'd ever called me beautiful. The only non-family member I'd ever vented my frustration to.

My first and only crush.

The minute I walked into a room, he'd stop fighting with my sister, but never hesitated to swear in front of me if he was pissed about anything else. He gave me crap about my dirty language, but always with a smile in his voice. He treated me like I meant something. Like I could do anything, and he fully expected me to.

I didn't know how any guy would ever measure up to him.

"You good?" Leo's voice startled me as he called down the short hallway. I'd been too busy daydreaming to even notice his footsteps.

"Yep, just getting my bearings," I answered, reaching out to run my hand along the wall as I moved forward. "Now that they're done with the downstairs, I'm going to have to come over here more often."

"Yeah, but Tommy's a fuckin' slob, so be careful even if you think you know where everything is," he warned me, laying his hand over mine on the wall as I reached him. "Come on, Dandelion, let's hit the road."

"You guys leavin'?" Tommy asked as we walked toward the front door.

"Yeah, gonna take her home," Leo replied.

"Better take her straight home," Tommy muttered, followed by an audible slap.

"Shut up, Thomas," Hawk scolded.

"Thanks for helping us get ready," I called to Hawk as Leo opened the front door. "Bye, shithead!"

"It was fun, you look gorgeous!" Hawk replied, just as Tommy yelled, "Get outta here, brat!"

Leo helped me down the porch stairs and stopped in the driveway. His helmet was placed on my head as I stood, my eyelids lowered.

"Gonna have to get a better helmet," Leo mumbled.

"I know you guys like these things," I replied as I slapped his hands from the straps so I could buckle it under my chin myself. "But this kind of helmet doesn't protect your melon for shit."

"Yeah, yeah."

"And the bugs. So many bugs hitting your face."

"It ain't that bad." Leo laughed.

"Bullshit. It's nasty. I've seen the shit caught in your beards."

"Not mine," he argued, helping me onto his bike. "I was too young for a beard back then."

"True." I got centered and waited for him to crawl on in front of me. "Poet's is the worst. So much beard. So many insects."

Leo laughed as he climbed on the bike, then reached back to pull me close and pull my arms around his waist. A few seconds later, the bike was rumbling under us, and for the first time in a long time, I felt an echo of the familiar rush of adrenaline.

I was too short to rest my chin on his shoulder as we pulled out of the driveway, so I tipped forward until my forehead rested against his back. He smelled like leather and cologne. His t-shirt was thin, and his chest and abs were tight under my hands. I could have sat that way forever, with the wind making my hair brush against my cheeks and his hand occasionally patting the tops of mine.

Unfortunately, our town wasn't very big, and only a few minutes later, he slowed down and turned into my driveway. We rolled to a stop, but neither of us moved as the night grew quiet around us.

"Looks like no one's home," he finally said, breaking the silence.

"It's cool. I've got my key." I pulled my arms from his waist and scooted back, waiting for him to climb off the bike so I could.

"I'm not leavin' you here alone," he said stubbornly.

"I'm sixteen," I reminded him. Wincing as I realized how young that must seem to him. "I'm home by myself all the time."

"Not—" he paused. "Not here. Can't leave ya here by yourself."

"You want to come in?" I asked, leaning forward a little.

"No," he replied instantly.

I laughed. "Well, I'm not sure what you want, then."

"Let's take a ride, yeah?"

The smile fell off my face and I leaned back. "Okay."

I waited while he fired up the bike and wrapped my arms around him as he backed up and turned around. Then we were off again, and soon we were racing down back roads. He must have forgotten that he'd said he'd go easy, because we glided fast around corners, the bike roaring loudly. I had no idea where we were going, no clue what direction we were headed, but I held on tight and kept my mouth shut anyway. Leo would never let anything happen to me.

Eventually, we slowed to a stop, near what I was pretty sure was a river.

"Where are we?" I asked as he turned the bike off.

"River," he answered, not really giving me anything as he got off the bike and helped me down.

"Yeah, I hear that. Why?" I took off the helmet and smoothed my hair down as best I could.

"I like this place," he replied, wrapping his arm around my waist to help me navigate over the bumpy ground. My footsteps were tentative as I shuffled forward toward the rushing water, stubbing my toes on roots just barely flowing out of the ground. "Here," he said, grabbing my hand and resting it on a rough tabletop. "Picnic table. Standard. Bench is about an inch below your knee."

I nodded and leaned over to find the bench, sidestepping a bit until I could sit down.

"You good? I gotta take a leak."

"Charming," I said drolly. "Yeah, I'm fine. Do your thing."

I was fine as he walked away, but the minute I couldn't hear him anymore I started to panic. I knew in my gut that he'd never leave me behind. That was unquestionable. But the idea of being in the middle of nowhere, near a large body of water, all alone, made my skin go instantly cold.

"Leo!" I yelled, embarrassed, but not enough to stay quiet. "Leo!"

"What?" he yelled, followed by crashing noises. "Dandelion?"

He was next to me in less than thirty seconds, his hands on my face and in my hair. "You alright? What happened?"

"I couldn't hear you," I said, shaking my head as my teeth began to chatter. "Stupid."

"Fuck, girl. You just took a year off my life."

"I'm sorry." My teeth chattered some more and my eyes started to water.

I hated feeling weak. I wasn't. I was strong. Independent. I stood up for myself and didn't take shit from anyone.

"Ah, sweetheart. Don't." He sat down next to me and put an arm around my shoulders, pulling me against his chest. "This wasn't my best idea, huh?"

"It was a good idea," I mumbled, gripping the t-shirt he wore under his leather cut. "I'm just an idiot."

"Pretty sure I'm the idiot," he said against the top of my head. "I just pissed all over myself when you yelled."

I choked out a laugh as he chuckled.

"I was actin' like a woman, wanted to make sure I went far enough away that you couldn't hear me pissin'. Shouldn't have gone so far."

"You realize I've heard you fart?" I replied, snorting.

"No you haven't!" He sounded outraged.

"Oh, yes I have!"

"Bullshit."

"My hearing is really good," I said with a shrug.

"Well, hell," he muttered, making me giggle.

He shifted on the bench and I leaned away, but his arm tightened around my shoulders until I was pressed up against his side.

"That douche is probably regrettin' not picking you up tonight," he said, leaning back against the table.

"I know, right?" I replied, nodding. "What a fucker."

"Better off knowin' what the guy's like now, before you spent all night alone with him."

"Alone and surrounded by the entire junior and senior classes?" I joked.

"There's a lot you can get up to surrounded by people who aren't payin' attention," he replied.

"True." I sighed. "I just wanted to do the whole prom thing with Rose."

"Still got next year, kid."

"Yeah, and next year I won't say yes to any dude that asks me. Hey, didn't you take Ceecee to prom?"

Leo stiffened slightly. "Yeah. Junior prom. We didn't stay long, though. Cut out early and went to a party."

"Sounds like Ceecee."

"Your sister's... wild. No other way to explain her. She wants what she wants the minute she wants it, and to hell with anyone in her way. Always been like that."

"Spoiled, you mean."

"Nah," he said, his knee started bouncing a little, just barely. "Your parents raised all you kids the same, yeah? You, Cam, Cecilia and now Charlie. Ceecee's the only one who's self-centered. It ain't cause she's spoiled."

"Are you guys still together? I can never tell." I hated that I'd brought my sister up. I hated that he was trying to be nice when we both knew she was a bitch to him. I hated that his arm was around my shoulders and that was the closest we'd ever be because she'd seen him first. They were closer in age. They had a history that I was too young to be a part of.

"You serious? Haven't been together in a long ass time, Dandelion," he replied, his head jerking back in surprise. "Years."

"Oh." I knew my face was screwed up in confusion, but his revelation was news to me. My sister talked about Leo all the damn time. As far as I knew, they still hung out regularly. I was pretty sure even my parents thought they were still a thing. "But don't you guys hang out all the time?"

"Sure, in groups," he said. "All us kids hang out. My sister and Cam, the Hawthorne boys and their women, Rocky and Mel, Ceecee."

"That wasn't the impression I had," I mumbled.

What the hell was Cecilia playing at? At least once a week, she was coming home late, saying she'd been out with Leo. It was always Leo—never the group. My parents were past the point of caring when she came in, as long as she let someone know she'd be late. No one in our family was comfortable hearing the front door open in the middle of the night.

I hadn't asked Ceecee about Leo in a long time. When I was younger, I'd craved news of him and what they were up to. Somewhere along the way, though, I'd realized that my older sister's comments had gotten more and more nasty until I finally didn't mention him at all. It was almost as if she'd been jealous, which made zero sense since I was so much younger than they were. We'd never hung out with the same crowd. Mick had been the only kid that could swing between the two groups of older and younger kids because he'd been right in the middle.

"She still givin' you shit all the time?" Leo asked, pulling his arm from around my shoulders as he reached for something in his pocket. A few seconds later, I heard the snick of his lighter and could smell that first scent of a lit cigarette.

"Not really," I replied, leaning back and crossing my feet at the ankles. "We get along pretty well, usually. I pretty much stay out of her way, though."

"Probably smart." He knocked his knee against mine.

"She's just…" I thought for a second about how to describe my sister. "Restless. It's like she doesn't know what she wants, and if she does know, she doesn't know how to get it."

"Ceecee in a nutshell," Leo joked.

"She loves me. I know she does. She'd walk through fire for me."

"True."

"But I don't think she likes me very much."

"She's jealous," Leo said seriously. "She's been burnin' bridges since she was fourteen years old. Goin' through friendships and boyfriends like steppin' stones across a creek. At this point, there ain't much for her here, and she knows it."

"What does that have to do with me?"

"Dandelion, can you think of one person who doesn't like you? One? I fuckin' doubt it. You got a personality that people flock to. They can't help themselves. Ceecee's got that same draw, but she can also cut someone down in a few words like it's nothing. People flock toward both of ya, but they *stay* with you."

"Yet, we never hang out," I said self-consciously.

"Yeah, cause you're sixteen and don't need to be hangin' out with men six years older." He scrubbed the top of my head, like a five year old. "Your pop would string me up by my nuts."

"No, he wouldn't."

"Oh, hell yes, he would." Leo laughed. "I'd do the same thing if I was him."

"He knows you."

"Exactly."

"You're a good guy," I protested.

"Bein' a good guy ain't got nothing to do with it, Dandelion. Bein' a good guy doesn't make it right for a man to be hangin' out with a teenage girl. Even if all they're doin' is hangin' out."

"Oh, whatever," I huffed. "That's stupid."

"Come talk to me when you've got kids runnin' around and tell me what you think about it then."

"Cam is way older than Trix," I pointed out.

"Trix was older when they got together." He paused to take a drag off his cigarette. "She was in college. That changes shit."

"I still think it's ridiculous."

"Course you do," he teased. "So anxious to grow up."

"Oh, shut the fuck up. You're not that much older than me."

"Fuck, the difference between me at sixteen and you at sixteen? Massive."

I was getting irritated, but I wasn't sure why. Was it because he was acting like I was a kid, or was it because I knew with a sinking feeling in my stomach that it was his super kind way of telling me that whatever crush I was still harboring would never amount to anything?

God, he was so sweet to me. He'd always been so sweet to me. Even when he was a dick to everyone else, he still went out of his way to be nice to me. It fucked with my head.

"I better get home," I finally mumbled, getting to my feet.

"What? You poutin'?" he asked as he stood up, too.

"I'm not pouting," I ground out, frustrated that I couldn't even walk away from him without falling on my face. "But you're right, my dad would flip if I stayed out late with you."

Leo huffed in irritation, but still gently led me back to his bike, handed me his helmet, and helped me sit. Always sweet, always helpful, even when I knew I was being a jerk.

He must have driven around for a bit on our way to the river, because the ride home took a lot less time. It still took long enough that by the time we rolled to a stop and the bike went silent, I felt like a complete ass. He'd been so cool, and he'd completely taken my mind off of being stood up, which I was sure was his intention.

"Looks like your parents are home now," he said as he got off the bike.

"I'm sorry," I said as soon as I had two feet on the ground again and started taking off my helmet. "I'm being an asshole."

"Nah, you're fine," he said carelessly. "Been a shit night for you. I get it."

"Yeah, and you made it a hundred times better. Thanks for the ride."

Just as I handed him the helmet, my dad called out from the front porch, making me cringe in embarrassment.

"The fuck? Givin' you a *ride*?"

"On his motorcycle!" I yelled back, my face on fire.

"Jesus," Leo mumbled quietly. "Point made, yeah?"

I snorted and laughed. "Yeah, I guess so."

"Chin up, Dandelion," Leo said, as I heard my dad's footsteps come close. "That kid ain't got no idea what he missed out on."

"Why aren't you at the dance?" my dad asked. "And why the fuck are you on this joker's bike?"

"My date never picked me up," I replied with a shrug as my dad's familiar scent wrapped around me.

"That little fucker."

"Gave her a ride home from Tommy's," Leo said. "Came back here, but no one was home and I didn't want to leave her here alone, so we went for a ride."

"She's sixteen," my dad replied flatly.

"I'm aware."

"Thanks, Leo," I said, cutting off the conversation that had suddenly become tense. "Come on, Dad, I want to go inside."

I heard Leo's bike fire up as we made our way onto the porch. Smiling a little, I braced myself. My mother was going to lose her shit the minute she knew what happened.

"Why are you home already?" Mom said as we walked into the kitchen. "Where's Rose?"

"Her goddamn date never showed and she spent all night with Leo," my dad growled.

"*What?*"

"It wasn't all night! And, yeah, my date never showed," I replied, sitting down in one of the stools at the counter. "He never even texted to say he wasn't coming."

"What a fucknut!"

"Truth. I had to force Rose to leave without me."

"I can't believe she actually went," my dad said. "Want a soda?"

"Sure." I waited until he'd set the can down in front of me, then kept talking. "I had to threaten to have her killed."

"Naturally," my mom said.

"It was so freaking embarrassing. Her date was just standing there for like an hour, waiting for Brent to show up."

"Eh, he probably didn't give two fucks," my dad said calmly. "Boy's waitin' on a girl that's all dressed up for him? He doesn't give a shit about anythin' else."

"Yeah, well, a few minutes after they left, Tommy and Leo showed up and Leo offered to give me a ride home."

"See? You should have gotten ready here," my mom said for the thousandth time. "I could have helped do something with your hair."

"I wanted my hair like this."

"Probably not exactly how it is now, it's sticking up all over the place. I assume you wore a helmet?"

"Of course."

"Of course," my dad scoffed, walking out of the room. "Fuckin' better have worn a helmet."

"Alright," my mom said quietly. "Now that he's gone, tell me the rest of it."

"Nothing much to tell," I replied, resting my chin on my hand. "We got all ready and Brent never showed. Jayden showed up on time, though. He brought Rose a corsage."

"I'm sure she loved that."

"Oh, yeah. He was practically tongue tied when he saw her. It was cute."

"Tongue tied? He won't last long if he can't keep up with Rosie."

"That's the exact same thing that Hawk said."

"Poor kid," my mom said with a chuckle. "So what's up with Leo?"

"Nothing."

"Don't lie to me, kid. I know every single one of your expressions, and you're currently wearing the Leo-did-something-sweet-for-me one."

She sat down beside me and shoved her toes under my thigh. I swear, my mom's feet were always cold, and she was always trying to warm them. I could remember her making me lay on them when I was six.

"He said he'd take me home, but no one was here when we got here, so we went for a ride to the river."

"The river, hmm?"

"Oh, whatever," I mumbled. "He pretty much told me that I'm awesome, but no way in hell are we ever going to hang out because he's too old and Dad would kill him."

"Hang out or *hang out*?"

"Friends, Mom. Jesus."

"Well! You have to put that shit in context."

"He was cool, just like he's always cool. That's all it was."

"It goes without saying, but you probably shouldn't say anything to your sister about it," my mom said with a sigh. "I wish things were different with her, but I'm not even sure what to do about it."

"Did you know that they haven't been together in a long time?" I asked. "Like, years, Mom."

"What? That can't be right."

"I don't think Leo would lie about it. He said they hang out in a group with all the kids, but they haven't been dating in a long ass time."

"That's weird. I wonder if your Dad knows."

Just as she spoke the last words, a loud crash came from the front of the house, and before I knew what was happening, I was on the floor and being shoved beneath our kitchen table.

"Don't fucking move, Lily," Mom hissed, before she left me.

My entire body shook as I pulled my knees against my chest and shut my eyes tightly. When they were closed, I could pretend that it was my choice that I had no idea what was happening around me.

I was curled into a ball for less than a minute when I heard my dad yelling from the entryway, his voice angrier than it had been in a very long time. "Are you fuckin' kiddin' me, Cecilia?"

I couldn't hear my sister's reply, but I climbed out from under the table anyway. Clearly, there wasn't an emergency, or my dad's tone would be completely different.

I'd heard his voice when shit hit the fan—tonight wasn't that.

"Your baby sister is sleeping, shut the fuck up," my mom ground out as I made my way into the entryway.

"Oh, whatever," Cecilia slurred, her volume not changing at all. By the sound of it, my sister was completely blitzed. She must have crashed into something as she came in the house, but I had no idea how much damage she'd done.

"How the fuck did you get home? Where you been?" my dad asked flatly.

"Out with Leo."

"Bullshit," my dad replied. "Leo was takin' care of your sister tonight."

"Charlie?" Ceecee asked in confusion. "When did Leo start babysitting?"

"No, *Lily*," my dad snapped.

"Of course," Ceecee said derisively. "Of course he was."

"My prom date stood me up," I said, joining the conversation. "Leo just gave me a ride home from Tommy's."

"Tommy couldn't drive you?"

"He didn't offer," I replied with a shrug. I wasn't sure what she wanted from me.

"I'm done, Cecilia," my mom said tiredly. "I'm so fuckin' done with this. Me and your dad don't ask for much, ya know? Clean up your own shit and don't be an asshole and you get to live here rent free."

"I'm twenty-one years old," Ceecee retorted.

"Exactly," Mom snapped.

"Ladybug, don't say anything you can't take back, baby," my dad warned softly.

"This is fucking ridiculous," my mom continued. "I'm cleaning up your shit all the time, you're comin' in late all the time, which is whatever, but half the time you're forgettin' your key and one of us has to let you in before you wake everyone up. And newsflash, Cecilia, you come into the house late, your dad and I are awake anyhow, because no way are we sleepin' through that shit. You do whatever the fuck you want and you don't give a shit who you inconvenience or that your dad is up at two in the fuckin' morning when you come in, and then getting' up four hours later to head to the garage!"

"Jesus, I'll remember my key next time! It isn't even that late!"

"Holy fuck," my mom muttered. "She's not hearing a word I say."

"Fine, you want me to leave?" Ceecee replied nastily. "I'll go."

She stomped away and I could hear her heavy steps all the way up the carpeted stairs.

"Where the fuck is she gonna go?" my mom asked my dad with a huff. "Your sister sure as shit isn't going to let her stay there."

"Leo's?" my dad asked.

"Not fuckin' likely," my mom replied with a laugh.

They weren't talking to me, so I moved silently toward the stairs and straight to my sister's room. Her door wasn't shut, probably because she wanted to make a big show of packing up her stuff. That was Cecilia. She'd leave, but she wouldn't do it quietly.

"Can I come in?" I asked, stepping into the room before she'd answered.

"Whatever," she snapped. Then her voice changed, just a little. "There's laundry on the floor. High-step it so you don't trip."

I nodded, and did what she ordered until I'd made it to her bed. Sitting down, I reached out, finding her open suitcase beside me.

"Where are you going to go?" I asked as she moved around the room.

"Anywhere," she mumbled. "Probably California."

"California?" I asked in surprise, my jaw dropping. "What the fuck are you going to do there?"

"I went to beauty school," she replied. "I can get a job cutting hair down there."

"But you don't know anyone down there."

"Exactly."

"Come on, Ceecee. How the fuck will you even get there?"

"Drive," she answered. "I've got plenty of cash saved up. It'll be fine."

"Come on, sissy," I said softly. "Think this through."

"I have," she said, startling me with a kiss on my forehead. "I've got no friends here, Lil. Mom and Dad are sick of my shit. Hell, *I'm* sick of my shit. I need a new reality."

"You're still gonna be the same you," I pointed out as she zipped up her suitcase. "It doesn't matter where you go."

"Maybe not," she said. "Maybe I'll be able to get my shit together down there."

Ceecee sat down with me on the bed then pulled me down to lie beside her.

"You remember when you used to crawl into bed with me at night?"

"Yeah. You always threw a fit until Mom made me get back into my own bed."

"And then you'd just wait until I was asleep and crawl back in," she said with a soft laugh.

"You never noticed until morning," I said with a shrug.

"I'm going to miss you."

"Then don't go," I said. My throat grew tight at the thought of her taking off to California all by herself. My sister was a huge pain in the ass, but she was still *my* sister.

"I won't yet," she replied. "I can't drive at the moment, anyway. Too much Jose."

"*Ew.* Tequila? You're going to feel like shit tomorrow."

"Truth." She scooted over and I could feel her pulling on the blankets beneath me. "Come on, climb in."

I kicked off my shoes and crawled under the covers beside her, the events of the day catching up with me. It had been so weird. First, getting ready for prom and being stood up, then Leo, and now Ceecee was telling me that she was leaving the state. Just like that.

I was pretty sure her decision wasn't a new one, though. Cecilia might be headstrong and self-centered, but she wasn't spontaneous. If she was leaving for California after a fight with our parents, she'd been planning on it for a while. The fight had just been the deciding factor.

"Your date stood you up?" she asked once we were situated under the blankets.

"Yeah. He didn't even text with a lame excuse or anything."

"I guess it beats the alternative. I mean, he could have brought you and then poured pig's blood over your head and ruined that hot crop top you're wearing."

"There is that," I replied seriously.

"I like that you went with the two piece," she said, rolling toward me. "That top looks good with your jeans, too, so you can wear it whenever. All of my formal dresses from high school are just taking up closet space now. It's not like I can wear them to the bar."

"But just think," I said with a smile. "In twenty years, they'll be vintage and you could sell them for a bunch of money."

"Start a retirement."

"Pay for Botox."

"Boob job."

"Braces for Timmy."

"Viagra for the hubby."

"Oh, *ew*!" I said, pretend gagging. "I hope I never sleep with a guy old enough to need Viagra."

"You will," she said with a small laugh. "But you'll be old, too, so you won't care."

"Do you think Poet needs Viagra?" I asked in disgusted fascination.

"That old goat?" my sister snorted. "No way in hell."

We laughed so hard that we barely made any noise, wheezing as we tried to catch our breath.

"Some day, kid, you're going to be married with a bunch of kids and I'm going to wonder where the fuck my gap toothed sister went," Cecilia said softly, running her hand over my hair. "And you have dad's gorgeous skin, so I'm also going to be completely jealous and petty that you look twenty years younger than me instead of just five."

"My hair will go gray way before yours, though," I replied with a yawn as she continued running her fingers through my hair.

"Eh, hair can be touched up," she said quietly. "I'll do it for you."

"I'm thinking of getting bangs," I murmured, closing my eyes.

"Oh, fuck no," she replied, giving my hair a tiny yank. "Do not cut bangs. You have a cowlick in the front and they'll look ridiculous. Plus, how would you style them when you can't see them? No. No bangs. You'll hate them and they take forever to grow back out."

"If you stayed, you could style them for me."

"I'm not staying to style your hair, no matter how much I love you," she said, running her fingers through my hair again. "But maybe you can come visit me sometime, you know? We can go to the beach and stuff."

"Where do you think you'll end up?"

"San Diego, probably," she said with a sigh. "I'm thinking that's a good place to start over."

I nodded, but her fingers in my hair were lulling me to sleep. I loved my sister. Even when I couldn't stand her, I loved her. I guess that was the deal with siblings. Even when you thought they were assholes, there was still that part of you that remembered sharing a bed with them when you were little. The part of you that loved when they ran their fingers through your hair. The part of you that knew they loved you with the same fierceness, even if they didn't show it most of the time.

"I love you, Bumblebee," I murmured, reaching out to rest my hand on my sister's thin waist.

"I love you, too, Lilybug."

I fell asleep within seconds, and it wasn't until a few hours later that I woke up again, when my sister left the bed.

"What're you doing?" I asked, my voice scratchy.

"I'm heading out," Ceecee whispered. "I'll call you later and let you know where I'm at."

"Aren't you going to say goodbye to everyone?" I asked, leaning up on my elbow. I couldn't tell where she was in the room, and I had no idea how much she had packed or how long I had before she walked out the door.

"No," she replied. "I'll call Mom later, but I want to get an early start."

"What time is it?"

"About four," she said, leaning down on the bed so she could plant a loud kiss on my forehead. "I'm going to go. Don't wake the 'rents, okay? I'll call them in a few hours. I promise."

"I—" my words cut off as I tried to think of something to say. If I didn't tell my parents that my sister was leaving, they'd be livid. If I did tell them, she was just stubborn enough that she'd leave anyway, and we wouldn't hear from her for months. "Okay," I said finally. "I'll give you a couple hours. But if you haven't called them by the time we have breakfast, I'm going to punch you in the face."

"Thanks," she said. I heard the swishing noises as she put her coat and purse on, and within seconds she was leaving.

"I love you, sissy," she said, her voice filled with excitement.

"I love you, too," I replied, falling back down on the pillow below me. "Drive careful, okay?"

"Always." She paused for a few seconds, and then, because my sister never could seem to help herself, she left her parting shot. "I can smell him on you, you know? His cologne. You might have fooled Mom and Dad, but no way do you smell like that if you were just pressed up against his cut on the back of his bike."

I opened my mouth to argue, but heard the quiet snick of the door shutting before I could say a word. It was exactly her style. Make an accusation, no matter how unfounded, and then bail before you could defend yourself. She'd been doing it since she was old enough to manipulate people. I shook my head as I scrambled further into the blankets, pulling them up and over my head.

A few minutes later, the door opened again.

"Where was she going?" my mom asked quietly, her voice tentative.

We should have known that my parents would realize the moment she left. If they were waking up every time she came home, it stood to reason that they'd wake up if she was leaving, too.

"California," I answered, throwing the blankets off my head. "She said she wanted to go to San Diego."

"Why?"

"I have no idea," I said honestly. "She said she wanted a new life."

"Christ. She'll be back," my mom muttered. "Get some sleep, kid."

I heard her step away from the door.

"Hey, Mom?" I called out. "Can you shut the light off?"

"What?" she asked in surprise.

"The light," I muttered back, pressing my face against the pillow. "Can you shut it off?"

Once the light wasn't burning my eyes anymore, I rolled to my back and lay there for a long time, my thoughts replaying the last twelve hours over and over.

## Chapter 3

# LEO

I WAS SWEATING like a pig as I tried to pry the engine out of an old El Camino that was brought in the day before. The thing was rusted and dirty as fuck, and I was pretty sure no one had been under the hood in at least ten years. Fucking nasty.

We had cars come in like that a lot—owners expecting us to rebuild on shit that wasn't even salvageable. The body of the El Camino was in pretty good condition, but asking us to work with the shit they had under the hood was ridiculous. Most things were going to need to be replaced on my current project. There was no coming back from the rust this piece of shit had going on.

"Hey, baby sister!" Cam shouted from across the garage. "Whatcha doin' here?"

I braced myself as I raised my head, expecting to see Cecilia sauntering in, but found Lily standing quietly in an open garage door instead. She never came inside, even if Rose was with her. The old timers had laid down the law when Lily lost her sight—Lily was no longer allowed inside the garage for any reason. There was just too much shit she could hurt herself on. Even if we kept shit cleaned up—which we didn't—the cars inside were changing every day. One day there could be a Volkswagen Beetle in the first bay and the next day it was a huge Ford pickup, and there was no way for her to know where everything was. The power tools left out could literally kill her if she fell on them wrong.

The garage went quiet as the guys realized it was Lily in the doorway. They stopped what they were doing out of respect, turning off their tools and pausing their movements so that she could hear what she needed to.

"Hey, Cam," Lily called back. "Dad asked me to come get you."

"Everything alright?" he asked as he moved toward her.

"Yeah, just… stuff he wants to talk to you about." Her voice grew quieter as Cam got closer to her, but she was still in the bay next to mine, so I could hear her pretty clearly.

"Alright," Cam said easily. "You comin' inside with me?"

"No." Lily paused. "Is Leo working?"

My head jerked back in surprise as Cam turned toward me, his eyebrows high on his forehead.

"Yeah, he's here," Cam said, jerking his chin at me.

I gingerly lowered the engine back where it was and flexed my fingers as I stepped away from the car and headed in their direction. I had no clue why little Lily wanted to talk to me, but I'd never tell the girl no.

I'd never been able to tell her no. She was just so fucking sweet. It would be like kicking a damn puppy.

"What's up, Dandelion?" I asked as I reached them.

Cam mumbled something and walked away, so I wrapped my arm around Lily's shoulder to lead her farther outside. The guys needed to get back to work, but they wouldn't as long as she was standing there.

"So, thanks for last night," Lily said. "I really appreciate it."

"Whatever," I mumbled. I slipped my hand off her shoulder and grabbed her hand, placing it on the top of the picnic table out front. I didn't have to tell her what or how tall it was, she could have made it to that table herself with no help from me. The forecourt was a little hard for her to navigate with the bikes and cars always coming and going, but the walkway in front of the building and the grassy area with the picnic tables were as familiar to her as her own house.

"I just wanted to let you know," she said with a sigh. "I figured I should tell you before it was all over the clubhouse."

"What?" I replied, grabbing my pack of smokes out of my pocket and lighting up as she climbed to the top of the table and sat down. "Your dad gonna kill me for havin' you on the back of my bike?"

"No." She snorted, making me grin. "Cecilia took off last night, *er*, this morning."

"Oh, yeah?" I asked easily, leaning against the table.

"She said she was going to California. San Diego," Lily said softly, like she was trying to protect me from the news. "She called Mom a little over an hour ago, and she's already halfway there. She hasn't changed her mind."

"Good for her," I ground out, trying and failing to keep the irritation out of my voice.

I didn't give a flying fuck what Cecilia did, but I knew why she was going to San Diego and it made me want to hit something.

"I don't know why she had to go so far away," Lily mumbled, resting her elbows on her knees and tipping her face toward the ground. "Jesus, do you have any sunglasses?"

I looked at her in confusion. "What?"

"Sunglasses," she said, shielding her eyes with her hand. "Do you have any?"

"I've got these," I replied, pulling a pair of tinted safety goggles from the neck of my undershirt.

She held her hand out expectantly until I'd handed over the glasses, then shoved them on her face.

"Jesus, are these safety glasses?" she asked as she ran her fingers along the edges. "I must be lookin' hot with these on."

"Oh, yeah, gorgeous," I replied distractedly, still staring at her. I opened my mouth to ask why the hell she needed shades, but before I could say a word, she was talking about Cecilia again.

"She doesn't even know anyone down there," Lily said in exasperation. "I mean, where the hell is she going to stay? Where will she work? How will she make friends? What if something happens to her? No one would even know for like weeks, because she's so far away!"

I knew she was worried. Everything about her body language and tone made that clear. But I couldn't help the derision that seeped into my voice as I replied.

"Your sister always lands on her feet, kid."

Lily stopped fidgeting with the bracelets on her wrist and turned her head slowly toward me, and for just a second, I could have swore that she was looking right at me.

"You're pissed," she said, her voice laced with disappointment. "I thought you would be."

"Not the way you're thinking," I argued, taking another drag of my cigarette. "I'm pissed for you. Pissed for your parents."

"That's not it," Lily replied flatly. "Just because I'm blind doesn't mean I can't tell when you're lying."

"I'm not lying."

"It's okay that you're mad. I would be, too, if I was you."

"The fuck is that supposed to mean?" I asked, standing up straight. I fucking hated being called a liar, and I really didn't like that this girl who wasn't even legal was talking to me like she knew something I didn't.

"I mean, you guys were together for a long time," Lily said. "I get it."

"You don't get shit," I snapped, the anger simmering beneath the surface coming up to raise it's ugly head. "Your skank sister went to San Diego because that's where Mouth is. Playin' doctor at the Navy base down there."

"Oh," Lily whispered, closing her eyes as she shook her head from side to side. "That makes sense."

"Dude left her and she goes chasin' after his ass," I said, trying to explain my anger as she climbed gingerly off the table.

"You know," she said, turning her head toward me as she faced the clubhouse. "I was always surprised when you never badmouthed my sister, even when I knew she was being a bitch."

She turned away. "Now I'm glad you hadn't. My sister isn't a skank, Leo. She just didn't want you."

My mouth dropped open as she walked away from me. Lily had never spoken to me with anything but adoration in her entire life. Hell, I remembered when she was a toddler, walking around the clubhouse singing my name. *Singing* it. It didn't matter what was going on, who was fighting with who, or how me and her sister were getting along, she'd still never said a nasty word to me.

Until now.

Pretty sure I'd deserved it.

Still, resentment built up as I watched her walk inside. Whatever. She could think whatever the hell she wanted, I wasn't going to try and change her mind.

I shouldn't have called Cecilia a skank, but I had a hard time keeping my mouth shut when it came to that woman. I'd always done my best when Lily was around, but Christ. No one knew all the shit that had gone down with Cecilia back when she was playing me and Mouth. They had no clue how deep that bullshit ran, because we'd kept it that way. A little rivalry between the club kids was one thing, planning on how you'd take out one of the brothers' kids was another, and I'd spent many nights planning exactly how I'd take Doc's kid out.

He was a piece of shit. He'd liked playing Cecilia, and that woman was all drama even as a teenager, so she'd played right along. She'd liked making me jealous, it was her thing, and for a while I'd gone along with it. So he'd been playing her and she'd been playing me and I'd been planning his death. That all ended abruptly when he'd left for the military, but he'd left me with his fuckin' mess to clean up. As much as I couldn't stand Cecilia most of the time, I hadn't been able to walk away from the mess he'd made. The motherfucker.

I ground my teeth together as I walked back into the garage, slamming my hand on the back of the El Camino as I passed it.

"Hey, now," Will called out with a laugh. "That's a prime piece of machinery you're abusin'."

"It's all good," I called back. "She likes it when I'm rough."

His laugh carried across the garage.

"As you were, then!"

I lifted my chin and moved around to the engine, staring at the block as I seethed. Cecilia was still chasing that piece of shit. Of fucking course she was.

I flexed my hands and got back to work. I was done worrying about Cecilia fucking Butler. I was done walking around on eggshells for her sister, too.

★ ★ ★

"NICE OF YOU to join us," my dad called out from his place at the table as Will pushed through the doorway. It was time for our weekly meeting, or church as we affectionately called it. I was nothing, a sergeant, but I still had a place at the table. My dad, Dragon, was president of our club and years ago when shit had gone down with the Russian mob trying to take out the Aces from the inside out, I'd made sure that I was right in the middle of the planning and executions.

Those motherfuckers had shot me in the face and killed people I'd considered family. I hadn't ended up pulling the trigger on anyone, but there was no way I would have let the elders leave me out. It wasn't how I was built.

Things had been quiet lately, but we'd heard a bit of chatter about some of the guys who'd been put away making deals for early parole. Casper had bankrupted and shut down most of their businesses and stolen the bulk of their alliances with people in the states, but there was always someone willing to get in bed with organizations ready and able to do anything to make it back to the top. He'd done everything he could to hobble the Russian's who'd come after us, but there was only so much you could do without taking out entire families.

*They* might have been cool with shooting at women and children, but that wasn't how we did business.

Luckily, the old timers had connections fucking everywhere, and usually had a lock on shit before it ever went down. We now kept an ear to the ground and our fingers on the pulse of the Russian organization. The shooting at Casper and Farrah's had been an anomaly, one that we wouldn't let be repeated.

"Reb was havin' a hard time leavin' for school," Moose mumbled as he dropped into his seat. "Had to give Molly a hand."

Grease nodded. "Got some news from inside. Looks like Karl Sokolov got his deal."

"Shit," Hulk muttered.

"Which one is that?" Moose asked, looking around the table.

"Big, bald guy," Casper answered, looking through some papers in front of him. "Owned a bunch of dry cleaning and carpet cleaning businesses that went belly up when he went inside. Feds closed them down once they realized how much money was being cleaned. Man has a wife and two sons back in the motherland. Hopin' that's where he's headed once he's a free man, but doubt it. Didn't care that he'd left them there for ten years before he got arrested, highly doubt he's anxious for a family reunion."

"Sokolov's a problem. Wasn't at the head of the food chain by any means, but he was high enough that he's gonna have friends if he goes lookin' for them," my dad added.

"You think he's gonna come here?" I asked, leaning back in my seat. I remembered Sokolov. He was a big bastard, almost as fat as he was tall. Looked stupid, but wasn't. He hadn't been directly responsible for the hits against the Aces, but none of us believed he'd been innocent. When Casper had started researching the faction of the mob that was fucking with us, he'd found Sokolov's meaty fingers in a whole lot of pies.

"Not sure what his plan will be," Grease muttered. "But if I was him, I'd be lookin' for someone to help me gain a foothold. Especially if I'd made a deal with the Feds. No way that asshole made a deal without approval comin' from the top, it'd be a death sentence for his family otherwise."

"Timeframe?" Hulk asked.

"Takes time, but he'll be out within the next month," Casper replied.

"Deal with that shit as it comes," my dad said, scratching his chest like the conversation was nothing. The man could look bored no matter what was being discussed. It was a gift I'd *almost* mastered.

"Has anyone heard from Cecilia?" Hulk asked, changing the subject. "She still hasn't called me back."

"Your sister's fine," Casper replied, scrubbing his hand over his shaved head. "Called your mother last night."

"She found a place to stay?"

"We done here?" I interrupted, making eye contact with my pop. I was all about discussing club business, but as far as I was concerned, Cecilia wasn't club business.

"Feelin' a little raw, Leo?" Grease joked, chuckling. "Cecilia ain't called you yet?"

I ground my teeth together to keep from saying anything that would get my ass handed to me. I was fine in a fight, but Grease was Cecilia's uncle. Will and Tommy were her cousins. Casper and Hulk were her dad and brother. If I said what I wanted to say, there was no way I was getting out of that room with all my teeth, and my dad wouldn't do a damn thing to stop it.

"Got shit to do," I finally muttered.

"We're done here," my dad announced, tapping his gavel once on the table. "Casper and Hulk are keepin' an eye on Sokolov and we'll let everyone know if anythin' new comes up."

I was out of my seat and out of the room before anyone else had pushed back from the table. Sokolov was going to be a problem. I could feel it in my gut. No man got out of prison so early unless he had a lot of shit he was willing to give the Feds, and no organization would let him give that information unless they had something big planned for him on the outside.

I was pretty sure the games we'd been playing with their organization were about to bite us in the ass. I didn't have time to worry about how Cecilia was doing in California. I also just didn't give a fuck.

# Chapter 4

# Lily

IT HAD BEEN two weeks since my sister left. Two long weeks where it felt like everything revolved around waiting for her calls home. Even when she wasn't in the same state, Cecilia still seemed to demand all of our attention. She never answered the phone when we called her, but at least she'd kept my parents updated on where she was and what she was doing.

According to Cecilia, everything was working out in San Diego. She'd found a job in some barbershop and was renting a room from a lady she worked with. She'd landed on her feet, just like Leo had said she would.

I hadn't talked to her since she'd left, but I was trying not to let it bother me. I had my own shit going on. The whispers about me and Brent had finally died down at school since he hadn't shown up at the prom without me. Apparently, he'd had a bad case of the stomach flu, at least that's what he'd been telling people. The excuse was a bit suspect since, according to Rose, he'd come to school the next week with a nasty black eye. I didn't really give it much thought beyond refusing to talk to him. Stomach flu or not, he could have at least texted me to give me a heads up.

Now I was just trying to focus on the college applications I was finishing up. I'd always been ahead of my peers in school, really far ahead. So far ahead that most of my teachers were clueless about how to teach me, especially after I'd gone blind. I'd felt like a freak when I was younger, but my dad had assured me he'd been the same way. His parents had shipped him off to boarding school when he was really young, though, and he'd refused to do that to me. So instead, we'd made sure that I was in every gifted class that was available, and that had been enough. I'd also used every tool available to work through my handicap, and to be honest, it hadn't slowed me down much.

Now, my SAT scores were near perfect, and my GPA was through the roof, and it was time for me to start deciding on colleges. We lived near the University of Oregon, so that was a safe bet, and so were some of the other private colleges in Oregon. Only my parents and Rose knew I was applying to other schools, too. Ivy League schools. Schools that I knew would challenge me and give me one hell of a leg up in whatever field I decided to study in.

More important than that, though, I'd also begun to see. Not clearly. Not yet. But for the first time since I'd gone blind, things were taking shape in front of me. I could see light and shadows, and large obstacles in my path.

I didn't tell anyone. Not even Rose.

My sight was too new. I didn't want to get anyone's hopes up, and I was terrified that the moment I said anything about it, the little vision I'd gained back would vanish and I'd be in the dark again. My family had been waiting so long for my sight to come back that I knew it would devastate them if I had it and lost it again.

"What's up with you?" Rose grumbled, elbowing me in the side. "You've been spacing out for like ten minutes."

I'd been trying to make out my dad's recliner in the corner instead of just a dark shape surrounded by the light coming through the windows.

"Nothing. These applications are boring as hell." I threw myself back against the couch and rubbed my eyes. "Let's go do something."

"Like what?" she asked with a sigh, slamming her textbook shut with a bang. While I'd been filling out applications for early admission, Rose was working on her calculus homework that had been due the day before. While I excelled in academics, Rose… didn't. It wasn't because she lacked intelligence; she just lacked the drive to do more than the bare minimum to graduate. She wasn't even applying to colleges. Instead, she planned to follow me wherever I decided to go.

"I don't know, river? The club? Movies? Anywhere."

"You know they're having a party at the club tonight," she replied. I knew without seeing it that she was rolling her eyes. "You really want to get into it with our brothers?"

"We'll just ignore them," I said, shrugging. Getting around our brothers had become a game when we were twelve years old. It didn't really matter how pissed they were, Rose and I usually got away with whatever we wanted. It just normally took a lot of fast-talking and innocent expressions, so we rarely went head to head with them anymore. It wasn't worth the hassle.

"I don't know," Rose said, completely out of character.

"What?"

"Last time, your mom was dancing on one of the pool tables," Rose grumbled. "Not something I want to see again."

"You know that doesn't happen very often," I replied, snorting. My mom had been dancing on that same pool table for years. She did it whenever my dad was pissed it at her. Without fail, he'd drag her off the table and into their room before she'd finished a single song and suddenly, their fight was over.

"Fine," Rose said, shoving me a little as she pushed off the couch. "Let's go then."

"I'm so glad Charlie's staying the night with Rebel," I replied as I followed her toward the front door. "Or else we'd be stuck here."

"Or we could've just taken her with us."

"Oh, right," I joked, setting my hand on her shoulder once we'd reached the driveway. "That would've gone over well."

"How many parties were we at when we were little?" Rose asked, leading me to her car. "A hundred? If you ask me, this younger generation is a bunch of wimps."

I climbed in and laid my head back against the seat, watching things go darker around me as the sun went down. "Pretty sure they just didn't have as many babysitters when we were little," I pointed out distractedly. "There was nowhere else for us to be."

"You're probably right."

★ ★ ★

My cousin Tommy threw his arms around our shoulders the minute we'd stepped through the clubhouse doors. We hadn't even made it two feet inside. "What the hell are you doing here?" he asked gruffly.

The music was loud and so were the people. It was slightly disorienting if I was being honest, but I still soaked it all in. The clubhouse was a safe place, at least for me. It was where we went if we were in danger, where my dad worked, where I could trip over a family member or longtime family friend if I took a step in any direction. Occasionally, if the guys were hosting other clubs, I steered clear, but for the most part, this place was an extension of my home and always had been.

"We were hoping to get laid and do some shots," Rose said dryly over the noise. "Point us in the right direction!"

"Also," I piped in, "if you could show us where the lines of coke are being drawn, that would be fantastic."

"Little sister," Cam said suddenly from right in front of me. "What the hell do you know about cocaine?"

"I'm almost seventeen," I replied in mock seriousness. "I know about all sorts of things."

"You better not!" He laughed, and suddenly I was pulled away from Tommy's side and wrapped up in my brother's beefy arm. "What're you doin' here, Lilybug?"

"Just wanted to get out of the house," I replied as he practically carried me across the room.

"Dad's gonna shit a brick when he sees you," he warned, setting me back solidly on my feet. "Gimme a bottle of Jack and a soda for the baby, here," he ordered someone.

"Aw, sweet of you to get me a mixer," I said, laughing when he pinched me.

"Jack's for me and Trix. Soda's for you, smartass."

"Trix is here?" I asked, smiling. The two of them rarely had a chance to be out at the same time since my twin nephews were born. Most of their potential babysitters attended the same parties.

"Yeah, Molly and Will have all the little ones tonight."

"Well, that's brave of them," I said as a cold can was pushed into my hand.

"Yeah, we said we'd take 'em next time, but you know how Molly is. Doesn't really like Rebel sleepin' at other people's houses," he replied as he guided me back through the room.

"It's because she doesn't *sleep*," I reminded him.

"Yeah, yeah. I know. Just hard for them, not bein' able to cut loose."

"I'm pretty sure they do just fine," I said with a smile.

Molly and Will were awesome parents. I knew that sometimes they were stressed about Rebel's limitations, but I also knew that they wouldn't have it any other way. Will had gotten in plenty of partying before he and Molly got together, and she wasn't really the type to 'cut loose,' as my brother called it. They were happy to stay at home.

"Lily, what the fuck are you doing here?" my sister-in-law asked, setting her hand on my arm in warning before pulling me into a hug. She was one of the only people I knew that gave me notice before she got all in my space. It was sweet. The rest of my family just went in for the kill without even thinking about how jarring it was to suddenly have someone wrapped around you.

It was pretty dim in the room, and as I hugged her back, I got a little pit in my stomach when I realized that what little sight I'd been enjoying was practically nonexistent without the presence of some relatively bright lights.

"Me and Rose were bored," I told her as she set my hand on the back of an empty chair. I sat down and gingerly set my soda on the table in front of me, right at twelve o'clock.

"I thought you were doing applications tonight?"

"I've sent most of them out. I was just finishing up the stragglers. It's fucking mind numbing."

"Yeah," she laughed. "I remember. College applications suck balls. I can't imagine trying to do it on that computer you have."

"Eh, I'm used to it. The only thing that gets annoying is trying to proof the essays when I'm done. The way it translates from voice to text isn't always super clear."

"You'd probably be a really good public speaker or speech writer," she mused. "You've been writing all of your papers orally for years."

"Truth."

Cam said something too quiet to hear, and I tuned them out as Trix said something quietly back. If they weren't raising their voices above the music and laughter, they obviously weren't trying to talk to me across the table. I took a deep breath and relaxed, listening to the people around me.

Old Poet's laughter came from across the room. Somewhere nearby, the president's old lady, Leo's mom, was talking about an extra keg stored in the garage storage room. Someone, I wasn't sure who, was singing really badly along with the music playing through the sound system. Glasses and feet were tapping around the room as people walked and talked and visited.

"You're supposed to be at home, Lilybug," my dad's voice said quietly in my ear, making me jump. "Pretty sure my little girl told me she was doin' schoolwork tonight."

"Hey, Daddio," I replied cheerfully, leaning into him as he kissed my cheek. "I was bored and almost finished with the applications anyway."

"Well, why didn't you just get 'em done, then?" he asked, pulling a chair close to mine with a screech against the floor. "Quit draggin' your feet. Deadlines are comin' up quick."

"I know. I just wanted you to look a couple of them over and then I'll send them off."

"Oh, so now it's my fault you're in the middle of a party instead of sittin' at home where you're supposed to be?" he laughed and yanked at the braid in my hair.

"It's not like I can see any of the bad things happening around me," I pointed out playfully, even though I knew I shouldn't. "Someone could be stripping on this table and I'd have no idea."

"Don't say that shit to me," my dad replied, his tone growing dark. "Your mother lets you get away with it, but you know I don't think that shit's funny. It ain't a joke to me, Lily."

My heart pounded as I nodded, instantly feeling like an asshole. I had my mom's sense of humor, completely. I made jokes at the most inopportune times, and they were usually offensive to at least one person around me. Not rude, exactly, but not in good taste, either. Where my mom would snort at one of my jokes about being blind, and give me shit right back, it affected my dad differently. He hated it. It wasn't funny for him in the slightest.

"Sorry," I said, remorse making my voice wobble.

It was hard for me to remember sometimes that I wasn't the only person who'd lost something when I'd gone blind. It just wasn't something that I thought about on a daily basis. Darkness was my reality. But for my parents, they'd lost something, too. Something they'd never spoken to me about, but I knew was there all the same. One day, they'd had a fully functioning eleven-year-old daughter who loved to ride and climbed trees like a monkey, and within hours they'd been parents of a completely different child. Oh, my personality was still pretty similar after I'd gotten over the trauma of that day, but my day-to-day life had changed drastically. Suddenly, they were watching me every minute, helping me learn how to do everything all over again in a different way.

I'd realized pretty early on that they were so grateful that I'd survived when others hadn't, that any frustration they had at my new disability had been quickly overshadowed by massive amounts of guilt, no matter how warranted that frustration was. They'd never said a word about any of it, but I knew my parents. Those first few years after the attack had been hard on them, not only as parents, but as husband and wife, too.

So, yeah. Jokes about my blindness weren't funny to my dad. I wasn't even sure if my mom found them funny, but she understood the need for sarcasm in a way that he didn't.

"Well, you're here now," Dad said, patting my thigh. "Might as well stay for a bit."

"Where's Rose?" I asked. Once Cam had separated me from her and Tommy, I hadn't heard her voice again. The clubhouse was one of the only places outside of our homes that she felt comfortable leaving my side for very long.

"Talking to Grease," Dad said with a laugh. "And he looks like he's about to break something."

"She's spent too much time with Mom," I replied. "She can pretty much talk circles around him."

"She's pointing over here," he murmured in amusement.

"Yeah, she's probably using you as an example. *See, Dad, Uncle*

*Casper isn't giving Lily a hard time."*

"You two are both little shits," my dad said with a huff. "I'm gonna go find your mother. You good?"

"Yeah. I'll probably just sit here for a while until Rose wants to leave."

"Got some boys from the Sacramento chapter here tonight," Dad said as he stood up. "Watch yourself."

"Always do," I replied as he rested a hand on the top of my head and then walked away.

As protective as my parents were, if things weren't particularly rowdy at the club, they didn't really mind if I hung around. There were times that my dad would have thrown me over his shoulder and carried me outside, but for the most part, he knew I could handle myself. Growing up in the club meant I'd seen and heard a lot of things that probably weren't age appropriate, but that was just the life we'd lived. Sometimes you got a huge dose of reality before you were particularly ready for it. Living through a shooting that killed some of your family was one of those things. I didn't think my parents were particularly concerned with me witnessing drinking or drugs or slutty women hanging all over the men after all the stuff I'd already been through.

"My dad is a pain," Rose announced a few minutes later as she dropped into my dad's empty chair. "I swear he still thinks I'm five."

"He's just protective."

"It's ridiculous. I'm *related* to most of these guys," she huffed.

"Not all of them." I turned my face in her direction and lowered my voice. "Dad said there's some guys from Sacramento here. Any good ones?"

Rose was quiet for a minute, then sighed. "Yeah, but just one. Messy blonde hair, some red in his beard, built like a wall."

"How old?" I asked, reaching for my drink.

"I'm guessing early twenties. Could be younger, I can never tell with this crowd."

"Clothes?"

"Gray flannel under his cut. They're pretty much all wearing long sleeves. Looks like the Cali boys can't handle the chilly spring we're having."

We both laughed at her ribbing. It was spring in Oregon, nearly summer, and from the minute the temperature rose above sixty-five degrees, all of the guys around here lived in short sleeve t-shirts. It was warm for us.

"I'm gonna go to the bathroom," I told her as she finished cackling. "Stay here so I can find you afterward."

"Oh, hell no," she argued. "There's shit all over the place. Nothing's where it's supposed to be. You're gonna fall on your face."

"I'll be careful," I ground out through clenched teeth as I used her shoulder to push myself to my feet. "The wall is two feet from me, I'll follow it to the fucking hallway and it'll be smooth sailing from there."

"Lil, there's a shit ton of people here," Rose hissed. "It's not a good idea."

"I'm fine," I snapped.

I walked away before she said anything else, but I could feel her eyes boring into my back as I reached the wall that would lead me to the archway that connected to the back hallway of the club. I knew it was taking all of her willpower not to follow me, but I really hoped she wouldn't. Ever since I'd begun seeing light again, the restraints I'd been living with for years had started driving me insane. I wanted to be able to go to the damn bathroom on my own. I wanted my sight back so I could learn to drive, and cook, and watch a fucking movie.

I breathed a little sigh of relief as I reached the archway that led to the hallway and bedrooms. There were rarely any people back there outside of the ones that I'd known since birth. The members weren't real willing to let outsiders go sniffing around in their shit, and they kept a lot of shit in their bedrooms that they weren't willing to bring home with them.

After knocking—a lot—I went inside my dad's room and the bathroom connected to it without any trouble. I wasn't sure where my parents were, but thankfully they weren't inside. I'd never walked in on them, but there had been a couple of close calls that I'd rather not remember or repeat. Their bathroom was always clean, though—my mother's doing—so I always felt safe going inside. I wasn't about to use one of the restrooms that the guys shared out in the hallway. Men were disgusting creatures and their bathrooms were usually vomit-inducing.

As I made my way out of the bedroom, I ran my hand along the wall on my left as I absently counted my steps. It was around fourteen and a half steps between my parents' room and the archway, but I only made it ten before an arm was wrapped around my waist and lifting me off the floor.

It startled me so badly that I didn't even scream.

## CHAPTER 5

# LEO

"Dandelion," I said cheerfully as I spun her around in a small circle. "What're you doin' here?"

I was drunk. Plastered, if I was being honest. And damn if it didn't feel good.

"What the fuck, Leo," Lily gasped as her nails dug into my forearm. "Put me down."

"Ah, don't be like that," I said, setting her back on her feet. "We're at a party!"

"You're drunk," she snapped, pushing away from me.

Her brows drew down in confusion as she reached tentatively out to her side until her hand met the wall.

"Feelin' good, yeah," I answered, even though it hadn't been a question. "What're you doin' here?"

"You already asked that."

"And you didn't answer me."

"I would have if—" she paused and her nostrils flared. "Where the fuck am I? Which direction am I going in?"

I realized then that I'd totally disoriented her when I'd swung her around. Whoops.

"Same direction you were headed when I found you," I replied uncomfortably. "About three steps from the main room."

"Thank you," she snapped, taking a step away from me.

"What?" I asked obnoxiously, irritated that she was walking away from me. "You still pissed about that Cecilia shit?"

"Are you joking?" she asked, turning her head toward me.

"Well, somethin' crawled up your ass."

"You just picked me up out without giving me any fucking warning!"

"You knew it was me," I protested, lifting my hands palm up, even though she couldn't see me. "Come on, it ain't like you didn't know."

"Actually, I didn't," she hissed, turning completely around. "There's a bunch of guys here that I don't even know, but since I was back here I wasn't paying close attention!"

Her arms flew out and one almost hit me in the face as she gestured, making me grin.

"Well, shit. You know it's me *now*."

"Whatever," she snapped, crossing her arms over her chest. "Did you need something?"

Her eyes were pointed right at me. I knew she couldn't see me. I knew it. But lately when they were pointed in my direction, it felt like she was looking at me. No shit. More and more, it seemed like her eyes were focused instead of staring into nothing.

"Just sayin' hi," I replied, stepping forward to I could throw my arms around her shoulders and turn her back in the right direction. "Wasn't expectin' to see you tonight."

"I'm surprised you aren't holed up with some skank," she said snarkily, making me chuckle.

"Nah, that was an hour ago."

"*Ew!*" She tried to pull away in disgust, but I pulled her tighter against me as I ushered her forward.

"What? You don't want any skank rubbing off on you?" I asked jokingly, scrubbing my hand up and down her bare arm.

"That's fucking disgusting," she replied, finally yanking herself away from me.

"Oh, now I'm disgusting?" I teased, stepping in her way before she could move out into the main room. "Thought you dug me?"

Her face turned red as she seethed, but I was having too much fun giving her shit to worry about it.

"Yeah," she said quietly. "I dig it so much when you tell me that you were just banging some nasty chick that's probably been with most of the club. That really does it for me."

I jerked my head back in surprise at the raw sound of her voice. I'd been joking. Teasing. But Lily wasn't. She was serious. And by the look on her face, I'd just seriously fucked up.

"Come on, Dandelion—"

My words were cut off when Cam's massive hand fell hard on my shoulder from behind, making me stiffen.

"What're you doin' back here, Lilybug?" he asked, shoving past me. "Ma's lookin' for you."

I stepped aside as they moved past me, but I didn't say another word and neither did Lily. I shook my head and leaned against the wall as I tried to figure out where I'd crossed the line with her. I'd always teased her. Usually not about the crush she'd been harboring for years, sure, but she was almost seventeen. Wasn't that a little bit old to be getting all wound up about shit like that? It's not like I was mean about it.

Whatever. She was probably still pissed that I'd called her sister a skank a couple of weeks before.

I strolled back into the main room and grabbed a beer off the bar top as I made my way over to where Tommy and Hawk were sitting with a couple of the other boys. The guys who'd come up from Cali seemed like good people and we'd been bullshitting with them most of the night. They were thinking about transferring north to join our chapter and my pop had asked if we'd get a feel for them and see if they'd be a good fit. So far, they seemed alright.

"What were you talking to Lily about?" Hawk asked as I flipped a chair backward and planted my ass. "She looked pissed."

"She's fuckin' moody tonight," I replied with a shrug. "Must be that time of the month."

Her hand came out and slapped the back of my head so fast that I didn't even see it coming. "The fuck?" I yelped.

"Don't be a dick," she spat.

"Tommy, control your woman," I ordered, glaring.

"Oh, fuck off," Hawk said, flipping me off. "I've cleaned your vomit off the floor of my spare room. I can smack you if I want to."

"Bullshit," I said, rubbing the back of my head. "Christ."

"Were you being a dick to her?" Hawk asked, not letting it go. "She never looks that angry."

"Who knows?" I mumbled back, dodging another slap. "I startled her in the hallway, she was probably pissed about that."

"Why?" she asked, staring me down even though I refused to answer. Finally, she scoffed and turned away from me in irritation.

I had no idea why I'd scared Lily in the hallway. It hadn't been my fucking plan, obviously. I'd just been happy to see her and I'd done what I would have done with any chick I was happy to see. I hadn't thought about the fact that she wouldn't know it was me. Hell, I could be walking across the floor any other time and she'd know me by the sound of my footsteps.

"You guys like it up here?" Copper asked as I started paying attention to the conversation going on around me.

"Don't know any different," Tommy replied, chuckling. "Grew up here, man."

"Wait, all of you?"

"Me and Tommy, yeah," I said. I pointed my beer bottle at Rocky, another member of our chapter. "Rock didn't, though. He came from Idaho, right Rock?"

"Yep." He nodded but didn't add anything else. Rocky's background wasn't really something we talked about.

"When'd you join up?" Copper's friend asked. I couldn't remember the dude's name. It was something forgettable like Bob.

"Grew up in the club," Tommy said, tilting his head a bit as he watched them. "Prospected at what? Seventeen?" he asked me.

"Something like that."

Copper looked between us, then started laughing. "Jesus Christ. Dragon's kid, yeah? And Grease's?"

"How'd you know?" I asked sarcastically.

Tommy and I both looked a shit ton like our dads. Tommy was way fucking leaner than his dad or brothers, but he still had the Hawthorne look about him in a big way, and if I didn't have the scar on my face, I would have looked exactly like my pop when he was my age. Our mothers must have been irritated as fuck when their kids came out looking everything like their men and nothing like them.

"Well, shit," Copper joked good-naturedly. "Why didn't I realize I was drinkin' with royalty?"

"Oh, God!" Hawk gasped, her eyes going wide. "I always knew I'd find my prince!" She looked at Tommy and batted her eyes. "Marry me and take me to your castle? Does it have a moat? It better have a moat!"

"Woman, I'm the one who does the askin'. Shit," Tommy replied, a huge ass smile on his face. "You didn't even get me ring. Your proposal blows."

"Let's have anal," Hawk said.

"I'll marry you tomorrow," Tommy said seriously before she'd even finished the last word of her sentence, making the entire table roar with laughter.

Hawk lifted her beer in salute, then sat back with a smug grin on her face.

I liked her. I'd wondered what the fuck Tommy was doing when he'd first gotten with her, since all of us had remembered her as his younger brother Mick's girl, but it didn't take long to see how well they fit together. Honestly, Hawk was the kind of chick that any guy would fit with—and I didn't mean that disrespectfully. She was fun, sweet when she wanted to be, smart as shit, and she didn't take crap from anyone. Girl was her own person and didn't give a fuck about what other people thought, and hell if that wasn't attractive as shit.

I glanced at Copper and noticed that he was probably thinking the exact same thoughts as I was, but his weren't quite as innocent. He'd better get that look off his face before Tommy saw him or we'd have problems.

"You got a woman back home?" I asked pointedly, making eye contact.

His lips tipped up a bit as he gave me a slight nod of acknowledgement. "Nah," he said with a shrug. "Free as a bird at the moment."

"Snatch he was with before was crazy," Bob—or whatever his name was—piped in.

"Hey," Copper said darkly. "She's none of your fuckin' business."

"Sorry," Bob said quickly, raising his hand in surrender.

"Had a girlfriend all through high school and for the past few years," Copper clarified simply. "Didn't work out."

"That why you're lookin' to change chapters?" Tommy asked.

"Part of it," Copper replied.

I barely paid any attention as conversation veered in another direction. I could understand wanting to move to a different state after being burned by a woman. Back in the day, I would have done anything to get away from Cecilia. I'd been too young and dumb to cut ties when I should have and that mess had gone on a lot longer than I should've allowed. Most of the hard feelings I had about Cecilia had pretty much disappeared over time—being around someone once you got out from under their spell does that—but I still fucking hated Mouth.

I looked around the room as the music got louder and found my sister and Cam mauling each other in the corner. It wasn't anything new. Going at it wherever they were was pretty standard on the rare nights that they didn't have my nephews with them.

Callie Hawthorne and Farrah were sitting with Lily and Rose at a table across the room, and it looked like Lily's mom was telling a story, because no one else was talking, just laughing as she waved her hands around in the air. Lily had a grin on her face as she leaned forward, her face tilted toward the table in front of her. She didn't look pissed anymore, but I was going to steer clear of her for the rest of the night, just in case.

She was turning out to be all kinds of gorgeous. I'd predicted it when she was just a little thing, but honest to God, she'd surpassed all expectations. She and Rose looked really similar, more like sisters than Lily and Cecilia, but where Rose's features and build were round and soft, Lily was delicate.

"Not sure if it would be better if you were eye fuckin' my mom and aunt or the girls," Tommy said derisively, kicking my chair. "Knock it off."

I spun my head in his direction, then took a second as the room seemed to tilt. Shit. Way too much booze. I was going to feel it tomorrow.

"What?" I asked stupidly, focusing on his face.

"Quit staring over there," he said, shaking his head. "My dad or Uncle Casper are going to see you."

"I wasn't staring," I mumbled, taking a drink of my mostly empty beer.

"Yeah, you were," Hawk said, chuckling. "I don't even think you blinked."

"Fuck off."

"Who're they?" Copper asked, glancing in Lily's direction.

He'd better turn the fuck away before I knocked his ass out.

"My mom, aunt, and baby sister and cousin," Tommy said, his voice filled with warning.

"Hey, just curious," Copper replied, raising his eyebrows in surprise.

"Keep your curiosity to yourself," I snapped.

"Jesus, Leo," Hawk murmured. "Go sleep it off already."

"I'm good." I shook my head slightly. "Gonna get another beer. You want one?"

"I want one," Tommy answered.

"Wasn't talkin' to you, asshole."

I got up and made my way to the bar, weaving through the crowd. The place wasn't as packed as it usually was during a party, but there were still quite a few people hanging out. Members and their old ladies or side-pieces, women looking to get laid, some hangers-on that were trying to weasel into the club and didn't realize that partying with us wasn't the way to do that. It took initiative, hard work, and loyalty. Loyalty was the most important.

"Hey, kid," my dad said as I reached the bar. My mom was standing between his knees as he sat on a bar stool, the back of her head leaning against his shoulder.

"Hey, Pop. Mom."

"You look like you're about to fall down," my mom teased as she poked me in the side. "Go easy, yeah?"

"I'm good," I assured her, catching the attention of the chick behind the bar with my raised beer bottle.

"Can you take your ma into town tomorrow?" my dad asked as I waited for my beer. "I got some other shit goin' on."

"Sure." I nodded my thanks for the beer set in front of me and turned to face my parents. "Where do you need to go?"

"I just have some errands to run," my mom replied. "But your dad wants someone with me while I'm stopping all over town."

"You're not getting your nails done or some shit, right?" I shook my head. "Last time, I had a headache for two days after sittin' in that shop."

"No," she laughed. "Just need to get some stuff at the store, stop by the post office, that kind of stuff."

"Alright. No problem."

I glanced over my dad's shoulder and caught a glimpse of Lily's long braid as she went back into the hallway I'd found her in earlier.

"I'm gonna hit the sack. Call me in the morning," I told my mom, leaning forward so she could kiss my cheek. "But not too early, alright?"

With a nod to my dad, I moved around them and followed Lily. She was just coming out of her dad's room when I stepped into the hallway, but I didn't say a word as she moved toward me. She was stuffing something into her pocket and didn't realize she wasn't alone until she had almost reached me.

"Leo?" she asked, tilting her head to the side.

"Hey, Dandelion." My voice was kind of scratchy, so I cleared my throat.

"What's up?" She didn't seem to still be pissed about earlier, but I wasn't taking any chances.

"We're cool, right?" I asked, taking a step forward.

"Yeah," she said easily.

"Okay, cause you were pretty pissed earlier."

"You were being a jackass earlier," she pointed out, making me grimace. "You aren't now."

"Alright, good." I reached forward like an idiot and ruffled her hair like she was a little kid. "Don't like it when you're pissed at me."

"Quit," she said in annoyance, pulling her head away from my hand. "I'm not a kid, you know."

"That's probably up for interpretation," I replied.

"Bullshit. I'm almost seventeen years old."

"Oh, so last month you were sixteen and now you're 'almost seventeen'?"

"Same shit. I'm not a fucking child. Don't treat me like one."

"Girl, you're young. Hella young. It might not seem like it to you, but you are."

"Then why the fuck did you follow me back here?" she asked, throwing her hands up in the air.

"Cause I was pretty sure I hurt your feelin's earlier!" I snapped back.

I didn't like her holding me under a microscope, especially when I had no idea what the fuck I was doing with her in the dim hallway. I had no business worrying about her feelings. None.

"Just—" She stopped talking and sighed. "We're good, okay? Go sleep it off."

"Hey," I murmured, grabbing her arm as she tried to pass me. "I know you're not a kid. Still way too fuckin' young, though. Way too fuckin' young."

"Well, that's not going to change tonight," she replied simply, pulling her arm from my hand. "I'll see you later."

I leaned heavily against the wall as I watched her go. What the fuck was I doing? Obviously, I was too drunk to be making any kind of decisions. I needed to stay the hell away from Lily Butler. The friendship I'd always had with the kid was getting blurred against my goddamn will.

I slid along the wall until I reached my room, and grabbed my keys from my pocket to unlock the door. I always kept my shit locked, even though a lot of the other brothers didn't. I'd seen too many things go missing for me to trust that no one would rifle through my shit when I wasn't there.

Pushing into my room, I tossed my keys on the floor and slammed the door behind me. I'd barely kicked off my boots and cut before I fell heavily onto the bed. I passed out within seconds.

## Chapter 6

# LILY

It was an ordinary Wednesday in the middle of summer. Not a holiday. Not even a weekend. It was just like any other day that I'd had that summer.

However, when I opened my eyes that morning, I could see clearly for the first time in six years. It wasn't light and shadows anymore. I could see everything—the blue curtains on my windows, the quilt on my bed that my great gram had stitched by hand, my dresser with the broken knob on the top drawer, the dirty clothes basket, my own hands—all of it was clear.

My heart pounded and I lay frozen for a long time, my eyes the only things that shifted as I heard my mom and dad downstairs talking to Charlie. Everything in my room was different than the last time I'd seen it, when I'd had toys and coloring supplies covering every surface. Now it was an adult room. I'd known it intellectually, but seeing it was like a kick to the face. *Seeing* it. I was seeing it all.

Charlie screeched downstairs, followed by the sound of her running, and I closed my eyes, picturing where she was by the sound of the floorboards under her feet. *No.*

No more closing my eyes. I didn't want to ever close them again. Not even to sleep.

Slowly, I pushed my quilt back and sat up in bed, growing dizzy for a second as the room tilted. That was normal. My point of view had changed. Holy shit.

I twisted my head from side to side trying to figure out what to do. My room didn't have a mirror in it. The bathroom did, though. I could go to the bathroom.

I pushed up from the bed and took a few tentative steps forward, looking at everything in my path. The walls were still the same light gray shade that they'd always been. My bedroom door was still white, but the doorknob was different because Rose and I had broken it a couple years before. It used to be gold, but now it was a dull silver color.

The carpet in the hallway was the same boring tan, but it was far more worn than it had been the last time I'd seen it. I hadn't noticed that it had felt any different as the years had gone on, but there were definite stains that Mom hadn't been able to clean.

My breathing was heavy as I reached the bathroom door, but right as I was about to swing it open, my dad's laughter drifted up from the kitchen, stopping me in my tracks.

I changed course and made my way to the top of the stairs. As I took the first step, I stumbled a little, miscalculating how far away it was. I grabbed the railing to keep myself from plummeting down on my ass. Okay, so my depth perception wasn't so good. That was probably pretty standard, right? Just something I'd have to get used to.

I walked slowly, taking in everything. So much was the same, and so much was different. My mom had repainted the downstairs so many times that there was probably an inch of paint on the walls, but the last time she'd gone with a pale blue, almost green. It looked good. She'd done a good job. There were new photos on the walls. Mom hung them up constantly, but I didn't let myself look at them. Not yet. I didn't want to see how people had changed in photographs.

When I got to the kitchen, I completely froze. I couldn't move. I could barely breathe.

My parents were standing near the stove with their backs to me.

Mom was stirring something and Dad was whispering in her ear, making her chuckle. She was wearing a purple robe that I'd never seen before and her hair was in curlers. She had a freckle at the nape of her neck. I'd never noticed that freckle before. I wouldn't have cared about it before.

Dad's hair was short, like he'd recently shaved it with a pair of clippers, and his jaw was scruffy with a mixture of grey and black hair. He was wearing a bright white t-shirt that I remembered wouldn't stay that way for long.

"What's up, Lilybug?" He turned toward me. "You're up early."

His eyes met mine, and things went blurry for a minute as tears filled my eyes. I took a step forward without even thinking about it. Then another one, and another.

"Farrah," he said, in a tone I'd never heard before.

He took a step toward me and I choked out a laugh, staring at his face. "You got old," I whispered, my eyes widening. He had wrinkles where there hadn't been any before. Little lines that spread out from the corners of his eyes and between his brows. The grooves on the sides of his mouth were even deeper than they'd been before, like he'd been smiling so much that they'd finally just decided to take up permanent residence there.

"Lily?" he asked in confusion, his eyes welling up. "Baby, can you see me?"

"Yeah." The word came out as a sob, and suddenly I was pulled against his chest, his arms so tight around me that I could barely breathe.

"Oh, God," he whispered, kissing my head over and over. "Oh, God. *Finally.*"

He pulled back and I laughed a little as he reached up and absently wiped the wet from his cheeks.

"Give her to me," my mom demanded, making him take a step

back.

Mom and I both froze as we stared at each other.

"If you tell me I look old, I'll shave off your eyebrows while you sleep," she said hoarsely, making me smile.

She didn't look old at all. Her eyes had some fine lines similar to my dad's, but otherwise she looked just like I remembered her. The skin of her cheeks and around her mouth were smooth and pale, her hair still the exact shade of blonde that it had always been.

"You look beautiful," I said honestly, my nose stinging as I tried to stop the tears rolling down my cheeks.

"I've taught you well," she replied, wrapping her arms around my shoulders and kissing the side of my face. "Smart girl."

"Holy hell," my dad murmured, wrapping us both up.

"When did it come back?" Mom whispered.

"I've been seeing light for a while," I answered, laying my head on her shoulder as we continued to stand in our little huddle in the middle of the kitchen. "But I could see *everything* when I woke up this morning."

"Why didn't you tell me?" Mom asked, squeezing me tighter until little arms started pushing in between us.

"What're you guys *doing*?" my five-year-old sister asked, trying to work her way into the middle of us. "I want a hug!"

My parents pulled back so she could wiggle her way inside our huddle, and the minute I saw the top of her dark head, I fell to my knees.

My baby sister was beautiful. When I'd lost my sight, my mom had been pregnant with Charlie. I could map out her chubby cheeks and sturdy arms and legs in my sleep, but I'd never actually seen her. Her eyes widened as I reached up and gripped both sides of her head with my hands.

"Oh, my God," I whispered.

She looked just like me. We had the same eyes and the same hair, and even though her skin was lighter than mine, she had our dad's olive skin tone.

"What's goin' on?" she asked, trying to pull away. "Quit it, sissy!"

I dropped my hands and sat back on my feet as she pulled away from me, pushing her hair back from her face in a dramatic show of irritation. She looked just like my mom when she did that.

"I can see you," I told her.

"No, you can't," she replied, sticking her tongue out. "You're blind."

Her words were so matter of fact that my mom and dad both gave watery snickers.

"Not anymore," I said with a shake of my head.

"*Uh-huh*! What am I doing, then?" she asked with her tongue hanging halfway out of her mouth.

"You're sticking out your tongue," I answered. "And you look like a llama."

"I do not!" She stared at me for a long time, then turned and glanced at me over her shoulder. "What am I doing now?" she asked as she shook her little booty.

"Shaking your butt at me," I replied, laughing as I swatted her. "Knock it off, weirdo."

"You can see?" she asked, turning back slowly, her eyes wide.

"Yeah," I whispered, raising my eyebrows as I smiled huge. "How cool is that?"

"So cool!" she screamed, launching herself at me.

We hit the floor with a clatter, and I laughed hysterically as she bounced up and down on my stomach.

"Look! I got a scrape on my elbow and I have a scar right here!" she said, as she pulled her knee up for my inspection.

"Whoa, cool scar," I said, watching her face as different expressions flittered across it.

"Did you know I got a purple skateboard? Curtis and Draco got boring black ones, but mine is purple 'cause Cam painted it just for me!"

"Of course he did," I said hoarsely. " 'Cause who wants a plain black one?"

"Right? Mine's way better!"

"You guys want some breakfast?" my mom asked, trying and failing to sound nonchalant. "I'm making pancakes."

"Mom's pancakes are always shaped weird," Charlie said under her breath. "But they taste the same as Dad's."

"Good to know," I whispered back, helping her up off the floor.

As I stood up, my eyes automatically went to the sliding glass door leading to our back yard, and my breath caught. I didn't even realize I was moving toward it until my dad came up next to me and put his arms around my shoulders.

"We changed it," he said quietly.

"I see that."

"Put in that fountain. Got rid of the horseshoe pit, since I hated that fucking thing anyway."

"The picnic tables are gone," I murmured, leaning against him.

"Yeah." He cleared his throat. "Needed space for the trampoline."

"And the flowers."

"Yeah, and the flowers. Amy helped with that."

"They look good," I said, tilting my head back to look at his face. "You guys did a good job." I'd known, of course, when they'd made changes. It was hard to avoid that kind of commotion when you were living in close proximity. However, *seeing* the differences somehow made them real.

"You think?" he asked, meeting my eyes before staring out at the yard again.

"Yeah. It doesn't even look like the same yard."

"That was the idea." He sighed and pulled me tighter against him.

"Food's ready," my mom announced. "Quit looking back there. It's morbid."

I snorted and took one last look around the backyard where so many things had changed for us. It didn't even look like the place we'd lost my grandpa, grandma, great gram, and cousin Micky.

Charlie scrambled into her seat at the table and without thought, I sat in the chair next to her while my parents grabbed the food and drinks. There were a lot of things around the house that I helped out with, but we'd learned early on that bringing food to the table wasn't one of my strong suits unless I was doing it all by myself. When there was another person helping me, it turned into chaos as we tried to move around each other without colliding.

Just as I realized my mistake and started to stand up again, my dad came in behind me.

"I can help—"

"Orange juice at your 11:30," my dad said at the same time.

We both went silent for a moment.

"Whoops," he said quietly, kissing the top of my head. "It'll take some getting used to."

I nodded around the lump in my throat and glanced around the table.

"I should probably start calling people," my mom said, smiling as she sat down across from me. "Or do you want to break the news? We could have some people over, or maybe go to the club? We should celebrate."

"Uh," I stuttered out. "No."

Mom's eyebrows rose.

"Can we just... not?"

"You don't want to tell anyone?" my dad asked incredulously.

"That's not gonna work."

"No, I just don't want a party," I mumbled, the thought filling me with mortification. "We can call people, but I'd like to talk to Cam and Ceecee first. And Rose should know, too. Then we can spread the word."

"Oh," Mom said softly, disappointment coloring her voice. "Sure. That makes sense."

The rest of breakfast was mostly silent as we tried to figure out our new normal. I was sure that my parents were filled with just as many questions as I was about how our lives were about to change once again. I could suddenly do so many normal things that I hadn't been able to before. I was seventeen. Most seventeen-year-old girls could drive. They went on dates. They had more responsibilities than I did, and weren't connected at the shoulder with their cousins every day of their lives.

After my parents went upstairs, Charlie helped me clean up the kitchen, and I realized just how odd it was to have my sight again when I reached down to turn on the dishwasher and couldn't remember which buttons to push. I glanced at my sister uncomfortably as she hung a dishtowel on the fridge, then quickly closed my eyes and felt my way to the correct buttons. Leaving my fingers where they were, I opened my eyes and took a mental note of the ones I'd pushed so I could remember them for later.

It was fine, I told myself. Growing pains.

"Come see my room," Charlie ordered, grabbing my hand with her tiny one.

"I've been in your room," I reminded her as she led me upstairs. "About a million times."

"But you haven't seen my dolls," she replied stubbornly.

"Hold up," I said as we reached her bedroom door. "Go in and get your dolls, I'll be there in just a second."

I left her in her room and walked down to the hallway to my parents' bedroom door. I felt bad that I'd told my mom that she couldn't call anyone, since I knew she was dying to tell my Aunt Callie the good news. Just as I raised my hand to knock, though, I heard their voices.

"Calm down, Ladybug," my dad soothed over the sound of quiet sobs.

"I don't know what to do," Mom replied, sniffling. "Do we act like it's no big deal? It *is* a big deal. Oh, my God, Cody."

"Act however you wanna act, baby."

"But I don't want to freak her out," she sobbed. "I don't want her to think that it's been this horrible life because she was blind. What if we act really happy and she thinks that? What if we act really happy and then it comes back? It would be so much worse for her!"

"It's not gonna come back."

"You don't know that."

"And I don't think that anything we're gonna do now will make it better or worse for her if it does come back," my dad continued. "She's gonna have to deal with that shit all over again, either way."

"Why now?" she asked, her voice so quiet I could barely hear her. "Why after all these years? The doctors said that therapy would help. It didn't. They said a calm environment would help. It didn't. They thought it would've been gone within weeks!"

That was news to me. The doctors and my parents hadn't told me a word about when they expected my blindness to disappear. I'd only ever heard vague promises that someday I would be able to see again and that there were no medical issues preventing me from regaining my sight.

"Who the fuck knows," my dad said calmly. "And who the fuck cares?"

"I care! I want to know why! I want to know why it took so long if it came back so goddamn easy!"

I stepped away from the door as my mom's angry words broke at the end.

The conversation wasn't meant for me. It was private between the two of them. I knew that. But even if they had been speaking directly to me, I had no answers to give them.

I'd been afraid of everything for a long time after the attack. Every little noise made me shudder in fear. A slammed door or the sound of a car driving down our gravel road had put me into a panic. I'd had nightmares and paranoia and I'd wet the bed. But all of those things had been gone for years. It made no sense that it had taken so long for me to see.

"Are you coming?" Charlie asked impatiently, sticking her head out her bedroom door.

I nodded and went into her room, smiling as I realized that my mom had painted it in a rainbow of colors, like she hadn't been able to choose which one she liked best.

★ ★ ★

"What's so important?" Rose asked later that day as she rushed into my room. "I know you haven't done anything but sit at home since I saw you like twelve hours ago."

I smiled and turned toward her, coming to a stop when I got a look at her face. My cousin was gorgeous. Really gorgeous. Like a woman who did makeup ads or something. She was curvy, which I'd already known, but her face reminded me of that saying, "The face that launched a thousand ships," or whatever. She was striking. She had large brown eyes, thick eyebrows that were perfectly manicured, high cheekbones, and one of the poutiest mouths I'd ever seen in my life.

"What?" she asked in irritation. Then her eyes widened so much they looked like they were going to fall out of her head. "You can fucking *see* me!"

"Surprise," I said, laughing uncomfortably.

"What the fuck?" she squealed, launching herself forward so quickly, she practically tackled me onto the bed. "When did that happen? Oh, my God!"

"This morning," I said, wrapping my arms around her as she squeezed my waist. "I just woke up and it was there."

"You just opened your eyes, thinking, 'I might as well just keep them closed,' and suddenly you could see everything?" she asked in awe. "Jesus, that must have been a shock."

"I thought I was going to have a heart attack," I answered honestly.

"I bet." She let go of me and fell onto my bed. "Tell me everything."

"Nothing much to tell," I replied, closing my bedroom door. "My parents are pretty freaked out, though."

"Well, *yeah*," she muttered. "Have you told your brother and sister?"

"They were the first calls we made."

"Hey!"

"Well, I wanted to tell you in person," I said, dropping down next to her. "I told my mom that she could call your mom as soon as you were here—so she didn't accidentally spill the beans."

"Oh, shit. She was on the phone the minute I walked through the door," Rose joked.

"Yeah, probably."

"This is so crazy."

"I know." I sighed.

"I can't pick my nose whenever I want anymore. That's going to take some getting used to."

"But, hey, you also don't have to lead me around like a goat anymore."

"A goat?"

"Do you have a different animal choice?"

"Lamb?"

"Fine, a lamb, then."

Rose smiled softly and lay down on her side, resting her head on her bent elbow. "I didn't mind."

"I know." I lay down next to her, my body a mirror of hers. "Thank you."

"Shut up."

"Whatever."

We both grinned. Rose had perfectly straight teeth, and her smile was so wide I could see most of them.

"You can do your own makeup, now."

"I wouldn't even know how," I replied. "Plus, my depth perception is a little off. I can't imagine how bad it'll be with a mirror."

"Wait," Rose said, dragging out the word. *"You haven't looked in a mirror yet?"*

I threw my arm over my face and shook my head, embarrassed. I didn't want to admit that I was too afraid. I knew that there was nothing wrong with my face. I'd felt every millimeter of it with my hands at some point. But knowing that there was nothing wrong with it didn't calm the fear that I'd look at myself and not recognize the stranger staring back at me. The last time I'd looked in a mirror, I was eleven years old.

"Get up, you wuss," Rose ordered, reading my mind. "It's not like you're a hideous beast."

"Thanks," I groaned as she pulled me to my feet. "That's reassuring."

She dragged me into the bathroom and shoved me in front of the sink with little fanfare.

"See? Beautiful."

I clenched my jaw as my brown eyes watered. I looked almost the same as I had before. Thank God. My cheeks had lost the baby fat they'd had before, making my cheekbones more prominent, and the little bit of a unibrow I'd had was plucked away, but beyond that, I looked like... me.

## Chapter 7

# LEO

After a week and a half on the road meeting up with some contacts and protecting a shipment into Montana, I was ready for beer and a bed. Even when things went smoothly, going on those runs was exhausting. Some of the guys lived for it, loved getting away from the daily grind and their wives for a bit, but it had never been like that for me. I loved being on my bike and planned on doing it every day for the rest of my life, but the human part of the runs wore me the fuck out. Talking to people and making nice wasn't my strong suit.

Thankfully, we rolled into the clubhouse midday, so there weren't a ton of people around. The guys in the garage didn't give a shit that we were back and most of the women and kids who spent time on the grounds were at work and school.

"Hey," my dad called out as I strolled through the door. "How'd it go?"

He stood from the stool he'd been sitting on and gave me a quick hug. He always hugged me when I got back. It wasn't the way my mother hugged me, though. It was more of a quick check that all of my parts were in working order and there weren't any new holes that shouldn't be there.

"Went fine," I replied as he let me go, pulling away to round the bar and grab a beer out of the fridge in the back. "Nothin' to report. Montana hasn't heard anything new about the Russians or Sokolov."

"Shipment get where it needed to go?"

"Yep."

"Good." He sat back down just as my Gramps shuffled in the front door.

"Thought you were back, boyo!" Gramps called out, smiling through his messy beard. "All's well?"

"Yeah, Gramps," I replied, meeting him at the edge of the bar so he could pull me into a hug. Gramps' hugs were more like my mom's.

"Poet," my dad called out. "You hear anything?"

"Not a word," Gramps replied gruffly. "Quiet out there."

"Fuck," my dad mumbled. "Gonna go talk to Casper."

"You stink," Gramps said cheerfully after my dad had gone. "Go bathe."

I laughed and agreed with him, slapping him on the back as I made my way toward my room. I didn't keep a place outside the club. Sometimes, I stayed in my old bedroom at my parents' house, but for the most part, I lived fulltime at the club. I didn't see any reason to waste money on a place when I didn't have a woman or kids. It seemed smarter to just bank the extra cash I didn't spend on bills or my bike. I figured that someday, if I needed it, I had cash on hand if I wanted to buy a house or something. I liked keeping things simple. Plus, some of the trusted chicks at the club made extra cash by doing laundry and cleaning the bathrooms and main room, so it was a pretty sweet set up.

Twenty minutes later, I was clean and in bed, with a few fresh beers on my nightstand and beautiful silence surrounding me. Finally.

A knock on my door had me groaning in irritation as I stood up and swung it open.

"What?" I barked, my mouth falling open in surprise when I saw Lily standing in the hallway.

"You—" She threw her hand in front of her face.

"What? What's wrong?" I looked around the hallway, but no one else was there and I couldn't hear anything coming from the main room.

"Clothes," she choked out. "No clothes."

I glanced down at my boxer briefs in confusion. It's not like I was free-balling it.

"The hell are you talking about?" I asked, losing patience with her. "Did you need something, Dandelion?"

Later, I'd see the scene in slow motion, the way her hand dropped away from her face and her eyes had tracked up my chest until they'd met mine. The second I came to the realization that she was *looking* at me. The way my gut had twisted at the realization and the split second of embarrassment as her gaze found the scar on the side of my face.

But right then, it all happened in seconds, and I was left standing there completely speechless.

"Surprise," she said awkwardly.

"You can see?" I asked incredulously, searching her eyes. "It's gone?"

She shrugged, like it was no big thing. "Yeah," she murmured, her lips tipping up in the corners. "It's gone."

We stared at each other wide eyed for a long moment, and then I was yelling, my arms around her waist as I lifted her up and swung her around.

"No shit?" I asked again, still holding her as I came to a stop.

"No shit," she confirmed, her smile huge.

I grinned and leaned back a little to get a better look at that smile, and that's when I fully noticed her hands, cool and soft on my shoulders. My bare shoulders. It wouldn't have been such a big fucking deal, I went without a shirt for most of the summer and I was sure she'd touched me before, but my hands were also on her, so low on her back they were practically wrapped around her hips.

Our torsos were pressed together like pieces of a goddamn puzzle.

"That's good news," I said quietly, trying to get my shit together. I didn't know whether I should shove her away or try to act like neither of us was noticing that within seconds, our friendship had turned into something far different.

"I told Tommy not to tell you while you guys were gone," she said, her voice losing volume, too. "I wanted to tell you myself."

"So happy for you, Dandelion," I replied.

Her hand barely moved at first, just barely twitched, but then it was sliding up my shoulder to my neck, and wrapping around the side of it.

"Not a good idea," I murmured. I didn't move, though. I should have fucking moved.

"I knew you were being a pussy," she said, ignoring my warning. "Back when I felt your scar, I knew it wasn't as bad as you thought."

I could feel my heartbeat in the base of my fucking throat as she reached up and drew one fingertip down the line of my scar.

"It's barely anything," she whispered, shaking her head like she thought I was an idiot.

I wished I could blame it on booze, but I'd only had one beer. And I wished I could blame it on exhaustion, but it was only two in the afternoon. I had no excuses. None.

There was no excuse for the way I'd reached down and grabbed her ass, boosting her up so she could wrap her legs around my waist. There was no excuse for the way I'd gone after her mouth, sliding my tongue inside without any preliminaries, and biting at her lip as she whimpered. There was no excuse for the way I'd carried her into my room and slammed the door behind me, or the way I'd pressed her up against the wall and proceeded to grind against her as she rolled her hips and scored her nails down my back.

I don't know if it was common sense or the sound of someone laughing outside my door that finally knocked me back into reality, but as soon as it hit, I almost dropped her to the floor in my haste to get away. Her hair was messy and she was breathing heavy and she was fucking gorgeous, but she was also seventeen years old.

I'd always assumed I'd die young, but I'd never imagined that it would be my own brothers who'd kill me. Looking at her flushed face as she tried to figure out why I'd stopped, I realized that being killed by my own was now a distinct possibility.

"You gotta get outta here," I said, glancing at the door behind her.

"What?" she asked as she looked around in confusion.

"You gotta get outta my room. Now." I reached past her and swung open the door, quickly checking to make sure the hallway was still empty.

"What the hell, Leo?" she said as I used a hand on the small of her back to practically shove her out the door.

"I'll be out in a minute," I replied. "Give me one minute."

I slammed the door in her face and strode to my dresser, pulling out a pair of jeans and a t-shirt so I could get dressed.

I'd fucked up royally. In five years, things might be different if I was super fucking lucky. I'd lost my virginity to her older sister, which was all sorts of fucked up, no matter how you looked at it, and I knew her dad and brother would never be happy if I tried to get in with their little princess. Hell, they'd been less than pleased when I'd got with Cecilia, and that was a completely different scenario. We'd been the same age, had grown up together, and they'd known that Cecilia was going to do whatever the fuck she wanted, no matter what they thought.

Lily was different, so different. She was a genius, had colleges knocking on her door even when she'd been blind, and treated everyone like they were her best friend. She was sweet, bone deep sweet. I knew that if I ever had a chance with her, I'd have to think long and hard about what that would mean. Lily wasn't ever going to be a woman you banged for a couple of months before moving on. She was old lady material, a woman you protected any way you could.

I smiled huge as I slipped my socks and boots on. The girl had finally gotten her sight back after all that time. It was goddamn miracle. The doctors had told her parents that it would come back at some point, but I think all of us had started to assume that the blindness was going to be a permanent thing.

I hurried through my doorway and out into the main room, then stopped dead when I realized Lily had bailed.

"You bein' an asshole?" my Gramps asked from his place at the bar. "Little Lily went running out of here like her arse was on fire."

"No," I replied, walking to the front door just to make sure that she wasn't waiting for me outside on a picnic table.

"Well, you did something," he grumbled.

"I told her to wait for me so I could get dressed," I snapped, frustration pounding at my temples.

"Opened the door in your birthday suit, eh?" He laughed. "No wonder she went running."

"Can it, old man," I joked, my lips twitching even though I was irritated as hell. "I had boxers on."

"That girl's always carried a torch for you," he said as I grabbed a beer and sat down next to him. "Even when you were with her sister."

"I know," I mumbled.

"Better not go there."

"Wasn't plannin' on it."

"Oh, you're plannin' on it," Gramps said knowingly. "I know the look."

I just shook my head. There was no use arguing with him when he got into one of his moods. He was going to school me no matter what I said. The man had seen and done everything at least twice.

"Got with Amy when she was just a kid," Gramps said, like he was telling me a secret, even though I'd heard it a million times. Their story was practically Aces folklore. "She had a crush just like Lily does."

"Yeah, I know."

"Thing about crushes, boyo, is they aren't based in reality."

"What?"

"That girl's been moonin' after you for years, yeah?" He bumped the back of his hand against mine. "But she ain't in any type of love with the man ya *are*. Just the man she *sees*."

"You're not makin' sense, old timer."

"Lovin' a man like a woman does is different than lovin' a boy like a girl does. Lily's still in the girl stage, ya see? Ain't old enough or seen enough of the world to love all the different sides of ya."

"I'm aware," I replied flatly.

"Just warnin' ya, is all." He took a drink of his beer and sighed. "Amy wasn't ready for a husband when I married her. Oh, she thought she was. *I* thought she was. But lookin' back, no way in hell. Give the girl some time, is all I'm sayin'."

"I wasn't plannin' on doin' anything."

"Not to mention her pop," Gramps continued like I hadn't even spoken. "He'd kill ya and we'd never find your body."

"She's too fuckin' young," I said. I took a long drink of my beer, and then another. "That ain't gonna change any time soon."

"It'll happen if it's supposed to," Gramps said, slapping me on the back. "Patience, boyo."

I nodded and stepped away from the counter, exhaustion pulling at me. I was going to sleep for a few hours and then I'd figure out what to do about Lily.

★ ★ ★

I WASN'T GOING to do *anything* about Lily. After waking up to someone pounding on my door and getting roped into helping my mom carry groceries in for a party I hadn't known was happening that night, I'd come to the conclusion that there was nothing I *could* do. Bottom line? She was seventeen. Clearly, I wasn't going to start anything up with her.

I just needed to find a distraction for a while, and eventually she'd get the message.

She'd probably hate me. I knew that. I'd crossed a line with her and we both knew it. The careful distance I'd kept between us for the last year had been completely annihilated. Treating her like a kid the way I always had wouldn't work anymore. She'd see right through me.

I realized that the party we were having wasn't just a normal get together to blow off steam when my mom handed me a cake with Lily's name on it. Of course it was a party for her. I couldn't catch a fucking break, and the minute I decided to stay as far away from her as I could, the universe decided it was time to practically drop her in my lap.

"Did she come talk to you today?" my mom asked as she followed me inside, carrying a bag full of streamers.

"Yeah," I replied. "I saw her when I got back."

"Pretty cool, right?" she asked, smiling. "I can't believe she can see again after all this time."

"Doctors said her sight would come back," I reminded her.

"Well, yeah." She shook her head. "But still, it had been so long."

"Shit happens." I shrugged.

"What's wrong with you?" Mom asked, dropping her bags on the bar top. "You're in a pissy mood."

"Was just looking forward to some time to myself," I grumbled, setting down the cake.

"Well, you came to the wrong place," she joked. "Maybe it's time for you to get an actual apartment, huh?"

"Maybe."

## Chapter 8

# Lily

"I TOLD HER I didn't want a fucking party," I muttered to Rose, tossing a pillow on my bed. "I was pretty clear."

"They're just excited," Rose replied, hanging up a shirt.

We were in the middle of cleaning my room, and I was pissed. After the shit with Leo earlier in the day, I wanted to just curl up in my bed and replay the interaction over and over to try and find where the hell it had all gone south. Instead, I was making my bed and putting laundry away before we left for a party that all the moms had planned for me at the clubhouse.

I didn't want a freaking party. I hated being the center of attention. It made my skin crawl. I hadn't even had a birthday party with anyone outside my close family since I was six years old. I had no idea why my mother had imagined that some huge celebration would make me happy.

"Well, it's annoying."

"What's got your undies twisted?" Rose asked, flopping down onto my bed.

"I'm just annoyed," I replied.

At any other time in our lives, I would have told Rose exactly what had been playing on repeat in my mind, but for the first time, I was anxious to keep something to myself. Everyone had always had an opinion about me and Leo. Since I was little, they'd teased and joked about how much I liked him and how maybe one day he'd come around. But that had been all it was, joking. I don't think anyone, not even Rose, had ever envisioned a scenario where Leo and I actually got together. It was too weird. He was too old for me, at least right now. He'd been with my sister on and off for years. I'd never had a boyfriend and Leo had been whoring around since he realized what his parts were made for.

Twenty-four hours earlier, I would have agreed with everyone's arguments. The age difference was too big and Leo was way too experienced for me. But then, he'd kissed me, and suddenly everything had made sense. All of the arguments had seemed silly. For the first time since I'd started mooning over Leo, I'd seen an actual future where he and I were together.

Of course, all that had come crashing down around me when he'd pushed me out of his room and slammed the door in my face.

"So what did Leo say when you told him the news?" Rose asked, shoving at one of the pillows under her head until she was comfortable.

"He was excited," I replied evenly, throwing some shoes into the bottom of my closet.

"Did you see the scar?"

"Yeah, kind of hard to miss."

"Word."

"But it's not as bad as everyone acts like it is. It's just a line."

"It used to be a lot worse," Rose said somberly, rolling to face me. "When it first happened, he looked like Frankenstein. It was scary."

"It couldn't have been that bad," I argued, shaking my head.

"It was, Lil," Rose replied. "I didn't see it when it happened because no one would let me, but Will said it looked like half of Leo's face was gone before they pulled it back together."

I shuddered and reached for another pair of shoes.

"Well, it's not that bad now," I said again.

"Nope, he's been back to dreamboat status for a while," Rose joked, lightening the mood. "The guy knows how to work a room, just wait until you see it tonight."

"I'd rather not," I griped.

"Oh, come on. You know you want to see Leo acting all broody in the corner, with women flocking to him asking if he needs anything."

"I thought you said he works a room?"

"He does," she laughed. "He doesn't even have to do anything. He just sits there and I swear to God, people go to him. It's the craziest shit."

"Oh, goody," I said under my breath.

★ ★ ★

"You don't have to stay long," my dad promised as he met me and Rose outside the clubhouse a few hours later. "I know this ain't your thing."

"And you couldn't talk Mom out of it?" I asked, letting him lead me toward the front door.

"Cut your ma some slack," Dad said, kissing the top of my head. "She's excited and she wants to celebrate."

"She could've done that without me," I pointed out.

"She wants to celebrate *you*, Lilybug. She's excited for you. Proud of you. She wants to show you off for a bit. Let her, alright?"

"Yeah, yeah, okay," I agreed, smiling as I walked in the room and saw how crowded it was. Did I love being the center of attention? No. But it was still kind of nice to see how many people had turned out to celebrate the fact that I'd gotten my eyesight back.

It had been six years since the attack, and even though some of the others had been far more injured than me, I was still the last person to heal. As I glanced around the room, I realized that it wasn't only me that they were celebrating. The entire club was finally celebrating putting the aftermath of that attack behind them.

We'd lost people, and the pain of that would never go away, but finally, we could try to move on.

A cheer went up around the room as everyone realized I'd arrived, and suddenly Rose's arm was around my waist and she was forcing me to take a bow with her.

"Knock it off, nutjob," I hissed.

"No way," she replied, smiling. "I'm milking this shit."

I laughed as we stood straight again, then let her lead me around the room. I'd visited most of the people in the crowd since I'd gotten my sight back, but it was still nice to be able to see their faces again. It was amazing to me that a couple of weeks before, I'd never even seen most of the kids. I'd been making up for lost time with Charlie, my nephews, and my cousin Will's daughter, Rebel, but most of the other kids still seemed brand new to me.

Even though I could see, I still couldn't look across the room and yell at the kids by name when they were being little shits. I had to be close enough to hear their voices in order to know who was who. It was weird.

Less than an hour into the party, I'd been pulled into a chair by one of my cousins and was busy watching and laughing as the boys in my family played a game of poker where the winner seemed to be the person who could cheat the best without anyone seeing them do it. We were crowded around the small table like sardines in a can, but no one left as the game got rowdier and rowdier.

"Oh, what the fuck, Willy," my brother Cam heckled. "That was fuckin' blatant. Are we just doin' whatever we want now? 'Cause if that's what we're doin'…" He reached for the deck in the middle of the table, and my cousin Tommy slapped his hand like an old woman.

"Don't touch that!" Tommy ordered.

"New hand!" Cam demanded, tossing in his hand of cards.

"You can't just decide for the table that we're startin' over," Will argued in disbelief.

"Oldest." Cam pointed his thumb at his chest. "Makes the rules."

"Oh, bullshit," Tommy yelled, throwing his hands in the air. "Foul!"

"Foul?" Will asked, his brows pulled in so far they practically met in the middle. "We're not playin' fuckin' basketball, ya pussy."

"Cam's fuckin' cheating."

"We're all cheating!" Will and Cam yelled at the same time.

Jesus, it didn't matter how old they got, if you put the three of them together, they turned into children again. I wondered how the dynamic would have been different if Mick was still around. I had a feeling most of their nitpicking would be directed at him, as the youngest. As it was now, the only person missing from their little group was Leo, but none of them said a word about him as Tommy reluctantly dealt the cards again.

I glanced around the room, but didn't see Leo anywhere. I was sure that he was somewhere around, though. He lived at the club, and I was pretty sure he wouldn't hide out at his parents' house even if he was avoiding me. That seemed a little immature for the guy who'd been so insistent that he was too old for me.

"You playin' this round?" Tommy asked me, pulling my attention back to the table.

"Sure," I replied. "Hit me."

"Hit me, she says," Cam joked, pulling at one of my braids.

I waited and watched as the hands were dealt, then laughed under my breath as I lifted up my cards.

"Two," Will ordered.

"One," Cam said next.

"I'm good." I shrugged as Tommy took two for himself.

"She's smiling," Will said, pointing at my face. "Why's she smiling?"

"I've been watching her. She's bluffing."

"Maybe," I said, leaning back in my chair. "But are you sure?"

The boys all stared at me, and Tommy winked.

"Call," he murmured.

I set down my cards face up and laughed as Cam and Will started yelling. Somehow, and I have no idea how he did it, Tommy had dealt me a royal flush.

"Ma!" Cam yelled over the noisy crowd. "Come get your daughter! She doesn't understand the goddamn rules of poker!"

"How the fuck did you do that?" Will asked in bewilderment, lifting up my cards and looking them over. It was like he couldn't even fathom that Tommy had been the one who'd cheated on my behalf.

"You win?" my mom asked, coming up behind me. "That's my girl."

"Take her over with the women," Cam ordered, "This is a man's game."

He dodged as my mom swatted at his head.

"And just like a man, he can't handle it when a woman beats him," she joked.

"I have to pee anyway," I announced, standing from the table.

"You just want to leave before we beat you!" Will called out as I walked away from the table.

It was so crazy being able to navigate the room without touching anything. I wound around tables and people easily as I made my way to the back hallway. Thankfully, when my mom had taken me to the doctor right after my sight had come back, they'd promised that my depth perception would correct itself, and it had. The first couple of days, I'd bumped into things as I'd misjudged how far away they were, but after that, it was pretty smooth sailing.

The bathrooms in the hallway looked like they'd just got a good scrubbing, so I slid into one and did my business. I probably wouldn't get so lucky the next time I was at the club, but it was kind of freeing being able to use any bathroom I wanted without the worry of stepping or sitting on something unpleasant. Plus, since they were having a family party that night, the chances of a vomit disaster were pretty slim, unless one of the kids had some sort of sugar overload.

I knew I shouldn't, but as I left the bathroom, I detoured toward Leo's room and knocked on the door. If he was hiding out in there, I wanted to clear the air. He really didn't have to avoid me, if that was what he was doing. I could be an adult about it.

When he didn't answer the door, I knocked again.

He'd kissed me and then changed his mind. Maybe he didn't like it or something. I mean, it was pretty damn good for me, but I really had no way of knowing if it had sucked for him.

My Aunt Callie came out of my Uncle Grease's room right as I turned to walk back down the hallway.

"Hey kiddo," she said, smiling. "Enjoying your party?"

"More than I thought I would," I said dryly as she wrapped an arm around my waist.

"What, you didn't want a big party to commemorate your sight?"

"It's weird," I said, rolling my eyes.

She squeezed my waist. "Your mom is just excited for you, sweetheart."

"I know, that's the only reason I showed up."

"Sometimes, you just have to grin and bear the shit other people do for you, even when it sucks." She grinned. "Your uncle fixes shit that doesn't need fixed all the time, and I just say thank you as he tears apart my kitchen to fix the dripping faucet that only needed a new washer."

"Thank God this party isn't going to take weeks, the way that kitchen remodel did."

"Amen, sister."

I laughed as we entered the main room, but as soon as my eyes hit a familiar figure, my entire expression dropped.

Leo was standing near the bar with a very pretty blonde.

I looked away and kept moving toward the middle of the room with my aunt, but I couldn't stop myself from glancing back at him.

His hand was on her back. Really low on her back. Almost on her ass, which is where I was sure it was headed. She was leaning against him easily, like she'd been there before, and she was talking to Rocky, another guy from the club, as if she knew him.

I swallowed hard and turned away, just in time to meet Rose's eyes. She was playing pool with my Uncle Grease as little Rebel walked around, picking up pool balls and setting them back down in random spots. I shook my head at Rose, and raised my chin.

I didn't want to talk about it. I didn't want to think about it or worry about it or even remember that he was there. I just wanted to enjoy the party that I hadn't even wanted to go to.

"Ah, the guest of honor," Uncle Grease said, wrapping me in a bear hug as I reached them. "I was wonderin' why I hadn't seen you yet. You been hidin'?"

"Nah." I hugged him back and grinned a little at the familiar feeling of his massive chest and arms. "I was playing poker with the boys."

"They teachin' you how to cheat?"

"I beat them."

"Thatta girl," he said, patting my back proudly before letting me go. "Now I'm gonna beat your cousin in pool."

"Dream on, old man," Rose said haughtily, strolling around the table. "Me and Reb are gonna take you down."

"Only way you could beat me is if I was drunk and had one arm tied behind my back," Uncle Grease boasted. "And neither of those two things are happenin' tonight."

"I don't know about that," Aunt Callie said, sliding onto a chair near the pool table. "How many beers have you had, handsome?"

"Two," Uncle Grease said, holding up five fingers.

I laughed and leaned against one of the tables against the wall. I glanced around the room, ignoring the spot where I'd last seen Leo. He'd made his point, bringing that woman.

He might have been the first guy I'd ever kissed, but I promised myself he wouldn't be the last. I was young, as he was so fond of pointing out, and there would be others. Of course there would. I had one more year of high school and then I'd be off to college, away from Leo and any reminders of him.

I just had to get through one more year.

Reaching up, I pushed a fist against my churning stomach, the soda I'd drank threatening to come up at any second. Unconsciously, my eyes moved toward the bar and met Leo's. Our eyes held for a long time until he tilted his head down in apology and turned away.

Just like that, it was over.

## Chapter 9

# LEO

"THE MOTHERFUCKER IS back in Oregon?" Will asked in disbelief, leaning forward in his chair.

Even though Will's road name was Moose, I never called him that in my head. I'd grown up with the fucker, had seen him piss himself and pick his nose. It was hard for me to see him as anything but Will.

"Word is, he's in Portland at the moment," my Gramps verified darkly.

"How'd you hear that?" Hulk asked, glancing around. "You sure?"

My dad shook his head. "Poet's contacts up there are trustworthy—haven't ever given us bad info. Had Nix check it out, he verified."

My Uncle Nix wasn't a part of the club, but was considered an honorary member, if there was such a thing. He was my Grandma Amy's son and lived up north. Clean cut, mostly, but he was always willing to help out when he could. Because his life was so different than ours and he'd gone to great lengths to keep it that way, we kept him as far away from the business as we could out of respect.

"It can't stand," Grease said quietly, staring at the tabletop. "Only one reason he'd come back here."

"Don't know his plans, yet," Gramps said.

"Doesn't matter," Tommy replied. "Don't need to know the plans to stop them."

Casper looked at the door and Will reached behind him, making sure it was latched tightly.

"Need to send someone up," Casper said, locking eyes with my dad. "Got no other choice that I can see."

"I'll go," I said, before anyone else could get a word in edgewise. "Crash with Uncle Nix for a few days and take care of it."

The old timers' eyes widened in surprise, but they didn't contradict me the way I was expecting. Instead, they watched me closely, until I felt the urge to squirm in my seat. Finally, after one of the most uncomfortable silences I could remember, my dad spoke.

"You can do it?" he asked. "Got one shot. He sees us comin', the man's gone."

"I can do it," I replied with a nod.

"We sendin' anyone with him?" Casper asked.

"Don't want a presence up north if we can help it," my dad replied. "Leo goin' up to spend a few days with his uncle ain't anythin' new—add a couple more Aces and things start lookin' squirrelly."

"We really want to send the sprout on his maiden voyage to deal with Sokolov?" Grease asked seriously.

"The boy can do it," Gramps replied gravely. "Of that I have no doubt."

After that, church went by quickly as we decided when I'd leave, and how long I'd stay in Portland before heading south again. Everything had to look like I was on the up-and-up.

As soon as we spoke to my uncle, everything was planned. I'd take one of the trucks up that night, stay with my uncle for a few days, then load his bike into the bed of my truck and bring it to the garage for some work. If anyone was watching, it gave me a reason to be in Portland.

As soon as plans were made, we went back to work.

October was always rainy as hell, and I threw my hood up as I went out back to get the truck I'd be taking to Portland. I bumped into someone as I stepped outside, and as I lifted my head to apologize, the words died on my tongue.

"I wasn't watching where I was going," Lily mumbled, trying to step around me.

"You okay?" I asked, sidestepping to stop her. "Why aren't you at school?"

"In-service day," she replied. She wasn't looking at me, and I wasn't surprised.

Since the night of her party, Lily had gone out of her way to stay as far from me as she could. I'd known she'd be pissed, but I'd seriously underestimated how far she'd go to punish me. It had been months since she'd said one word to me. I was pretty sure we'd never gone that long without talking before—it was almost impossible to do when our lives were completely intertwined.

"How you been?" I asked, wincing as soon as the words were out of my mouth. I sounded like an idiot.

"I'm fine, Leo," she replied. "I'd like to go inside, though."

The rain was completely soaking us both, but I still didn't move as I stared at the side of her face. She looked older, if that was possible. Her cheeks had thinned out or something.

"Are you wearing makeup?" I asked stupidly.

"What?" She looked at me in surprise. "Yeah."

"Why?" I blurted.

"Why wouldn't I?"

"You never did before."

"I couldn't see my face before."

"You looked better without it," I said truthfully.

Her eyes widened and she shoved at my chest, pushing me to the side. "You're an asshole."

"Shit," I mumbled as she walked through the door behind me. "I didn't fuckin' mean it like that!"

I spun and followed her into the clubhouse, grateful that the place was pretty much deserted. As soon as she began to pass the door to my room, I wrapped an arm around her waist, and lifted her off her feet as I shoved my key into the lock.

"Leo," she hissed as I carried her through the doorway. "What the fuck are you doing?"

"You know I didn't mean it like that," I replied, slamming the door behind me. "You don't get to be pissed because I said you were prettier without makeup."

"Are you fucking with me right now?" she asked incredulously. "Fine, you didn't mean it. Bye, Leo."

"No," I said stubbornly, leaning against the door.

"Jesus Christ," she muttered.

"You haven't talked to me," I said, pointing at her until she slapped my hand out of the air. "You've ignored me for fuckin' months."

"That's what you wanted," she replied, throwing her hands in the air.

"No, it isn't."

"I'm not your goddamn pet, Leo," she said, her eyes so dark they were almost black. "I'm not gonna follow you around like a puppy."

"I never asked you to follow me around."

"No, you wanted the opposite, right?" she asked, taking a step forward. "You started fucking someone else so I'd get the picture, *I got it.*"

"You're too fucking young for me," I yelled.

"Fine! Then leave me the fuck alone!"

"You've always been too young for me, why the fuck is anything different now?"

"Because you kissed me, you fucking idiot," she hissed. "You changed the rules, not me."

"That was a mistake," I ground out.

"Agreed," she snapped.

I could say it was a mistake. I could, but she couldn't.

"Oh, you think so?" I asked, my voice growing soft.

Her eyes widened as I moved toward her, but she refused to take a step back.

"You know it wouldn't work," she said quietly, as soon as our faces were just inches apart. "We both know it."

"You movin' on then?" I asked, reaching up to run my finger down the braid lying over her shoulder. "Gonna pretend like we weren't ever friends?"

"We weren't friends," she said, her voice barely audible. "You put up with me, but we were never friends."

I inhaled sharply, and shook my head. Resting my forehead against hers, I remembered all the times over the last two years when she'd shown up at my worst moments. Swear to God, the girl knew just when I was feeling lowest, she had a radar for that shit, and she'd show up with a smile on her face and a funny story about God knows what, and I'd instantly feel better. She had that effect on people. Without fail, Lily—with her filthy mouth and dirty sense of humor—could completely change someone's mood.

"We were friends, baby," I whispered, hating that she thought anything different.

"I don't want to watch you with someone else," she said, her mouth curling up on one side in a sad smile. "And I have to *watch* now. It's better if I just stay away."

"Not better for me," I argued.

"It's better for *me*," she said.

I couldn't argue with that, so I didn't stop her as she turned and left the room.

★ ★ ★

"Time to run the gauntlet, huh?" my Uncle Nix said, handing me a beer that night.

The drive to Portland had been easy. Driving one of the trucks wasn't my preference, but considering the fact that it was pissing rain, I wasn't going to complain. Sucked that it gave me so much time to think, though. My mind raced between the way Lily had looked at me in the clubhouse, and how I was going to get to Sokolov without anyone noticing I was at his hotel. I hated to say it, but I thought of Lily a fuck of a lot more.

"I volunteered," I told Nix, nodding my thanks for the beer.

"Why?"

I watched my uncle as he dropped onto the couch next to me, trying to figure out how to explain it to him. He was different than us—not in a bad way—he just was. He didn't live life by our rules, didn't spend his life looking over his shoulder or figuring out new ways to stay off the government's radar. He was a good guy, and definitely one I'd trust guarding my back, but he didn't have the instincts or drive that the rest of us had.

"If it wasn't me, it'd be someone else."

"I'd rather it was someone else," he replied seriously.

"Yeah, yeah," I joked, grinning. Sometimes the guy reminded me of my mom, which was weird considering that they hadn't even met until they were adults.

"You got everything you need?" he asked.

"Probably better, the less you know."

He nodded and turned up the TV, ending the conversation. It was as easy as that.

I SPENT THE next day hanging out in Nix's apartment while he was at work, and driving across town to check out the hotel Sokolov was staying at. It was a shit hole, in a nasty part of town, but the place was pretty much deserted in the middle of the day. I knew the man's room number, and tried to check it out as I drove past, but there really wasn't anything to see. All the rooms looked the same, shitty doors that would be easy to kick down, and old as hell windows.

I parked a few blocks over and threw the hood of my sweatshirt over my head, thankful for the rain. Umbrellas were rarely used by anyone except out-of-towners, so my hood would go completely noticed. If you were an Oregonian, you pulled up your hood, tilted your head toward the ground, and dealt with the fucking weather.

I could hear a few people in their rooms, TV's blaring and a couple fighting, which made me a little nervous. Thin walls were a pain in the ass when you were trying to get shit done without noticing.

I clocked Sokolov coming out of his room around lunchtime, and the fucker strolled down the street to a diner like he didn't have a care in the world. The man was still as fat and bald as the last time I'd seen a glimpse of him, but the years in prison hadn't treated him well. The guy's skin was gray. Not just pale, actually fucking gray, like a corpse.

As soon as he was in the restaurant, I went back to his room and jiggled the handle until it opened. The locks on those rooms were a fucking joke. They probably hadn't been changed since the seventies.

The room stank like some nasty aftershave, and as soon as I'd done what I needed to do, I got the fuck out of there.

I spent the rest of the day watching cable at my uncle's and eating most of the leftovers he had in the fridge. The guy never cooked for himself, so the fridge was always filled with takeout from the week. He was anal about throwing shit out, though, so I knew none of the food was too old. He was the only person I'd ever met that wrote the dates on top of the boxes, so he knew how old the food was. Smart, but also a little pathetic. Uncle Nix was obviously going through a dry spell, because every guy he'd ever been with could cook, and there was nothing homemade in the fridge.

I fell asleep from boredom around four and didn't wake up again until Nix was pushing through the front door that night with a bag of takeout in one arm and his ratty old briefcase in another. I raised my eyebrows in surprise as I glanced at my phone, realizing that it was almost eight o'clock.

"Work late?" I asked, sitting up. Shit, my eyes were blurry from sleep and I felt groggy as hell. I hated that feeling.

"Yeah," he said, dropping the food on the coffee table. "New assistant at work fucked a bunch of shit up that I had to fix before I left."

"Is she hot?"

"He's not, no. The kid's young and an idiot, and if he does this shit again, he's going to be unemployed, too."

I laughed and took the fork he was handing me, shaking my head at the beer he offered. I wasn't having anything to drink when I needed to be sharp in just a few hours.

"Thai," he said motioning to the bag of food.

We dug in and I almost groaned. Nix knew the best places in Portland to get food. He always found the hole-in-the-wall restaurants where you worried you'd get food poisoning, but decided it would probably be worth it.

"I'm gonna load up your bike in the morning," I said, my mouth full. "Grease is gonna take a look at it."

"You're not?"

"Nah, I'm in the middle of a project." I shook my head. "Grease has some time, so he'll work on it, and one of his boys'll drive it back up at the end of the week."

"That's some good service," he said with a sigh, leaning back in his seat.

"Family, and all that." I grinned. We both knew there was no way I'd be carting his bike around if I hadn't needed the cover. For longer than I could remember, he'd been bringing it to Eugene himself whenever it needed work. It gave him a reason to visit with my grandparents and see the rest of the family.

The next few hours flew by and around eleven o'clock, I got up and went to the bathroom to get ready. I threw on a set of clothes that I wouldn't mind losing and pulled a hat down low on my head, leaving my wallet on the bathroom counter as I left.

Identification was only good for the cops, and they had my fingerprints on file anyway.

"Leo," Uncle Nix called out as I reached the front door. "I'm setting the alarm."

My eyes widened in surprise.

"Setting the alarm in about two minutes. When you get back, come through my bedroom window. It'll be open. That alarm's not gonna show anyone going through the front door until seven tomorrow morning."

I nodded and left, thankful that even though I was hours away from my club brothers, I still had family watching my back.

The hotel was a lot more crowded that night, but there wasn't anyone outside beyond a couple hookers that were smoking as they left a John's room. They didn't notice me as I walked up the stairs across the breezeway from them, and I used their chatter to hide the sound of my footsteps as I made my way to the window in Sokolov's room that I'd left cracked open earlier in the day.

Slowly, so fucking slowly, I pushed it open, listening to the TV he had going. The curtains were thick, and I didn't have a problem as I made an opening large enough to fit through. Pulling my pistol from the holster under my hoodie, I stepped one foot inside and quickly brushed the curtains back. I was inside in one fluid movement, the curtains and window closed behind me before anyone could see my shadow from outside.

Sokolov was lying on the bed with his back to the door, like a fucking idiot, and he didn't move even as the window made a small snick as it latched behind me. I figured that was probably a good thing, since he hadn't started yelling the place down yet, but I got really fucking confused when he still hadn't moved as I stepped through the room.

It wasn't until I'd seen his face that I cursed.

Dude was already dead.

I couldn't see any wounds. He didn't have a single scratch on his bare torso or arms, but the man was definitely dead. His eyes were wide and unseeing, and his mouth was slack.

I huffed in disbelief.

Someone hadn't gotten there before me, the dude had just fucking *died*.

I shook my head and looked around the room, but everything was the same as the last time I'd left it. His open suitcase was on the chipped old table, and there were two pairs of shoes sitting by the door instead of the one pair that had been there earlier. It looked like he'd gotten back, stripped off his clothes and folded them neatly into his bag, and got into bed.

I checked out the window, making sure the parking lot was still deserted, put my pistol away, and walked out the door like I had every right to be in that room.

Jesus.

I laughed as I got to the truck a few minutes later. If I didn't know better, I'd think my Gramps had come up and done the job before I could get to the guy—but I knew that wasn't his style. Gramps worked with knives. If Sokolov had died from anything but natural causes, it would have been poison, and that shit was a woman's weapon.

I climbed in my uncle's window a few minutes later, and froze just inside.

"You took less time than I thought," he said nonchalantly, setting his gun back on his nightstand.

"You don't even want to know," I huffed, laughing a little.

"Nope, I don't," he replied. "Want me to help you load up the bike in the morning?"

"Nah, I got it." I strode to his bedroom door and paused in the opening. "Thanks, Uncle Nix."

"No problem, kid," he said with a nod. "Hit the light, would ya?"

I reached out and flipped the switch and closed the door behind me, realizing as I left that his eyes hadn't even searched my clothes for evidence or my face for some kind of guilt. He'd treated me like I'd been out partying and he'd covered for me, nothing more, nothing less.

★ ★ ★

"I'M BACK," I yelled to Grease after I'd backed the truck up to one of the garage bays.

"Church!" he ordered, lifting his chin at me. "Ray, come get this bike off the truck, yeah?"

The guys followed me inside the clubhouse, and we all quickly piled into the small room and sat at our places at the table. No one spoke until my dad came in behind us and sat at the head, slamming the gavel down once.

"How'd it go?" he asked, looking me over.

"Fucker was dead," I said, shaking my head.

"That was the general idea," Casper said.

"No, he was dead before I fuckin' got there," I clarified.

"Say what?" Grease asked, leaning forward to rest his elbows on the table.

"Went during the day, saw him walkin' to a restaurant down the street. Went inside his room to check shit out, and everything was cool. I went back last night, and the motherfucker was dead already."

"Someone get to him before us?" my dad asked.

"No, dude was just dead. No wounds. Died in his ratty ass hotel bed." I lifted my hands in confusion. Even after laying awake most of the night, and hours of going over it in my head as I drove, I still couldn't figure out how the fuck it had happened.

Casper coughed, and then suddenly, every man around the table was roaring with laughter.

"No shit?" Grease gasped.

"No shit," I replied, a small grin pulling at the corners of my mouth.

My smile got wider as they continued to laugh. "And I did good, too," I said over the noise. "I was like fuckin' James Bond."

That made them laugh even harder.

"In and out, easy."

"That's what she said," Cam muttered.

"Alright," my dad yelled, lifting his hand for silence. "Alright, enough." He shook his head and wiped a hand down his beard. "Everyone back to work. I gotta go tell Poet this shit."

I stayed in my seat as everyone left the room, slapping my shoulders and giving me shit for my botched first kill. Technically, it wasn't my first, but pre-meditated was different than shooting back at someone trying to take you out.

"You good?" my dad asked, laying his hand on the top of my head.

"Are you kidding?" I asked, scoffing. "I didn't do anything."

"Right." His lips twitched, and he slapped the back of my head lightly as he kept walking. "Take the day off, anyway."

I leaned back in my chair and stared at the ceiling as the clubhouse grew quiet through the open door behind me. Now that I was done doing what I needed to, my thoughts went right back to Lily.

## Chapter 10

# LILY

"WHAT THE FUCK, Lily?" Rose hissed as she slammed open my bedroom door. "I waited for you for like half-an-hour!"

"Oh, shit," I said, sitting up in bed. "Sorry, I skipped last period and came home early."

"You could have *told* me." She threw her backpack on the bed and huffed in frustration. "How the hell did you get home?"

"Brent drove me."

"Say what? Brent, the guy who stood you up at prom last year?"

"He was leaving anyway, so I caught a ride." I shrugged. I didn't have to explain myself. I had a few classes with Brent, and he was actually a pretty nice guy. We hadn't ever talked about the prom disaster, but he really didn't seem like the type to stand someone up without a good reason. If he was choosing not to tell me why, I wasn't going to push it. It was obviously private.

"You're being crazy," Rose said, looking at me in confusion. "This is like the fourth time you've skipped this month."

"Oh, whatever," I mumbled. "You skip all the time."

"Yeah, but you don't."

"I've already gotten in to most of the schools I applied for," I said, pushing her bag off my bed with my feet. "And it's not like I'm going to fail any classes. I'm so far ahead, I could stop going altogether and still pass."

"You've bailed on me a bunch of times," Rose said darkly, pushing at my feet. "What the fuck?"

"Are you pissed that I skipped today, or are you just feeling left out because I don't follow you around anymore?" I asked.

Rose jerked like I'd slapped her. "You're an asshole," she said tightly. "Fuck you, Lily."

She quickly picked up her bag and threw it over her shoulder, not even bothering to look at me again before she left my room.

I just sat there like an idiot, resentment not letting me open my mouth to apologize. I was so frustrated that I was pretty much treating everyone around me like crap, and I couldn't seem to help it.

After years of relying on everyone so much, I wanted to do shit on my own. I wanted to be by myself once in a while. I didn't want to tell people where I was every second of every day. I didn't want Rose to wait half-an-hour after school because she just assumed that I'd be riding home with her.

No one asked me what I wanted. No one thought about how I might want to do my own thing. Everyone just acted like I was the same Lily, and I wasn't. I didn't need someone to lead me around anymore. I didn't need help the way I used to, and no one seemed to notice. They just kept helping and hovering and treating me like a little kid.

I growled in frustration as I got up and slammed my bedroom door. No one was home to hear it anyway, thank God.

I'd been pushing to get my license for the past month, and I still didn't have a straight answer from my parents. It was like they couldn't deal with the fact that I wanted to be independent, so instead of answering me when I asked, they talked in circles about it until I finally gave up. That had happened at least four times, and I was so goddamn sick of it.

I'd had no control over my life for so long, and it was as if it was all bearing down on me at once. I wanted to do all of these things that other people my age were doing, but I couldn't, and it just underlined the fact that I had no control. None. Zero.

I needed to be able to get myself around. I wanted to drive myself to school and to friends' houses. I mean, I didn't really have any friends besides Rose, but maybe if I had a car, I could make some. I was so tired of being the blind girl that could see. I just wanted to be Lily, and I just wanted to be able to do normal teenage shit that everyone else got to do so I could distract myself from Leo.

It all came down to Leo, and I knew it and hated it.

His girlfriend's name was Ashley. She was blonde, gorgeous, and nice. I fucking hated that she was nice. I hated that everyone seemed to like her, even his mom. I hated that he seemed to come up in conversation, even though I did my best to avoid any mention of him.

More and more every day, I was beginning to remind myself of Cecilia, and I hated that, too.

I was just so frustrated. It went beyond the normal level of frustration that I assumed everyone felt once in a while. No, this was a frustration that colored every single thing I did. I couldn't sit and play with my baby sister or let my mom do my hair—which she loved—without wanting to scream.

Every day, I felt more and more alone. Like I was in the middle of this thick gray fog all by myself, and I had no idea how to find my way out.

I shut off my light and crawled in between my sheets.

An hour later my mom and Charlie got home, and within minutes my mom was flipping on the light as she came into my room.

"Get up," she ordered, pulling the blankets off me.

"What's wrong?" I stretched and sat up slowly, irritating the hell out of her, if her expression was anything to go by.

"Nothing's wrong." She threw her hands up in the air. "But even though you seem to think the world revolves around you, it's time you started helping out around here."

"Fine," I mumbled, getting to my feet. "What do you need?"

"Clean the bathrooms," she said flatly. "Then you can vacuum the stairs and do the kitchen floor."

"Is that it?"

"For now." She turned to walk away.

"Are you mad at me?" I asked, throwing on a sweatshirt. "Or just in a bad mood?"

"Seriously, Lil?" Mom asked, turning back around. "You've been moping around for weeks, and I have no idea what you said to Rose, but you're going to have to grovel like hell to get back into her good graces."

"Maybe I don't want to get back into her good graces." I tried to scoot around my mom in the doorway, but she stopped me with a hand on my arm.

"Get your shit together, Lily," she said softly. "Rose is your best friend in the entire world, and you're treating her like garbage."

"Is that what she said?" I asked mutinously.

"No." My mom let go of my arm and crossed hers over her chest. "She hasn't said shit. I've *seen* you doing it. I know stuff has been hard for you lately. All of us are adjusting, and I don't think it's easy for any of us. But is this really the type of person you want to be?"

I turned and walked away without answering her.

Of course it wasn't the type of person I wanted to be, I just didn't know how to stop it. Part of me wanted everyone to leave me alone, and part of me wanted someone to make everything go back to the way it was. I never wanted to be blind again, but God, I hated feeling like this. I couldn't get a handle on it.

Maybe chores would help. I was willing to try anything.

"Can I help you?" Charlie asked an hour later, bouncing into the bathroom after me, taking up what little space was left beyond where I knelt on the floor.

I wanted to snap at her, and that made me feel like shit. She was grinning and kind of swaying from side to side, and I could see how sweet she looked, but part of me wanted to yell at her to get out and let me do my chores.

"Sure," I choked out, turning back to the tub. "Grab all the dirty towels and bring them to the laundry."

"Okay!" she said happily. Then she started pulling the towels from the racks.

"Just the dirty ones," I snapped.

"Oh." She looked over at me wide-eyed, and swallowed hard. "Sorry."

Inhaling through my nose, I fought the tears that threatened. "It's okay," I said finally. "Just put the clean ones back on the shelf, okay?"

She nodded and I went back to what I was doing, forcing myself not to look back at her to make sure she was doing what I'd asked. My annoyance had been so illogical that I was ashamed. It took about one minute for her to put the folded towels away, and then she was leaving the bathroom, dragging the dirty towels down the hall to the laundry room.

I was glad when she was gone. I felt like an asshole and I just wanted to be alone while I tried to get my temper under control. I assumed she wouldn't be coming back, since I'd totally yelled at her, but a few minutes later, I froze when I heard her little voice behind me.

"Now what, sissy?" she asked, shifting from one foot to the other.

I burst into tears.

★ ★ ★

I'D DONE ALL my chores and had just dropped onto the couch for a break when I heard my dad's bike roll up to the house. It was still a little early for him to be home, but I didn't think anything of it. I was sweaty and kind of tired, and the only thing I cared about was making sure he didn't walk over the clean floors in the kitchen.

"Let's go, Lilybug," Dad called from the front door, not even bothering to step inside.

"What?" I replied, turning my head to look at him.

"Put some shoes on," he ordered. "And a coat."

He closed the door between us, and I huffed in annoyance as I dragged my ass off the couch and slid some sneakers on my feet. Mom and Charlie were doing something upstairs, so I didn't bother telling them I was leaving as I grabbed a jacket and went out front.

My dad was standing next to his bike, and when I reached him, he handed me my mom's helmet without a word. As I put it on, he turned away and climbed on the bike, waiting patiently for me to climb on behind him. Once I was situated, we were off. I stared over his shoulder as we flew down the road and tightened my arms around his waist.

I loved my dad. He was the best man I'd ever met. As we cruised down winding roads, I felt my body begin to relax for the first time in months. It began in my shoulders and worked its way down my back until I was comfortably leaning against him, my helmet resting against his cut. I closed my eyes, and just for a second, I was thirteen again, disoriented but oddly unafraid as my dad took me on my first ride after the attack.

As we began to slow, I opened my eyes and realized we were at the gate outside the club's property. We didn't stop as the prospects on the gate opened it wide enough for us to pass through, and then we were gingerly riding down the smooth gravel until we'd reached the forecourt.

My shoulders were tight again by the time my dad had parked the bike.

"Follow me," he said gruffly as we climbed off the bike.

He didn't say another word as I followed him around the side of the clubhouse. Once we were in the grassy area out back, he kept walking. Half a football field from the back of the building, he stopped and turned to me, pulling a pistol from the holster under his cut and holding it out to me.

"Uh, what?" I asked in confusion, glancing back at the building behind us.

"Take it."

I reached out and gripped the handle the way I'd been taught, then dropped my arm down so it pointed toward the ground, still staring at him in confusion.

"See that log?" he asked, pointing toward a downed tree. "Go to town."

"Uh, what?" I asked again.

Dad sighed. "You got a lot of anger in ya, a lot of frustration," he said quietly, reaching up to run his hand down the back of his head before crossing his arms over his chest. "Don't know what's causin' it. Don't know how to help ya. Figured we could start with this."

I just continued to stare at him.

"Shoot, Lilybug," he ordered, lifting his chin at the tree. "Get it out, baby."

I swallowed hard and turned toward the tree, widening my stance the way I was supposed to. Then I aimed and started firing. The first recoil took me by surprise, but I didn't pause as I continued to shoot, making adjustments as I went until I could see the bark flying up off the log every time it was hit. It didn't take long before I was out of bullets.

"Hand it here," Dad said, gesturing for the gun.

As soon as I'd given it back, he pulled a box of ammo out of the front pocket of the hoodie he was wearing under his cut. He reloaded slowly so I could see how it was done, then handed the gun back to me.

We did that four times. By the fifth, I could barely raise my arms and finally stopped.

"You wanna talk?" he asked, dropping to his ass on the wet ground.

I followed him down and wrapped my arms around my knees. I wasn't sure what to say. I barely knew why I was so angry all the time, and I had no idea how to explain it to someone else. All of the things that pissed me off seemed so small when I looked at them logically, but I couldn't help the way I felt.

"This about Leo?" he asked, shifting to get more comfortable, but not looking at me.

"No," I said quickly.

Silence surrounded us.

"Maybe some," I clarified finally.

"Makes sense," Dad said. "Not the man I'd choose for you, but I know you've always liked him."

"He's too old for me."

"Glad you see that," Dad said, humming a little in agreement.

"I can't talk about this with you," I said, leaning my chin on my knees.

"Sure you can," he argued. "You can talk to me about anything."

"And then watch you flip out? No, thanks."

"Lily," he said with a sigh. "Baby girl, I love you. There's no one on this earth that loves you more than me."

I swallowed against the lump in my throat.

"I can tell you're hurtin'. It's festerin' and tearin' at you. If I gotta hear shit I don't wanna hear so that you can finally say whatever it is you need to say—I can do that. Gladly. Ain't nothin' in this world that you can't tell me. Can't promise that I'll like it, but I can promise that it'll go no further than this field. I'm not gonna fly off the handle or bring shit up later when you piss me off, that ain't my style."

"I'm tired of everyone babying me," I said when he was finished, emotion making my voice wobble. "And I feel like an asshole because I know everyone's just trying to help."

"But you don't need help anymore," he said understandingly.

"No." I stared at the open field. "And I hate that I'm so far behind everyone else."

"How so?"

"Everyone else has their license. They go to parties and have boyfriends and jobs. And I'm over here like I'm fourteen and I still need my parents to tell me when to go to bed at night."

"Gotta be frustrating," he said quietly.

"I'm just—" I clenched my hands against the urge to scream. "I'm so fucking *pissed*."

Dad nodded.

"They fucked up my life!" I growled, tears filling my eyes. "And my own fucking mind betrayed me for years. And now I'm behind and everyone acts like I'm a little kid still, and it's not fucking fair! It's not fucking fair that I didn't get to see Charlie until she was five years old. It's not fucking fair that Mom watches me like I'm going to break at any second. It's not fucking fair that Leo looks at me like he doesn't know if he should pat me on the head or tell me he's sorry every time he sees me, when he's the one who kissed *me*!"

Dad made a surprised noise, but didn't say a word as I seethed.

"I hate that no one takes me seriously. I hate that I've become some freak show at school, like Lazarus risen from the dead. I hate that no one will leave me alone for five fucking seconds. I just want to climb into bed and sleep. Sleep is the only time that I can shut my mind off. Nothing is normal anymore. Everything is different."

I finally grew silent, my breath coming in gasps as tears ran down my face.

"Now's probably when I tell you somethin' that fixes it all," Dad said, reaching out to rub my back.

"That would be nice," I choked out.

"Yeah," he said, nodding. "Can't, though."

"Why not?"

"Nothin's gonna fix it, Lilybug," he said gently, still rubbing my back. "You think I ain't angry? Hell, you think your mom ain't been right where you're at? We've all been there, Lilybug. Life is *not* fair, you're right about that. You just gotta find a way to get rid of that anger, so it don't eat you up inside."

"I don't know how," I whispered.

"You push through, kid," he said. "You let your old man take you out to shoot at a tree stump for an hour. You start running, or break some plates, or take a baseball bat to an old car, or fuckin' talk about it. Whatever works for you."

"Do we have an old car?" I asked.

"Hell, I'll get you one—that's what you want to do. Not the point, though." He tugged on one of my braids. "You gotta stop takin' that anger out on the people who love ya, Lil. Ya gotta stop, honey. The only solid thing we got in this life is family, you don't ever want to push them away."

"I'm trying," I ground out, swiping at the tears on my cheeks. "Maybe I'm depressed."

"Maybe," my dad said. "That's the case, maybe you should be talkin' to that doctor you used to see."

"I hated therapy."

"Could help, though."

"I doubt it. This sucks."

"It does." He got to his feet and reached for me, pulling me up to stand beside him. "I've been waitin' for you to flip out for years, kid. You took everything too easy, let everything slide for too goddamn long. I know part of that was just *you*. You're not the type to wallow—never have been. But it's just been building, waiting for a time you felt comfortable to lose it."

"I don't want to feel like this."

"I know."

We made our way back to the clubhouse and changed out of our soaking wet clothes.

"Lil?" Dad called from outside the bathroom. "I gotta take care of some shit before we head home, you cool to hang out for a bit?"

I stared at myself in the mirror and tried to re-braid my tangled hair. My face was a mess from crying and I looked like a drowned rat.

"Sure," I replied. It wasn't as if I had anywhere to be. If I was home, I'd probably just be sitting in my room doing nothing.

A few minutes later, I left my dad's room and walked out to the main area of the club. There was usually someone out there to talk to, and I knew I should probably start mending fences where I could. People had started steering clear over a month before, and I grimaced as I realized that everyone had noticed that I was being an asshole.

No one had said anything, but everyone had seen it.

"Hey, there," Poet said as I grabbed a soda from behind the bar.

"Hey, Poet." I smiled easily for the first time in a long time. "Do you ever leave that bar stool?"

Poet chuckled. "Not if I can help it," he replied. "Everyone comes in here at some point and I can get a good visit in without getting off my arse."

"Smart," I said, sitting down beside him.

"How you doin'?"

"I've been better," I told him with a rueful smile. "How are you?"

"Better now that I've got a pretty girl sittin' next to me."

"Flatterer."

"Always." He smiled, making his beard twitch. "You and your pop get things figured out?"

"He made me shoot at a tree stump for an hour."

"Felt good, huh?"

"Yeah." I sighed and leaned on the bar top. "It did."

"Lots of changes, yeah?" he said, nodding a little. "You'll find your footing. Just takes a bit."

"I've been kind of an asshole," I confessed.

"We've all been there," he said with a guffaw. "You ain't done nothin' but be in a pissy mood, girl. Come to me when you've actually done somethin' worth bein' sorry about."

As he finished speaking, Leo came in the front door, sliding the hood of his sweatshirt back and shaking the rain from his shoulders.

"It might happen sooner than you think," I mumbled, the anger inside me rising up again as I met Leo's gaze.

"I'll leave you to it," Poet said with a soft pat on my shoulder. He got up from his stool and ambled away, disappearing into the back hallway.

"Hey, Dandelion," Leo said as he walked toward me. "Haven't seen you around in a while."

"On purpose," I replied, turning away from him.

"Come on," he said in frustration. "Still?"

He sidled up to the bar next to me, and leaned down so he could see my face.

"You still banging that blonde chick?" I asked, staring straight ahead. When he didn't answer, I scoffed.

"I'm fuckin' sick of this," he snapped, turning my barstool until I had no choice but to look at him. "Grow the fuck up, Lily."

I jerked back in surprise at his tone, but as soon as his words sunk in, anger like I'd never known hit me so hard that it took my breath away. My hands were shaking as I shoved at his chest, forcing him back a step as I slipped off the stool. It felt so good to shove him that I did it again.

"Fuck you, Leo," I said quietly through my teeth. "I am grown up. You walk around like you have it so bad because you have a scar on your face. Poor Leo, his pretty face isn't perfect anymore."

Leo's nostrils flared as he reached out and grabbed my arms so I couldn't shove him again.

"Poor, poor, Leo," I said nastily. "Give me a fucking break."

"You're bein' a bitch," he said, his fingers tightening on my arms.

"You're a fucking joke," I hissed, leaning forward. "You have a scar on your face? I went blind for *years*."

"This isn't a goddamn competition," he said, giving me a little shake. "What the hell is wrong with you?"

"You." My shoulders relaxed suddenly, like all the fire inside me had suddenly been extinguished. I'd blown up, and now I was left with nothing but an ache in my chest.

"I've been nothin' but good to you for your entire life," he growled, shoving me a little as he let me go. "You wanna act like I'm some monster, that's on you."

"You know," I said, shaking my head. "You *know* how I feel about you."

"You're seventeen years old!" Leo yelled, throwing his hands in the air. "What the fuck do you want me to do?"

"Wait," I yelled back, the word falling between us like an anvil.

"Lily," he said quietly, his eyes sad.

"It was like the moment I got my sight back, everything changed," I said, taking a step backward. "One minute I had you in my corner, and then when I needed you, you were gone."

"That's not how it happened," he replied, taking a step forward every time I stepped back. "You know it's not."

"All of a sudden, we were different," I said softly, lifting my hands palms up. "You kissed me and everything imploded."

"It didn't have to," he argued.

"How can I go back?" I shook my head. "I can't watch you with her. Why would you make me?"

"It's nothin'," Leo murmured, reaching for me but not making contact as I shrugged him off.

"You changed everything right when I needed you the most," I choked out as my eyes began to water. "And now, I don't know what the fuck I'm doing."

"Stop it," he growled, yanking me against his chest. "Stop. I've been right here. You know that I've been right here. Goddamnit, Lily."

"I hate this," I rasped against his cut.

"I know."

His hand went to the back of my head and pressed until my face was tucked into where his shoulder met his neck, and his other arm wrapped around my back, pulling me as close as I could get. I tried not to cry as my hands found the bottom of his sweatshirt and burrowed inside, but I couldn't stop the small sobs as I pressed my fingers against his smooth back.

I hadn't realized how much I'd counted on Leo's friendship until it wasn't there anymore. I was close with Rose, so close that we could finish each other's sentences, but Leo had always been the person that I could tell anything to and not feel judged. I could complain about my mom helping me without feeling guilty. I could tell him about how frustrated I was that other kids got to do so many things that I couldn't, and he wouldn't feel guilty the way Rose would.

He was a vault, and I was pretty sure he was only that way for me. I couldn't see Leo having the patience to listen to anyone else's complaints the way he listened to mine.

He held me tight against his body until my hands stopped shaking and my tears subsided, but he didn't completely let me go even after the storm had calmed. Instead, he just stood there in the middle of the room, running his rough fingers through my hair over and over again.

"I accidentally told my dad that you kissed me," I said apologetically, tightening my hands against his back as he stiffened.

"Jesus. You *are* pissed," he replied. He continued to run his fingers through my hair.

"He took me out back and we shot at a stump for an hour."

"Oh, yeah?"

"He thought it might help me get my anger out."

"Did it?" he asked, resting his cheek against the top of my head.

"Not as much as yelling at you," I confessed.

Leo laughed and kissed the top of my head.

"I'm sorry if telling him causes you problems," I said, tipping back my head so I could meet his eyes. "That's not why I did it."

"It probably will," Leo replied, as his hand shifted and his thumb rubbed gently along my cheek. "But he's the one that told me you were in here, so I think we're okay for now."

I smiled and rolled my eyes.

"You don't need to worry about seein' me with anyone else," Leo said after a long moment of silence. "Alright?"

"What?"

"That's over."

My eyes widened in surprise and I sputtered.

"If you start seein' someone else, though—"

"I don't want anyone else," I interrupted.

The wicked smile that appeared on his face was the best thing I'd ever seen.

## Chapter 11

# LEO

I WAS IN over my head and I knew it. I climbed off my bike in front of Ashley's apartment and glanced at the door I'd been using as my escape hatch for months. Ashley was a sweet girl and fun, too. She didn't want me all up in her business all the time, but was around when I wanted to hang out, and was cool about it when I was busy. We were no great love story, and both of us knew it, but we'd had a hell of a good time.

And I was going to end all that because a seventeen-year-old girl asked me to.

I scrubbed a hand down my face and sighed. I wasn't doing it because she asked me to. Not really. I was ending it because I didn't really care either way about Ashley, but I'd kill for Lily. It was tearing her up, and no matter how I rationalized that Lily's feelings were over the top and weren't my responsibility, I couldn't keep hurting her.

It pissed me off. I was a grown ass man. I did what I wanted, when I wanted. But somehow, watching Lily as she slowly faded over the past few months, my priorities had shifted. As Lily had gotten angrier and more withdrawn, I'd become the opposite. I'd gone out of my way to help out my brothers in the club. I'd always pitched in where I could, but I'd never been as outgoing and interested in others as I had been over the last month.

I knew, without consciously thinking about it, that I was going to need their support soon. I wasn't going to be able to let Lily keep spiraling, and the minute I stepped in, I was going to cause a shitshow.

I didn't for a second think that Lily's anger was all about me. Hell, I was pretty sure that I was just her scapegoat. No, sweet Lily was going through some shit that didn't have anything to do with me or anyone else. I'd been in her shoes. After the Russians had executed the attack on the club, I'd been livid. Yeah, I'd been pissed about my face, but it had been everything else that had set me off. We'd lost people. Friends and family that I'd grown up with and loved had been gone in less than five minutes, and there hadn't been anything I could do to stop it, even though I'd tried.

But the difference between me and Lily is that I hadn't had a single person to be pissed at. Sure, I'd done everything I could to take out as many men in the Russian organization as I could, but I hadn't had that single person to work out my frustrations on. One person that I could vent to and rail at, and at the end of the day known that they weren't going anywhere.

For better or worse, I could be that person for Lily. I could be the one to take that bullshit from her and get rid of it. I could shoulder that, easy. If she needed me to take her shit and come back for more, I'd do it. Gladly.

I took a deep breath and knocked on Ashley's door. Time to man up.

"Hey," Ashley rasped as she opened the door. "Did we have plans?"

"You look like shit," I said, pushing inside her apartment. "You alright?"

"Yeah," she shuffled toward her couch and climbed under the wadded up comforter she had stashed there. "I think I have food poisoning or something."

"Damn," I sat down at her feet and tucked the blanket around her legs. "Where did you eat?"

"Leftovers," she groaned. "Probably should have thrown them away last week."

"Damn, girl." I chuckled. There was no pretense with Ashley. She wasn't embarrassed that she'd eaten leftovers that had been in her fridge for god knows how long, just matter-of-fact about it.

"What's up?" she asked, turning her head toward me.

I rubbed a hand uncomfortably down the back of my head. I needed a haircut.

"So it's like that, huh?" she asked knowingly.

"Just not workin' out anymore," I said kindly. Breaking up with a sick person was a shitty thing to do, but I couldn't put it off. I'd already told Lily that I was done, I had to *be* done.

"Okay," she said simply. She watched me closely for a moment before closing her eyes. "It was fun while it lasted," she said with a small grin.

"Fuck yeah, it was," I replied, squeezing her foot through the blankets. "We good?"

"We were never going to last forever," she said. "That's not what this was."

I nodded and got awkwardly to my feet. As I rounded the couch, I let my hand rest on her head for a second.

"I'll steer clear of the club," she said, scooting farther into her cocoon of blankets. "I'm guessing me showing up there would cause problems for you."

"Appreciate it," I replied, sliding my hand off her tangled blonde hair as I moved toward the door.

I didn't ask how she knew. She was friends with a lot of the old ladies and some of the brothers in the club, and even though we'd never talked about it, there was no way that she would have missed my relationship with Lily. It was clear to everyone, even when Lil and I hadn't been talking. It was like an elephant in the room any time we were within fifty feet of each other.

I left her apartment feeling lighter than I had in months. I was bummed that I wouldn't see Ashley again, at least not for a while, but I was also a bit relieved that it was over. She'd been a placeholder and we'd both known it. And while I didn't think she cared, I'd still felt a bit like an asshole any time we'd been together. The sex was off the charts hot, and we'd had a good time, but I'd never been fully there with her, and I was sure she'd been able to tell.

★ ★ ★

"It's been months," Casper said a few days later as soon as we'd all sat down and my dad had pounded the gavel. "And I haven't heard shit."

"All's quiet," Grease said, picking at the grime under his fingernails like he was bored.

"Is there any way that Sokolov was let out because he was sick or some shit?" my dad asked, turning to where my gramps sat.

Gramps didn't have a seat at the table anymore, by his choice. He'd once been the vice president of the Aces, but when our president Slider had died in the Russian attack, he'd stepped down. He didn't want to be in charge without his best friend at his side, and I couldn't really blame him. The man was old as dirt, and he just wanted to spend his last years loving on his wife and hanging with his family. He still had some irons in the fire, though. He might be retired, but those irons were there until he was dead.

"No," Gramps said simply. "Sokolov cut a deal. Gotta man at the DEA that verified for me. Couldn't get the details, but he didn't go free because he was dyin'."

"And they're still sayin' it was natural causes?" Will asked.

"Yeah." Tommy nodded. "They're sayin' he died in his sleep."

"Leo's face scared him to death," Cam mumbled.

"Shut the fuck up," I replied.

"Children," Casper snapped in warning.

"So we're in the clear?" I asked, glancing around the table. It didn't seem possible, not after everything.

"We're never in the fuckin' clear," my dad said tiredly. "But for now, it looks like Sokolov is a non-issue."

The conversation moved to other shit, and for the next hour, we discussed schedules and truck routes and other business as usual. It was cold as fuck outside, and we usually slowed down a bit in the winter and early spring, but the work never stopped. The New Year usually had Casper in his office, crunching and rearranging numbers so that we wouldn't go down the way Al Capone did, while the rest of us worked our asses off in the garage so that later in the year, we had a little cushion to take time off.

A few hours later, I wasn't surprised to find Casper striding toward me as I finished up the oil change on a Ford Focus.

"Got a minute?" he asked, not bothering to wait for my answer before he was walking away again.

I cleaned off my hands as I followed him into one of the back offices, then stuffed the rag into my pocket as he shut the door firmly behind me. All of the old timers were impossible to read, but I planted my feet anyway, waiting for a blow. There was only one reason why he'd singled me out, and it wasn't for a civil conversation.

"What's your plan?" he asked as he leaned against the desk behind him.

"My plan?"

"Yeah, your plan." He crossed his arms over his chest.

"Uh, I was gonna finish up with the Focus and then I figured I'd start on that BMW that came in a couple hours ago," I replied in confusion.

"You playin' with my little girl?" he asked, his face hard. "Cause I've seen ya with her. We've all seen ya. Hell, I've been watchin' ya chase my daughters since you found out the difference between girls and boys, so

I'm wonderin' what your plan is."

"I don't have one," I replied honestly, straightening my shoulders.

"You don't have one." He reached up and scratched at the tattoo on the side of his neck.

"I care about Lily—"

"You love her?" Casper asked, cutting me off. "Don't bullshit me, kid. I ain't goin' in circles with you."

"She's too young for me."

"Good thing you know that." Casper nodded. "But that's not what I asked."

"We're friends."

"I know that," he said conversationally. "That's not the discussion we're having."

I clenched my jaw and stared at his emotionless face. "Yeah," I said finally.

"Yeah?"

"Yeah, I love her."

I braced for impact, but Casper didn't move.

"Good," he said. "You love someone, you do what's best for them. You put them first, yeah?"

"Right."

"Then you'll keep your hands to yourself, your dick in your pants, and you won't stand in her way when she goes off to college in the fall." He walked around the desk and sat down. "You can get the fuck outta my office now."

I walked away in a daze, wondering what the fuck had just happened. Any other father I knew would have given me the touch-her-and-I'll-kill-you speech. Put the fear of God into me, and sent me on my way wondering how he'd kill me when the time came.

Casper had just mind-fucked me instead.

It was both completely fucked up and impressive as hell.

"Hey, you good?" Tommy asked as I tripped over a creeper in the middle of the garage.

"I—" Looking around at all the guys working, I wondered how I should answer him. "Yeah, man," I said finally. "All good."

"What did Casper want?" he asked nosily, following me to the bay I was working in. "He warnin' you off Lily?"

"Why the fuck does everyone think it's their business?" I asked, rounding on him. "I wanna get with Lily, what's it to you?"

Tommy's eyes widened in surprise, but he didn't back down. "She's my baby cousin, so I've got an opinion," he said seriously. "And if you don't want everyone else up in your shit, you'll stop yellin'."

I huffed in frustration and clenched my fists to keep from shoving him out of my face.

"You think I'd ever do anythin' to hurt her?" I asked.

"Not on purpose."

"Then back the fuck off."

"You're a dick," Tommy said, throwing his hands in the air. "I wasn't givin' you shit, idiot. I was just wondering what the fuck that meeting in Casper's office was about and if I should start lookin' for places to hide your body."

He stalked off and I turned back to the Focus I needed to finish up, my mind reeling. I wasn't sure how everyone knew that shit had changed with Lily, but they did. It was like I had a neon sign above my head telling everyone that I was about to start World War Three in the clubhouse.

I'd promised Lily that there wouldn't be any other women, but I hadn't made any promises about her and I getting together. I still didn't see how that would work. Important or not, she was still young. She was going off to college in six months, who knew where, and I'd be left in Eugene. Whenever I said that in my head, I wanted to punch something. It made me sound like a pussy, or that I hoped she would stay in town, when that wasn't the case. I wanted her to go off to school. She needed that experience, and a mind like hers didn't deserve to go to waste at some random community college.

I was an adult. I had my shit figured out and I knew what I was going to do with the rest of my life. I was happy with the choices I'd made and I was happy with where I was at. Lily wasn't there yet. She was still in high school, for fuck's sake. She had all these opportunities spread out in front of her, just waiting for her to choose them.

Did I want to be with her? Yeah.

Did I think being with her now would be fair to her? No.

I finished up on the car, grateful that I could change the oil without paying much attention. I needed to talk to Lily and see where her head was at.

## Chapter 12

# LILY

IF I THOUGHT that my parents had forgiven and forgotten how I'd been acting, I'd been sadly mistaken. Even after I'd gone shooting with my dad and we'd talked everything out, I'd still been on my mom's shit list.

I couldn't blame her, really. She'd put up with my sister's shit for so long, she'd finally snapped when she'd had to start dealing with mine. It wasn't that my mom was an asshole, far from it, but she didn't have much patience for people that were being jerks. If I needed her, she'd be there in an instant. If I fucked up, she'd help me clean it up. But if I treated my family like garbage, there wasn't anywhere that I could hide from her.

I'd spent the week grounded from my phone and doing manual labor around the house. I wasn't sure why, after months, they'd decided to punish me, but I didn't complain. I was finding that pulling weeds and scrubbing baseboards was oddly therapeutic. Working out frustrations was actually a thing, and I was doing it. It didn't matter how small the tasks were, finishing one gave me the sense of control I needed.

It also helped that I knew that wherever Leo was, he wasn't hanging out with his girlfriend. Maybe she was his ex-girlfriend already. I wasn't sure. I'd never broken up with someone before, so I wasn't super clear on how that all worked.

I was grounded from pretty much everything, but there was one person that my parents would never forbid me from seeing.

Rose had come over every day of my punishment. My mom's only rule for her was that she couldn't help me with what I was doing that day. When I pulled weeds, she sat in a lawn chair. When I cleaned baseboards, she laid on the couch or sprawled out on the floor near me. The day I had to clean out the garage, she sat on the bumper of my mom's car and watched. Unfortunately for me, the garage was a catchall for shit that needed to be sold or donated since my dad had a shop on the property where he did all of his tinkering, so I had to sort through years of old clothes and broken toys.

"I'm glad you're not being a bitch anymore," Rose said conversationally as I stacked another pile of clothes into a garbage bag. "I didn't want to hurt you, but I would've."

I snorted. "No, you wouldn't have. Too many years of conditioning—you'd never be able to do it."

"Oh, I don't know. I almost decked you when you let Brent drive you home."

"Sorry about that," I said, throwing my sweaty braid over my shoulder. It was cold as shit outside and I was sweating like a pig. There was something wrong with that scenario. "I was having a moment."

"You were having a lot of moments," she said dryly.

"I know. I already had a come to Jesus talk with my dad, remember?"

"I get it, you were frustrated," she said, coming inside the garage as it started raining again. "But I'm your best friend, dipshit. I'm the one you're supposed to talk to about that stuff."

"I know, I just felt guilty about it, which pissed me off more. I didn't want to complain."

"That's stupid."

"Yeah, yeah—hey, you're not supposed to be helping me," I said as she grabbed a pair of jeans off the floor and stuffed them in the garbage bag.

"What's Aunt Farrah going to do? Ground me?" she laughed, even though we both knew it was a possibility. Our parents had pretty much shared responsibility for punishing us since we were little. We were together so often and they trusted each other so much that usually if one of us was in trouble, they just punished both of us at the same time. The worst part about it was that Aunt Callie could take away TV at their house and my mom would enforce it at our house. It sucked.

"Brent's actually an okay guy," I said, reaching around her for another stack of clothes. "I'm not sure why he stood me up, but I don't think he wanted to."

"Dude had a pretty solid black eye when he came to school, so you could be right."

"Do you think he got jumped or something?" I asked, marking down the clothes I'd just packed. My mom liked to have exact numbers so she could write in the donations on her taxes.

"Nah, not with only a black eye. He seemed fine otherwise. That's how I knew that none of the guys got to him."

I laughed. "You actually thought that?"

"I wondered," she said. "Especially after Leo swooped in and spent the night cheering you up."

"Good grief."

"Well, he did magically show up to save the day," she said, elbowing me in the side.

"Coincidence."

"What's going on with you two?"

"Bravo," I said, laughing.

"What?"

"You held out for an entire week before you asked about it." I clapped like I was giving her a round of applause.

"I was too busy letting you grovel to ask you about the gorgeous older man you've been lusting after for years."

"Not years," I argued.

"At least two years," she countered.

"Fine."

"Well?"

I sighed and fell back onto my ass. I needed to take a break anyway. "We got into a fight."

"You're not still fighting, I can tell," she said knowingly.

"Nope." I grinned and rolled my eyes. "He said he's going to stop seeing the blonde girl."

"Ashley?"

"Is that her name? I didn't ask," I said, even though I was perfectly aware of her name.

I started to fold more clothes, but stopped when Rose smacked a shirt out of my hands.

"What does that mean?" she whispered, glancing at the closed door between the garage and the house. "Are you two a thing now?"

"I don't know," I replied, shrugging. "We didn't really work that part out."

"Well, what did he say?"

"That I didn't have to worry about seeing him with other people as long as I wasn't with other people."

"Holy shit," she breathed. "Leo's the jealous type."

"Are you surprised?" I asked dryly.

"Not at all. But still, that's nuts. I mean, I knew you guys had a thing, but I didn't realize it was going to be a *thing*."

"Why do you and my mom think that changing the tone of your voice changes the meaning of a word?" I asked.

"Stop changing the subject. What are you going to do?"

"I don't know," I said truthfully. "I haven't talked to him since I've been on house arrest, but the ball is in his court."

"Uncle Casper is going to flip."

"I accidently told my dad about the kiss—"

"Wait," she yelled, her eyes wide. "Back up. *What kiss?*"

★ ★ ★

AN HOUR LATER, Rose had finally worn my mom down enough that I could actually leave the house.

"You can go with Rose to Tommy's," my mom said, crossing her arms over her chest. "Then straight home."

Rose raised her fist and knocked her knuckles against mine as we hurried out the front door. Her car was parked haphazardly in the driveway, and we scrambled to get inside before my mom changed her mind. In less than a minute, we were barreling down the highway.

"I'm not sure who's going to be there," Rose warned. "You might want to fix your hair."

"Good call." I reached up and tried to get my mop of black hair into some sort of a style. Thankfully, I'd had years to perfect styling it without looking in a mirror, so by the time we parked on Tommy's street, I was reasonably sure that it looked okay.

"Whoa," I murmured as we stepped onto the sidewalk. "There's a ton of people here."

"Yeah, I think it's Hawk's birthday. We're having dinner at my house in a few days to celebrate."

Rose strode toward the front door like she was meant to be there, when I knew for a fact that she hadn't been invited. She'd overheard her brothers talking about it a couple days before, and as soon as I'd given her the story about Leo, she'd become convinced that we needed to go to the party and make sure he hadn't brought his girlfriend.

My cousin wasn't exactly trusting of the male gender when it came to fidelity. We knew a lot of men who were faithful to their wives, but I couldn't argue whenever she pointed out that wives were different than girlfriends... or whatever I was. We'd been around too often when her brothers and other guys from the club had been complete man-whores.

"Dang," she said quietly as we pushed our way into the house.

The music was loud, and the people were even louder as we made our way toward the back of the house. I didn't know anyone in the living room or the entryway, but they still gave us space to move between them as Rose navigated through the mass of people.

When we finally reached the kitchen, we found everyone we'd come to see. They were standing around the counter laughing as they took shots of tequila. My sister-in-law Trix's face screwed up in disgust, but she didn't quickly chase the booze with something softer the way Hawk and Molly did.

"The party can start," Rose announced, getting everyone's attention. "I'm here!"

She was so much like my mother that I sometimes wondered if we'd been switched as infants.

"The hell are you doing here?" Will growled, looking past Rose to scowl at me.

"Hey, I'm just along for the ride," I protested, trying not to laugh. He looked so pissed, and I'd always had a hard time keeping a straight face when the older boys got angry. They were all bark and absolutely zero bite when it came to me and Rose.

"Baby sister," Cam said, stepping around Trix. "Ma know you're here?"

"Actually, yes," I answered as he pulled me under his arm.

"Does she know there's a party goin' on?"

"Well," I hedged. "I'm not sure if Mom knows or not."

"Uh-huh."

"You drinking?" Hawk asked, lifting the tequila bottle and shaking it from side to side.

"No!" almost every voice in the kitchen answered.

"Well, that's not very hospitable," Rose complained.

"You're lucky we're not tossing your little asses out," Tommy replied, pointing his beer bottle at her.

"We can stay?" Rose asked, a huge grin on her face.

Instead of answering her, he hopped on the counter and stood there with his head brushing the light. It was a good thing their ceilings were so high, or he would have knocked himself out.

"Hey," he yelled, grabbing everyone's attention. "I see anyone givin' either of these girls a drink or *anythin'* else, you'll deal with me." He looked around the room, making eye contact with people. "And then I'll hand you off to my brother."

"Oh, my God," I mumbled in embarrassment as my brother's body shook with laughter.

"How's all that hard labor been treatin' ya?" Cam asked, giving my shoulder a little shake.

"Sucks," I replied as Trix handed me a soda and conversations started back up around us. "But I think she's letting up."

"Honestly, I think she's just been worried," Cam said, kissing my head. "Grounding you meant she could keep an eye on you."

"You think?"

"Yeah." He nodded. "Callie went off the deep end when they were younger, and I know Ma did, too. She's just trying to make sure you don't."

"I won't."

"You've been moping around since you got your sight back," Trix said, cocking her head to the side. "Seems like you'd be doing cartwheels."

"I'm happy about it," I protested, looking around the room. "I'm just having a hard time with all the shit that comes with it."

"Big adjustment," Trix agreed.

"I'm just like everyone else now," I said, saluting her with my soda.

"But, *not*."

"That asshole have anything to do with your whining?" Cam asked, nodding toward Leo.

"Oh, shut it."

"Cam," Trix scoffed.

"What? He keeps lookin' over here. You think I don't know what's goin' on? I see that Ashley's missin' tonight."

"She better be," I mumbled.

"What's that, baby sister?"

"Mind your own business."

"You are my business," he said, wrapping his massive arm around my head in an annoying version of a headlock. "You'll always be my business."

"Get off of me," I screeched, pulling at his arm.

"Make me."

"Oh, good. We've reverted back to grade school," Trix said in annoyance. "Leave her alone, Cam."

"Such a baby," Cam complained as he let me go.

"I'm sorry, your brother's a pain in the ass when he's drinking."

"Yeah, no shit."

"I'm a pain in the ass, huh?" Cam asked, taking a step toward Trix. "You poor thing."

"Don't do it," Trix warned, laughing as she stepped backward. "Cameron, I'm not joking."

"You're not?" he asked, raising his eyebrows. "You sure?"

I slipped away as Cam threw Trix over his shoulder and strode out of the room, her screams getting lost in the music and people.

The rest of the group was still standing around the counter talking as I found a spot between Leo and Molly. Will was telling a story about something that happened in the garage that week, but I barely paid attention as Leo's eyes found mine.

"Hey, Dandelion," he said quietly, a small smile making his eyes crinkle at the corners. "They finally let you out, huh?"

"Yeah." I leaned a little closer until our arms were barely touching.

"Everything good?"

"You're here alone?"

"Yeah." He gave a decisive nod.

"Then everything's good."

He chuckled under his breath and winked at me, and it was like the freaking sun had come out for the first time in months.

"Hey, now," Tommy said, pointing at us. "What I said goes for you, too."

"Shut up, Tommy," I ground out.

"I'm not gonna be givin' her anythin'," Leo said in disgust.

"Better not be," Will said.

"Oh, whatever," Rose piped in. "Hey, where's that hot blonde guy that was hanging around the club for a while?"

"Say what?" Will asked, glaring at his sister.

"Think she means Copper," Leo answered, his lips twitching.

"Oh, fuck no," Tommy yelled.

"What?" Rose asked innocently, meeting my eyes for just a second in solidarity. "He's one hot piece of male meat."

"Word," Hawk agreed, nodding.

"You'll stay the fuck away from him," Tommy ordered.

"Eh, we'll see." Rose shrugged.

As they argued, I felt Leo's hand tangle with mine, giving it a squeeze before he rested it back on the counter. A few minutes later, I slipped away and outside onto the small back porch. Tommy's house looked brand new, but his huge yard was still an overgrown mess. He was planning on working on it next summer, and I was pretty sure by the time he was done with it, it would look like something out of a magazine. My cousin never did anything half-assed.

"I wondered where you'd snuck off to," I heard behind me after just a few minutes.

I smiled as Leo came up beside me and rested his elbows on the railing next to mine.

"Having fun?" I asked, glancing up at him.

"Night's better now that you showed up."

"Of course it is. I'm awesome."

"You sound like Farrah."

"I'll take that as a compliment."

"I meant it as one."

We went silent then, and I had no idea what to say. Things had always been so easy between us, but now it was as if we had all of these unsaid things making it impossible to chatter about nothing.

"How have you been?" he asked quietly, reaching into his pocket for a cigarette.

"Better." I watched him out of the corner of my eye as he lit up and took a deep drag. "My dad thinks that I should go back to therapy."

"Might not be a bad idea," he pointed out. "What do you think?"

"I think I've had enough therapy to last my entire life."

"Could help, though."

"Maybe."

He was quiet for a minute, then turned his head to look at me. "You can talk to me, Dandelion. You know that, right?"

"I know."

"About anythin', any time."

"I know."

"So what's new, then? You get into all the colleges you applied to?"

"Most of them," I answered quietly, my stomach clenching at the thought of going anywhere. "Now I just need to figure out who will give the best scholarship."

"Gettin' scholarships, too?" He whistled quietly like he was impressed.

"Of course," I grinned proudly. "I applied for every one I could think of. Grants, too."

"Smart."

"I just don't want my parents going into debt so that I can go to some fancy school." I shrugged.

"You know they'll do whatever they have to. Ain't every day that you raise a genius. You gotta nurture that."

"Yeah, yeah." I'd been hearing different versions of that my entire life. I knew my family was proud of me, but honestly, I'd never really felt any different than my siblings and cousins. I had my parents to thank for that.

"So, what schools are at the top of your list?" Leo asked, looking away.

"U of O, of course."

"Of course," he said with a smile.

"But, the University of Washington, too. And Yale. Did you know my dad went to Yale? He's pushing for that, even though the tuition is ridiculous."

"Yale." Leo shook his head. "What a trip."

"I got in to three Ivy League schools," I confessed with a sigh. "But even if I got the scholarships I applied for, I'd still have massive amounts of tuition to cover."

"Worth it, though."

"I'd also be across the country." The thought of that made my chest ache.

"Only for a few years."

"Only?"

"You could do it," he said seriously, elbowing me gently. "You'd have the whole damn world at your feet with a diploma from a school like that."

"What if I don't want the world at my feet?"

"Can't imagine why you wouldn't."

"Maybe I just want you," I said quietly. I was watching him so closely that I knew the second he stopped breathing.

He turned to me, the light from the windows illuminating the scarred side of his face, and I tipped up my chin as he leaned forward until our noses were nearly touching.

"You've got me," he said, his hand sliding across my belly until it reached my hip. "Don't matter where you are, beautiful."

"Leo," I groaned into his mouth as his lips finally met mine. His hands stayed where they were, one gripping the railing and the other wrapped around my hip, but the kiss was just as overwhelming as our first. I inhaled the scent of him, my hands resting on the sides of his cut, and I let the feeling of his mouth on mine seep into every pore of my body. The kiss was a promise, it was reassurance and possession all at once.

It was everything I'd been waiting for and something I hadn't even known existed.

"Hate to break up the party," Rose called quietly from the back door, breaking the spell. "But Cam and Trix must be done bumping uglies because he's searching the house for you, Lil."

I pulled my lips from Leo's and made a noise of disgust. I didn't want to ever hear about my brother bumping anything.

"Thanks, Rose," I mumbled, dropping my head against Leo's chest.

"I'll just hang out here until you decide to go in," she said, closing the door behind her. "No need for blood to spill."

"It's all good," Leo replied, kissing the top of my head before pulling away. "I'm gonna head out."

"What, no," I protested.

"Yeah." He leaned down and gave me a quick peck on the lips. "We can finish this conversation later."

I stood there dumbly as he hopped over the railing and made his way around the side of the house.

"Damn, that guy is hot," Rose said, wrapping her arm around my shoulder as we stared at where Leo had disappeared. "I mean, I always thought he was, but the way he looks at you makes him a thousand times hotter."

"I think," I said roughly, clearing my throat. "I think that was the beginning."

"Of what?"

"Of everything."

## Chapter 13

# LEO

EVERY TIME LILY smiled, I felt it in my chest. The feeling reminded me of the few times I'd had the wind knocked out of me. That split second of almost panic before I'd realize that I just had to give my body a second to adjust.

I'd seen her a lot in the last month, and I swear whenever people saw us together, they watched us like animals in a zoo. The boys couldn't believe that Casper was letting his baby spend time with me. Hell, I couldn't believe it either.

I also couldn't believe how innocent our time together was. We went for rides. She sat next to me while I worked. We listened to music in my room, with the door open. I took her out to eat, took her to the pumpkin patch and let myself get lost in a corn maze with her. I even picked her up from school a few times and took her home when I knew that I wouldn't be able to see her otherwise.

We were dating like middle schoolers, and I didn't give a single fuck. My hand was taking care of business downstairs for the first time in years, and it didn't bother me a bit. I was just happy to spend time with her.

I couldn't get over the way her mind worked. She was always thinking ten steps ahead of everyone else. She saw shit that other people never noticed, and it was like she filed it away in case she'd need the information later. It was really similar to the way I'd seen Casper figure shit out, but I had a feeling that in a few years, after Lily had a bit more life experience, she'd leave her dad in the dust.

I'd done okay in school and I'd never had a hard time as long as I finished my assignments, but Lily was in an entirely different league. It was so fucking cool to watch. I had no idea how our school system had kept her engaged as she'd gotten older. I was almost positive that she could think circles around all the teachers in her high school.

I'd become one of those guys that noticed every single brush of skin. I'd never really thought about it before, but now, I knew the second that Lily's hand brushed down the back of my arm. I noticed any time her knee bumped mine underneath a table, or her shoulder rubbed against my chest as she brushed past me. All of those touches meant something. We were in a dance. I was the person standing in the middle of the room and she was the person spinning in front of me, crooking her finger to try and tempt me into movement.

She reached up and ran her fingers over the back of my neck when I was focused on something, rested her hand on my thigh when I drove her somewhere in my old truck, gripped my fingers in hers if we were walking side-by-side.

I never discouraged her.

I also never instigated more.

I could hear Casper's voice constantly reminding me that if I loved her, I wouldn't hold her back. I wouldn't give her a reason to bail on school or choose a lesser school just to be closer to me. It was my job to make sure that she knew she should go to the best school, not the one that kept her near me, but the one that would help her build a future. If I wanted to be with her, and I did, it was my responsibility to make sure that she picked wisely and for the right reasons. Because of that, I kept our touching to a minimum, no matter how badly I wanted my hands on her.

It was only a few months until she turned 18, but at that point, it no longer mattered. Sex changed things, especially sex with someone you cared about. It made feelings stronger and connections tighter, and that would be multiplied for Lily because she'd never been with anyone else.

I couldn't tie her to me like that. Not yet.

So, like Casper had told me to that day in his office, I kept my hands to myself and my dick in my pants. It was easier than I'd thought it would be.

Loving her made everything easier.

"Guess who," Lily whispered, covering my eyes with her slender fingers as I sprawled out on a couch reading. I swallowed hard as she bit gently on my earlobe.

"Mom?" I asked, feigning confusion.

"Oh, gross!" Her hands flew off my eyes as I laughed.

"What're you doing here, gorgeous?" I asked, shifting a bit as she sat down. I was laying lengthwise across the cushions, and her ass was half in my lap and half between my hip and the back of the couch. It felt a little too good.

"Got out a bit early, so I came here instead of going home. Why aren't you working?"

"Slow day." Resting my hand on her thigh, I allowed my thumb to smooth back and forth across her jeans, but no more than that. "I'm flush, so I took the day off to let some of the other guys work."

"That was nice of you," she said, smiling.

"Worked out well for me," I pointed out, shaking the book in my hand. "Gave me some time to read."

"I love it that you read."

"Everyone reads."

"Not everyone reads for pleasure."

Listening to her say pleasure was the highlight of my week.

"Most people just haven't found the right book yet," I said, dropping my paperback on the floor so I could fold my arm behind my head. "Or they have a hard time reading, but that would get better with practice."

"What's your favorite book?"

"Don't have one."

"Bullshit," she said, pinching my chest.

"I'm serious," I argued, grabbing her hand. "I have a bunch of books I re-read, but I don't have a single favorite. Depends on what I'm in the mood for."

"I like romance novels."

"I've read a couple 'a good ones," I agreed, nodding.

"No way!"

"Yes, way." I laughed. "You'd be surprised at how many romance novels are floatin' around inside. I musta read like ten of 'em last time I was in."

"How long were you there?"

"Just the weekend."

"That's a lot of books in one weekend."

"What the fuck else was I supposed to do?"

"Good point," she said, nodding.

"Like this better," I said quietly, grabbing my book off the floor. "Sittin' here on a couch that smells like stale beer and weed, with a little sci-fi novel and you in my lap."

She blew me a kiss, then leaned back and yanked her backpack from behind the couch.

"I'll make it even better," she said, lifting her eyebrows up and down.

She turned and slid until her head was on the arm of the opposite end of the couch, wiggled her ass until it was between my knees on the cushions, then brought her feet up and rested them on my belly, crossed at the ankles. A few seconds later, she had her own paperback in her hands and was happily ignoring me beyond the hand that was softly rubbing circular patterns on my shin.

"Jesus Christ, you're perfect," I said hoarsely, staring at her.

"I've been telling you that for years," she said without taking her eyes off her book.

After an hour of silence, Casper came in the front door looking for her.

"Time to go, Lilybug," he called, his eyes tracking from my end of the couch to hers. He paused and stared at the way my hand was wrapped around Lily's foot, my thumb massaging the arch, but he didn't say a word.

"Okay, Daddio," she replied, wiggling her toes before lifting her feet from my belly and spinning in her seat until they landed on the floor. "Be right out."

"We should do this every day," Lily said quietly, glancing at me as she stuffed her book back into her bag.

"I can make that happen," I said, watching as her braid fell over her shoulder and she absentmindedly threw it back behind her.

"You're the best part of my day," she said, looking quickly at her dad across the room before she lowered her voice even further. "I wish—"

"Come on, kiddo," Casper called, cutting her off.

I never knew what she was going to say. She hopped off the couch and gave me a huge smile before spinning toward her dad and following him out of the clubhouse. If I'd known what would happen the next morning, I would've stopped her. I still don't know what I could've said that would have made what came next any easier, but I would've said something. Maybe told her I loved her, no matter what. That I believed that she was going to do big things with her life. That she was the smartest person I'd ever met. That if it was up to me, she'd never hurt or want for anything for the rest of her life.

Instead, I just watched her go, my lips twitching as she bumped her dad with her hip as she passed him.

★ ★ ★

"WE'RE GOING TO that bar Trix likes tonight," Cam told me as he helped me jack up a Corolla. "Hopefully, the place won't be packed."

"You know it's gonna be," I replied, shaking my head. "That place is always crowded on Fridays."

"The things I do for my woman," Cam grunted.

"You know my sister leads you around by the short and curlies," I huffed back. "Jesus, this car is a pain in the ass."

"Why the fuck are they trying to salvage this piece of shit?"

"Nostalgia, I think. The guy that came in said his wife has had it since she started drivin'."

"Cheap ass doesn't want to upgrade," Cam said derisively.

"Could be."

"So you comin' tonight?"

"Probably not." I laughed at his scowl. "I stopped havin' to do what my sister said when I got bigger than her."

"You know that ain't true," Cam joked. "I'll just make sure she asks you directly."

"I won't answer my phone," I warned. He knew that I had a hard time telling my sister no about anything.

"Yo, Leo," Tommy called, his tone off somehow. "You got a visitor."

"Christ," I mumbled, grabbing a rag to wipe my hands. "What now?"

I turned and walked toward the front of the garage, pausing in surprise when I saw Ashley standing there awkwardly. She wasn't wearing any makeup, but she wasn't really a woman who needed it anyway so that didn't really alarm me. It wasn't until I saw the scared shitless look on her face that I wanted to spin on my heel and run in the opposite direction.

If the woman gave me some fucking STD, I was going to lose it.

"Hey," she said, glancing over my shoulder at the guys. "You have a minute?"

"Sure." I didn't look behind me at the men I knew were watching every move I made. They knew the situation with Lily—or at least thought they did—and I had a feeling that none of them were pleased that Ashley was showing up to see me.

"Come on," I said, ushering her toward the front door of the clubhouse. "Let's get out of the rain."

"I'm sorry I'm bothering you at work," she said as we hurried inside. "I didn't want to show up, you know, when she was here."

"Not sure showing up in the middle of the day was any better," I replied. "It's fine, though. What's up?"

We stood awkwardly right inside the door, but I didn't offer her a seat. I didn't want to give the impression that her visit was welcome. I knew that made me an asshole, but fuck, the minute Lily heard about this she was going to flip. It didn't matter how innocent Ashley's visit was, if Lily heard I was hanging out with her, she'd lose her mind. After all the times she'd seen me whoring around while she waited on the sidelines, I couldn't stomach the thought of her worrying about that shit now.

"I'm so sorry," Ashley said, crossing her arms over her chest. "I'm so sorry, Leo."

"For what?" I asked in confusion. My mind raced. "What the fuck did you do?"

Thoughts of her in bed with our enemies or even worse, the police, made me stare at her in horror.

"I swear to God, I was on birth control. I had an IUD, you know? They put it in and it was supposed to work for like five years. They said it would work."

Black edged at my vision and I shook my head to clear it. No. No fucking way.

"I didn't have to take pills or anything, so that way I knew I wouldn't forget."

"No," I mumbled, unable to take my eyes off her face, even though I wanted so badly to look around the room for someone to save my ass.

"I was going to get an abortion—"

My stomach pitched like I was going to be sick.

"—but I couldn't do it. I'm so sorry, Leo."

"You're sure?" I rasped out. She nodded. "You're sure it's mine?"

She winced, but nodded. I hoped she saw it as a fair question. We'd been with each other a lot, but neither of us had made any promises. For all I knew, she'd been seeing other people.

"Fuck me," I breathed, finally able to look away. The room was spinning as I stared at my work boots, trying to make sense of the epic clusterfuck my life had just become.

"I don't need anything from you," she said quietly, her voice wobbling. "You didn't ask for this and—"

"You didn't ask for it either," I cut in, wiping my hand down my face as I tried to find some sense of control.

"I didn't want to say anything. I have a good job, and I've got this. But telling you was the right thing to do," she said, shrugging. She brushed at the tears on her face.

"Thank you," I replied, meeting her eyes again. Even if it was the most unwelcome news I could've imagined, the thought of having a kid out there that I knew nothing about was abhorrent.

"You're welcome," she said, shuffling her feet a little. "The doctor said I just hit my second trimester, so I've still got a long way to go before it gets here."

I nodded dumbly, wondering what else I should say. What the fuck was I supposed to say?

"Okay, well," she said, sighing. "I'll keep you updated, okay?"

I nodded, my tongue glued to the roof of my mouth, making speech impossible.

I stood there silently as she left, and then I stood there some more, my eyes so wide that I was sure they looked like they were going to pop out of my head at any second.

I swayed on my feet, but didn't reach for anything, kind of hoping I'd go down and knock myself out.

"Whoa, kid," Casper said from behind me, his hands grabbing my shoulders. "Take a seat."

As soon as I'd dropped into a chair and he saw my face, he jerked back.

"You're pale as your mother," he said. "Never thought I'd see that happen. You okay?"

"Ashley's pregnant," I replied.

I saw his fist come at my face in slow motion, but I didn't move, just closed my eyes and let it come.

"Goddamn it, Leo," he said as I recovered from the punch that had rattled my jaw.

"What the fuck am I going to do?" I whispered, clenching my jaw against the very real urge to cry.

"Shit," he said softly. Then, without any warning, Lily's dad was hugging me tight, his hand on the back of my head, pushing my eyes against his shoulder. "It's alright, son. It's gonna be alright."

I didn't really see how that was possible.

# Chapter 14

# LILY

"You don't know me," I yelled at Rose as she tried to steal my Spanish homework so she could copy it. "Don't tell me how to live my life!"

"You're such an asshole," she laughed. "Hand it over."

"Why don't you just do it yourself?"

"Because I want a good grade and you're the one who got into Yale!"

"*Shh*," I warned, smacking her with the paper. "I haven't told my parents, idiot."

"Well, why not?" she asked, snatching the paper out of my hand.

"Because my dad really wants me to go there, and I don't want to hear it."

"You're going," Rose said, shaking her head. "You're not stupid enough to give up Yale."

"I got into plenty of other schools."

"Yeah, but *Yale*."

"It's really expensive."

"So? Dude, if you graduate from Yale, you can pay off all your loans with the fancy ass job you get."

"I think I want to stay in Oregon," I said quietly, not meeting her eyes as I pulled my calculus book out of my backpack. "In-state tuition is way cheaper."

"Oh, bullshit," Rose said, slapping my bed. "You just don't want to leave Leo."

A knock on my bedroom door silenced me before I could protest.

"Lily, you've got a visitor downstairs," my dad said through the door.

"A visitor?" Rose asked as his footsteps grew faint. "Who'd come to see you? I'm already here."

"No idea." I rolled off my bed and soothed down my braid. "I'll be right back."

I jogged down the stairs and came to an abrupt stop when I saw Leo standing in the middle of our living room. He looked like shit. His eyes were bloodshot as hell, and his face was paler than I'd ever seen it. He looked sick.

"What's wrong?" I asked, fear making my voice come out high.

"Lily," he said, taking a step forward.

"You never call me Lily," I replied, watching him carefully.

"You're the most—"

"You never call me Lily," I said again, suspiciously, my heart beginning to race.

"Baby—"

"Why are you calling me Lily?"

"Dandelion," he said softly, taking another step toward me.

"No," I ordered, raising my hand. "Stop."

Leo's shoulders dropped, and I felt everything inside me, everything that made me *me*, begin to shake. That's when I noticed that my dad had left Leo and I completely alone.

"What did you do?" I asked, my eyes beginning to burn. "What did you do, Leo?"

"I love you."

"*What did you do?*"

"Ashley's pregnant."

"No, she's not." I shook my head.

"I didn't know," he said, his voice pleading. "I swear, I didn't."

Everything inside me quieted to nothing.

"You're going to have a baby," I said flatly. "With someone else."

"I'm so sorry, Dandelion," he said, coming even closer to my spot at the bottom of the stairs.

"Babies aren't something to be sorry about," I replied, lifting my chin. "Don't say that again."

"That wasn't what I meant—"

"Thanks for letting me know," I cut him off. I tried to smile, but that small prevarication was impossible. "Congratulations."

"What? No." He finally reached me, but his hand on my face brought none of the familiar feelings that I'd come to expect. I was numb with disbelief. Numb with horror. Numb with the realization that the man I loved was going to be building a life with someone else. I felt nothing.

"I think you should go," I said softly, pulling his hand off my face. "Good luck, Leo."

"I'm not with her," he argued, reaching for me again. "This doesn't change anything."

"It changes everything," I replied incredulously. "I'm seventeen."

"I know how old you are."

"You're going to be a dad."

"I know."

"I'm *seventeen*," I said again, swatting at his hands.

"It's time for you to leave, Leo," my mom said kindly as she stepped into view.

His arms dropped to his sides in defeat as he stared at me like he didn't even know me.

"I was there for you," he said so quietly that I almost didn't hear him. "I've always had your back."

Then he turned and strode out the front door, closing it respectfully behind him, though I knew he'd wanted to slam it.

"You did good, Lilybug," my mom said gently. I stiffened as she hugged me. "You did the right thing."

"Does everyone know?" I asked dully as she let me go.

"No. Just me and your dad. Leo wanted to tell you first."

"Okay." I nodded. Swallowed. Nodded again. "I got into Yale."

I was already turning toward the stairs when my mom finally said, "You did?"

"Yeah." I looked over my shoulder at her and smiled wanly. "We should probably start figuring out finances if I'm moving across the country."

"I'm so proud of you, Lily," she called as I forced myself up each stair.

"Thanks, Ma."

Rose was at my door, her arms wide with welcome and understanding as I stumbled toward her. Thank God, my cousin always eavesdropped. She knew exactly what I needed and I hadn't had to say a word.

"We're going to fucking *own* New Haven," she whispered into my ear. "I hope you didn't think you were going without me."

# Part 2

## Chapter 15

# LILY

Two years and three months in New Haven, and the place still didn't feel like home. The weather was too harsh and the humidity killed, and I couldn't stand all the people. I was making it work, I even had fun with Rose on occasion, but living there still felt like a shirt that wasn't sewn correctly and pulled in all the wrong places.

I was doing it, though. I'd been plugging along, doing my schoolwork and tutoring for extra cash, like my dad had advised me to. Well, he'd *actually* told me to write papers for the rich kids, but I figured my way was a bit safer for my scholarships with the ethics clauses. As long as I planned everything down to the hour and stuck to my schedule, I did alright. I even had time to hang out with Rose, even if it was just sitting at the bar where she worked, watching her sling drinks for frat boys and trust fund babies.

The first year had been hard because I'd had to live in the dorms while Rose shared an apartment with five other people, but we'd made it work. Eventually, we had been able to get a place together. We had to share the two-bedroom apartment with two other people in order to afford it, but since we'd been living in each other's pockets for our entire lives, sharing a bedroom wasn't too bad.

I groaned as I hit the first flight of stairs in our building and readjusted my messenger bag across my chest. Early morning classes sucked ass, but I'd realized in my first year that it helped to get a jump on everything if classes were knocked out first thing and I had the rest of the day to actually do the work. Rose worked so late most nights that she was rarely awake by the time I got home, so I usually had a couple of hours of quiet before she climbed out of bed and started jabbering.

I was contemplating an hour-long nap as I opened our front door, but all thoughts of rearranging my schedule completely flew out of my mind when I found Rose waiting for me, two duffle bags at her feet.

"What happened?" I asked instantly, letting the door swing shut behind me. It was Friday. She'd worked the Thirsty Thursday shift the night before and there were very few things that would wake her at ten in the morning the next day.

"You have your wallet?" she asked, searching my face.

"Of course. What the hell?"

"First, you have to know that he's okay," she said, picking up the bags at her feet. "But we need to leave right now to catch our flight home."

"Who's okay?" I asked, starting to panic as she moved toward me.

"Come on," she said as she steered me back out the front door, moving ahead of me as she practically jogged forward. "Your dad was in an accident last night."

"Oh, God," I murmured, stumbling as I tried to keep up with her descent down the stairs.

"He was in your mom's SUV," she clarified, instantly calming me a little. Motorcycle accidents were almost always significantly worse. "He was t-boned by some old guy that had a heart attack. Your mom called this morning. He's in the hospital, and he'll be okay, but she said it's pretty bad."

"How bad?" I asked as she climbed into the back of a waiting cab that I hadn't even noticed as I'd entered our building five minutes before.

"Broken pelvis, broken ribs, broken arm and shoulder," she said as I sat down next to her. "They're doing surgery this morning to fix some internal bleeding."

Her hand reached for mine and squeezed it hard as I tried to make sense of what she was telling me.

"Jesus Christ," I rasped as she told the driver where to go. "The guy must've been going a hundred miles an hour."

"Close to it, I think," she said quietly, buckling my seatbelt as I sat there stunned.

I stared out the window in a daze as we cruised down now-familiar streets toward the airport. I'd gone home as often as I could afford, saving and scrimping so that I could spend Christmas and the summer with my parents, but all of a sudden, it felt like I'd abandoned them completely. I knew in my gut that a part of me had.

I'd been home. I'd celebrated holidays with them and had video chats with them at least once a week, but I'd made it very clear from the moment I left that I'd only wanted to see or hear about our little family. I hadn't let them discuss the club with me, even though it was a huge part of their life.

I had to do it. I had to cut that part out completely, or I wouldn't have been able to leave, and once I'd gotten to New Haven, I wouldn't have been able to stay.

Over the past couple of years, I'd grown. I'd had a couple casual boyfriends. I'd dated and been to parties with Rose. I'd even lost my virginity in a lousy attempt at sex with a guy who lived in my dorm my freshman year. I'd done my best to move on and move forward, something I'd have been incapable of doing with constant reminders of what I'd left behind.

My parents understood. I think they'd even been proud of the decisions I'd made. However, thinking about the way I'd left almost everyone behind made my stomach tighten into knots. It had been self-preservation, plain and simple, but I couldn't help but wonder if somewhere along the line it had turned into something else. Maybe it had just become easier to pretend that half of my life didn't exist anymore.

I'd grown comfortable with the absence of people that had loved me for my entire life, and I was suddenly ashamed of that. I knew with a certainty born of eighteen years of support that in that very moment, there were people flooding the waiting room of the hospital waiting for news, and for the past two years I'd completely ignored those people's very existence.

Rose kept up with all of it. I'd overheard her regular calls home to the people I'd ignored. Even Trix, my sister-in-law that had loved me for as long as I could remember, had felt the sting of my indifference. She was Leo's sister, and though I'd been kind and had always been happy to see her and my nephews, looking at her was just plain painful for me. I hadn't been able to pretend.

It took us two hours before we were on our first flight, and I'd spent most of the time quietly stuck in my own head. I couldn't stop thinking about how my dad would look, what he was going through, and whether he was in any pain. I'd tried to call my mom twice, but her phone must have been turned off. I called my brother and got no answer.

As we'd boarded the flight, Rose was able to get a hold of Aunt Callie, but she didn't have any more news for us. My dad was in surgery and they didn't know when he'd be done.

We just had to wait. Wait and worry. Switch planes. Call home again. I finally got in touch with my brother, but he didn't have anything new to tell me, and his voice sounded off, like he was carefully planning his words. He told me that he was sitting in the waiting room with everyone else and hadn't been updated in hours. My mom was somewhere in the bowels of the hospital waiting for my dad's surgery to be over, but unsurprisingly, no one had seen her in a while.

The next flight was longer. Rose played games on her tablet, but I couldn't seem to do anything but stare at the seatback in front of me. I ignored her attempts at conversation and the new romance novel she dropped in my lap.

I couldn't focus. I could barely breathe. The longer it took to get us home, the harder it got to wait. I needed to be there. I needed to hold my mom's hand and reassure her. I needed to make sure someone had called Cecilia because I didn't even have her new phone number.

I needed to get off that fucking plane.

Eight hours later, my hair was greasy, my stomach was churning, and my hands were shaking as we taxied down the runway to our final gate.

"Lil," Rose said quietly, turning her head slowly to face me. "I didn't tell you everything."

I stopped breathing.

"Your dad," she grimaced. "He was driving Ashley home from a party at the club."

"What?"

"Leo's Ashley."

The in-flight soda I'd choked down threatened to come back up.

"She didn't make it," Rose said softly.

"What?" I asked again, dumbly. "That doesn't make any sense."

"He wasn't drinking and my mom said that he offered to take her home since she was pretty blitzed and didn't want to stay the night."

It felt like a betrayal. The emotion hit me so hard that I had to deliberately hold back a gasp. I'd spent so much time pretending like she didn't exist, like neither of them existed, but my family had clearly been close to them and I'd never known. I'd made my opinion clear about any news on Leo, but I still couldn't believe that my parents maintained some sort of relationship I didn't know about.

I didn't say any of that out loud. I couldn't. She was dead. She was dead and my dad was in the hospital, and my hurt feelings didn't matter to anyone. Guilt hit me hard as I realized how very self-centered my reaction was.

Somewhere at the end of our flight was a child without its mother. Leo, a man that I'd tried and failed not to love, had lost someone important to him. I didn't know if they were together, though I always assumed they would be, but even that didn't matter. She was the mother of his baby. He must be devastated.

I closed my eyes, deliberately picturing Leo's face for the first time in years, and fought tears as my chest tightened with a sob. It was awful, all of it, and for the first time in a long time, I wanted my mom.

When we finally made our way out of the airport and into the Oregon rain, my uncle was waiting. He didn't say much, that wasn't his style, but he pulled us in for a group hug the minute he saw us and held us tightly for a long moment. His big arms and solid chest were the most comforting thing I'd felt since I'd woken up that morning, and I swallowed down the lump in my throat as he let us go.

"You girls hungry?" he asked as he threw our bags in the trunk.

"We can eat at the hospital," I said, not even glancing his way as I climbed into the backseat.

It only took seconds before he and Rose were climbing in the front, but it felt like an eternity.

The scene at the hospital was exactly like I'd imagined. Aces stood around, filling the tiny waiting room on the surgical floor, while their wives and girlfriends sat in small clusters of chairs talking quietly. I let my eyes flicker over every face as we got off the elevator, but I didn't meet anyone's eyes until my brother, Cam, took a step away from the wall he'd been leaning on.

My entire body sagged as he moved toward me on steady feet, his boots making little noise as he crossed the floor. I let out a breath of relief when he hugged me tight.

"Dad's out of surgery," he said quietly, his hand smoothing down the back of my hair as I shook. "Mom came out and updated us just a little while ago. She told me to wait for you so I could bring you back when you got here."

"Does Ceecee know?" I asked, my voice tight with relief and anxiety.

"Yeah, I got a hold of her after I talked to you. She might be heading up here."

Half of me was relieved and the other half concerned that my sister might be coming home for a visit for the first time in so many years, but I brushed those thoughts away as my brother led me down the corridor toward my dad's room.

I tried to brace myself as he pushed open the door, but the sight of my dad laying there with tubes and IVs everywhere made me lightheaded. He was unconscious, and monitors were beeping and whooshing like some sort of weird symphony.

"You're here," my mom said in relief, giving me a small smile as she got out of her chair. "Wasn't sure if we could pull you away from all that higher learning."

"I was getting bored anyway," I shot back, wrapping my arms around her waist and pulling her fully against me. "It's hard being smarter than everyone."

"Of course it is," she replied, giving me a squeeze. Then her voice changed, and the exhaustion leaked through. "I'm glad you're here, baby."

"Me, too."

She pulled away and gave my brother's bicep a squeeze before walking back to her place beside my dad.

"How's he doin'?" Cam asked.

"They said everything went well," Mom answered, laying her hand gently on my dad's thigh. "They set his arm while they were in there, but I don't think they can really do anything for the rest."

"Probably just dope him up," Cam said, agreeing.

"Wish they'd dope me up again," Mom mumbled dryly.

"Wait, what?" I asked, making my way slowly to my dad's side.

His arm was casted and his skin was paler than I'd ever seen it, but if I ignored all the tubes and wires, he almost looked normal. He didn't have a single scratch or bruise from the neck up.

"They gave me something to calm me down when I got here last night," Mom said, dropping her head back against the chair.

"Causing a ruckus, were you?"

"That bitch of a nurse at the front desk wouldn't tell me a goddamn thing and wouldn't fucking let me see him," she replied. "I may have gotten a little belligerent."

"You're lucky they didn't call security."

"Molly showed up while we were arguing and took care of it," Mom said. "Everyone loves her here."

"Everyone loves her, period."

"You need anything, Ma?" Cam asked, still standing uncomfortably by the door. "I was gonna run home and shower."

"I'm good, son," mom replied gently, her eyes soft on his face. "And Dad's just going to sleep it off for a couple more hours. Go home, give the boys and Charlie some kisses for me."

Cam nodded. "She's gonna want to come up here."

"Tell her she can come up tomorrow," Mom said tiredly and gestured toward my dad's bed. "Hopefully, some of this shit will be gone by then."

"Will do."

He left without giving either of us a hug, anxious to leave the room.

"Your brother might be built like a bull, but he's got the heart of a lamb," my mom joked as I ran a finger softly over my dad's hand. It was the only place that felt safe to touch him and let him know I was there. "I think seeing your dad laid up shook him more than he'd like to admit."

"He's always been good with this stuff," I replied.

"Yeah, but it was never your dad," she pointed out. "He's been pretty lucky. The last time your dad was hurt, we didn't have any of you kids yet. I guess it was his turn."

"That's a morbid way to look at it," I argued, meeting her eyes.

"Gotta find some reason for this shit," she said softly. "Otherwise, you'll go crazy."

"You look exhausted—"

"Hey!"

"Still beautiful," I corrected. "But tired."

"I am, kid." She nodded. "He was awake, you know, when they put him in the ambulance."

"Really?" I looked him over and couldn't imagine how he'd stayed conscious.

"Yeah." She sighed. "He called me on his way here. He knew before the paramedics showed up that Ashley was gone and he wanted to make sure I knew it wasn't him."

"Jesus," I breathed.

"The guy hit her side." My mom shook her head and squeezed her eyes tightly shut. "She didn't have a fucking chance."

"But he's going to blame himself," I replied quietly.

"Yes."

"What happened to the guy?"

"They think he was dead before he even hit them."

"What a fucking nightmare," I mumbled, scrubbing my hands over my face.

It felt like an eternity since my alarm had woken me for class. I didn't even remember most of the day, but it felt like it had dragged on forever.

"You should go home and get some rest," Mom said, eyeing me.

"*You* should go home and get some rest. Were you up all night?"

"Yeah. I passed out for a couple hours once we knew he was going to be okay, though. Whatever they gave me made sure of that."

"Why don't you go home and I'll stay?" I offered.

"I love you for offering," she replied with a smile. "But as long as he's here, I'm here."

"Stubborn."

"Where do you think you got it?"

"You know he's going to make you go home when he wakes up."

"He can try. For now, though, he doesn't have a choice."

Since there was only one chair in the room, I found a spot against the wall and settled in on the floor. There was nothing that I could do, but I wasn't ready to leave my dad yet, either. Just knowing that I was only a foot away from him calmed me. I'd always been close to both of my parents, but my dad and I had a special bond. It was different than either of my sisters or brother had with him. From the minute I could walk, I'd followed him around, asking questions and soaking up everything he said. I think that's how they'd originally known that my intelligence wasn't quite the same as other kids my age. When I'd wanted to know how an engine worked, he'd explained it, then had watched wide eyed as I'd asked him detailed and specific questions about what he'd told me. That's the story I'd heard growing up, anyway. I'd only been three at the time.

Mom and I chatted quietly to pass the time, but we didn't hit on any particular topic. Instead, we just talked to listen to each other's voices, trying to drown out the beeping that was inescapable. Nurses came and went, and the night grew darker, but we didn't move until someone came in to tell us that visiting hours were over.

They'd been over for hours, but I guess they wanted to make sure that I wasn't planning on sleeping on the floor like a hobo.

"I drove your dad's truck," Mom said, digging the keys out of her purse. "You can still drive a stick, right?"

"Pretty sure it's like riding a bike," I replied. The summer before I'd left for college, my parents had made sure that I had my license and knew how to get myself around. It was a little ironic, since I didn't end up doing any driving in New Haven.

My ass was numb as I grabbed my bags and Mom's keys, kissing her and then my dad as I left the room. There was always stuff happening at hospitals, people moving around and working and worrying, but there was something eerie about a hospital at night. Everyone talked quieter and stepped lighter, making everything seem hushed.

There were still people hanging out in the waiting room when I got there, and I made the rounds as they stood up to greet me. Molly and Will hugged me and asked me how I was. Poet's wife, Amy, grabbed me gently with a hand on each side of my head and kissed my forehead, but didn't say a word. Poet didn't notice me because he was dozing in the corner. I made my way around the room, letting them know my dad was doing okay and was still sleeping.

As I stepped onto the elevator, they all sat back down in their seats and resumed what they were doing—reading, playing cards, messing around on their phones. They were standing vigil, and I knew that wouldn't stop, not until my dad was completely out of the woods. The people would change, more would show up and others would leave, but there would always be someone there, waiting in case my parents needed anything.

When I got to the front doors, I groaned and pulled my hood up. It was cold as shit in Connecticut, so I'd thankfully been wearing a jacket, but I was not looking forward to trying to find my dad's truck in the dark and pouring down rain. I settled my bags more firmly over my shoulders and trudged outside, then almost peed my pants as a voice barked my name in the darkness.

## Chapter 16

# LEO

SHE LOOKED THE same.

She looked different.

She looked exactly how I'd imagined she would.

I called her name just once, but it was enough to make her turn in my direction and freeze.

"Leo?"

I couldn't reply.

I couldn't say a damn thing as she moved toward my spot against the building, just outside the halo of light coming from the building's entrance and barely beneath the overhang.

"Are you okay?" she asked, her face screwed up in confusion. "Do you want me to get someone for you?"

"What the fuck are you doing out here alone?" I barked.

It wasn't what I wanted to say. I wanted to ask her how she'd been, if she liked school, if she ever thought of me, if she knew that my entire world had just been upended. I wanted to tell her that the short haircut she was sporting suited her, that she looked older without the long braid hanging down her back. I wanted to ask how Casper was doing and if her mom needed anything.

"I'm going home," she said, stopping a few feet from me. "I just need to find my dad's truck."

"You shouldn't be out here by yourself. It's fuckin' pitch black."

"The parking lot is well-lit," she replied softly. "Are you okay?"

She stepped even closer, and I panicked.

"Stop."

"Leo," she said softly. "You look like shit."

"I'm fine."

"No, you're not. Why are you standing out here?"

I couldn't tell her that I'd been too afraid to go upstairs. That I knew Casper was laid up there because I'd gotten into a huge fight with Ashley about Gray, and when she'd stormed outside, I'd been too fucking wasted to drive her home. I couldn't tell her that the thought of seeing her for the first time in over two years when we were surrounded by people made me break out in a sweat, so I'd just been standing outside the hospital for an hour like a lunatic.

"I'll walk you to the truck," I said instead, ignoring her questions.

I moved forward, but stumbled back when she reached for me.

I was too fucking raw for her to touch me. I'd let a lot of shit go over the past couple of years. I'd come to realize that she'd been completely right when she'd ran across the country to get away from me. She'd done the only thing she could have, and what I'd wanted for her all along, even if her execution had left a lot to be desired.

But I knew if she touched me, the tight leash I'd been keeping on my emotions since Farrah had gotten that ambulance call from Casper after the accident would completely snap. I'd fucking lose it, and I'd lose it in a way that wouldn't be good for either of us.

"Don't," I warned with a tight shake of my head.

"I'm so sorry about—"

"*Don't.*"

She nodded and let me move around her. I'd seen Casper's piece of shit truck when I'd parked earlier, so I led her in that direction. It was still weird to me that she could follow me without actually touching me. She'd been able to see for a long ass time, but I still remembered when she'd stand perfectly still in a place she wasn't familiar with, afraid to move.

"Thanks," she said as we reached the truck.

I stood there silently as she threw her shit in the passenger side and slammed the rusted door shut. She was so self-assured now, so confident in the way she moved. It was like watching a completely different person, and also someone I knew better than myself at the same time.

"Do you need me to get anyone?" she asked as she moved toward the tailgate where I was standing. "Will's upstairs."

"No," I said simply. "Careful drivin' home."

"I will. It's been a while, so I'll probably go ten miles under the speed limit until I get the feel of driving again."

I wanted to ask her why she wasn't driving around in Connecticut, but I didn't.

I stepped back and let her go around to the driver's seat, not moving again until she fired up the truck. Then I headed toward my bike that was fucking soaking wet from the rain. I should have driven the Suburban I'd bought when Gray was born, but I hadn't had the stomach to climb in there without him.

Following Lily home felt familiar and also weird as fuck. I'd never seen her drive before. She was good. She didn't seem nervous or anything, but still really cautious. As we wound through town toward her parents' place, I ground my teeth together to keep myself from screaming into the wind.

My life was fucked. Once again, it had flipped on its axis in a single moment, leaving me grasping at anything that would right it again. And just like before, there wasn't a single thing I could do to change the situation.

I stopped at the end of Casper and Farrah's driveway and watched as Lily carried her bags onto the porch. She must have known I was waiting, because she moved quickly, but she didn't acknowledge me. Once I saw the light flip on and the front door shut behind her, I took off again.

I had an apartment about ten minutes from the club, but I couldn't make myself go there. I'd needed a place of my own once I had Gray, and the place suited me, but I had no desire to be there alone tonight. I hated sleeping there without his little body curled up next to me.

I knew he had a bed at his mom's. I'd seen it a million times. But I'd never felt the need for him to sleep anywhere but beside me. He loved climbing into dad's bed to fall asleep, even if I wasn't there yet. He was the type of kid that put himself to bed when he was tired, and more than once, I'd found him curled up under the covers with sticky hands and a thumb in his mouth before I'd even thought to put him there. He knew what he wanted, and did for himself. I loved that about him.

It only took a few minutes to get to the clubhouse and when I got there, the place was crawling with people. I wasn't surprised. When something big happened, we congregated there, always. Losing Ashley and having Casper laid up in the hospital was big.

When I got inside, I was surprised to find that the entire place had been cleaned from top to bottom. There was no evidence that we'd had a party the night before. Not a single beer bottle or dirty glass.

People sat around the room, talking and hanging out, but I didn't see anyone drinking. Tonight was a coffee night, if there was such a thing.

Fuck. Fuck. Fuck.

My chest tightened and I searched for anything that would distract me.

"Hey," I said as I dropped into a chair across from Hawk and Tommy.

"Leo!" Hawk blurted, jumping up from the couch. "Dude."

Before I knew what she was doing, her arms were wrapped around my neck, and my head was pressed against her tits as she hugged me.

Because I was sitting and she was standing, there was no way to return the hug without touching something Tommy would knock me on my ass for, so I just left my arms at my sides and allowed her to hug me.

"Come on, Heather," Tommy said gently. "Let him go, baby."

I jerked when Hawk pulled away and I saw the tear tracks on her cheeks. She hadn't made a sound or given any indication that she'd been crying.

"I'm sorry," she mumbled. "I just can't believe this shit is happening."

"Me, either," I replied with a sigh.

"How're you holding up?" Tommy asked, pulling Hawk into his lap.

"Barely," I replied, staring at my feet. One of my boots had a streak of green paint on the side from when I'd spray painted Gray's trike a few weeks ago. "I'm fuckin' barely holdin' up."

"How's Gray?" Hawk asked.

"Fine." I shook my head. "He doesn't know shit, and even if he did, he wouldn't understand it. Tonight, he was just happy he got to stay with Ash's mom."

"Is she going to be a problem?" Tommy asked reluctantly. I knew he hated to ask, but fuck, I understood why he was. Ashley's mom didn't like me, and she wasn't going to be happy that I was Gray's only parent now.

"Right now, she's just devastated about her kid," I said softly. "Happy to have Gray there with her, givin' her a reason to keep her shit together."

"Makes sense," Hawk said. "He's her only link to Ashley now."

"That's what I'm worried about," Tommy replied quietly.

"I'm not," I said with a shrug. "She can hate it all she wants, man. I'm Gray's dad. She wants to fight me, she'll lose."

"Ash wouldn't want her to give you grief," Hawk said seriously.

I nodded. We may have had a casual relationship in the beginning, but as we'd worked together to raise Gray, Ashley had become one of my closest friends. I thought that it probably helped that neither of us was looking for more. There were no hard feelings that we weren't a typical couple with a baby, no resentment or jealousy when one of us hooked up with someone else. I knew that the way we did things and the way we'd parented wasn't the norm, but it had worked for us.

We'd rarely fought about anything, and honestly, we'd gone out of our way to help each other out when it came to Gray. If I was on a run, she'd let me have him the minute I got back into town. If she had plans to go camping or out with her friends, I rearranged my schedule so that Gray could stay with me. It worked for us because we'd worked at it. Gray was the most important thing in our worlds, and we'd done the best we could to give him the most drama-free life that we could.

I clenched my fists and breathed deep, fighting the tightness in my chest at the thought of never seeing her again.

"I'm gonna hit the sack," I mumbled, not meeting anyone's eyes as I stood up from the chair.

I didn't even wait for their responses before I was striding toward my room. I needed to get away from everyone.

The minute I closed the door behind me, a shudder wracked my frame, almost bringing me to my knees. I struggled to inhale air into my lungs, and the moment I succeeded, a sob broke from my throat. I stumbled to the bed and landed hard on my ass, my hands covering my face, trying to keep everything inside.

Jesus, I couldn't believe that she was gone.

I couldn't imagine my life without Ashley in it. I couldn't imagine a life where Gray didn't light up at the sight of his mom's face, or fall asleep curled against her chest as she laughed. I couldn't imagine not having that one person in the world to talk to that loved my son as much as I did.

I didn't know how to be a parent without Ashley. We'd figured out shit together. If I wasn't sure how to deal with something, we talked it out. If I was feeling overwhelmed or freaked the fuck out, she calmed me down.

I didn't want to try to explain to my two year old that his mama wasn't coming back. I didn't want him learning about her secondhand and only remembering her face through the photos we had. He'd never remember how much she'd loved him and how much he'd loved her. I fucking hated that.

I let the tears fall down my face, thankful that I'd made it to my room and locked the door before I'd lost it. No one would judge me, I knew that, but I didn't want anyone's sympathy. I didn't want them comforting me and smothering me with their good intentions. I just wanted to get it out. Purge the awful feeling in my chest that had gotten tighter and tighter as the day had gone on until I'd felt as if it would completely suffocate me.

By the time my lungs had stopped heaving and my face was dry, I had a hard time keeping myself vertical. I'd been awake since the morning before, and exhaustion hit me hard.

As I kicked off my boots, I let my mind drift beyond Ashley and Gray, looking for a reprieve, but the first thing I thought of was Lily walking out of that hospital in her brown coat, exhaustion and the bags she was carrying making her shoulders sag. She was as beautiful as I remembered. Her face looked older, more refined and mature, but she was still the beautiful Lily that I'd watched grow up.

The irony of her coming home during one of the worst days of my life wasn't lost on me. If I'd had any doubts that the universe had a fucking sick sense of humor, those doubts were gone now. The chance of something happening to Casper and Ashley at the same time was so fucking miniscule that it hadn't been something I could have ever imagined. Sure, Casper was one of the brothers, and in that way we'd always be close, but Ashley barely knew him. We didn't spend much time with the old timers outside of club parties and the garage, and it was pretty rare that Ash would even come to an event at the clubhouse.

It had been the perfect storm, Ashley at the club for a party, our argument about Gray's potty training that had turned into both of us pissed and defensive about our parenting, Casper deciding early-on not to drink because he'd had some stomach bug the night before. The scenario was so fucking unlikely that I couldn't have seen it coming.

And now Lily was back, fucking with my head even though I barely had the energy to think of her. It shamed me to say it, and I would have never admitted it out loud, but in those moments when she'd looked at me the way she used to, I'd felt for just a second like everything would be okay.

## Chapter 17

# LILY

I SPENT THE morning after my mostly sleepless night in my childhood bed on the phone with Yale, trying to get shit sorted so that they wouldn't boot me out. Unfortunately, it didn't matter what department I tried, everyone was out for the weekend. Eventually, I just left messages for all of my professors letting them know that I'd had a family emergency and promising to be back in a week. I just hoped that worked and I wouldn't get punished. There wasn't a whole lot I could do until the following Monday.

I was proud of myself for taking care of things, especially when Yale seemed so far away and completely unimportant. From the moment I'd stepped off the plane yesterday, everything seemed to have shifted, and somewhere between then and when I'd woken up that morning, I'd come to the scary realization that I wasn't sure if I could make myself get back on a plane to Connecticut.

I'd just gotten out of the shower and was towel drying my hair when my mom came home looking strung out.

"Not a word," she ordered tiredly. "Cody's awake and made Callie drive me home. I swear to God, that man is bossy."

"He's awake?" I asked, a small smile pulling at my cheeks.

"Yeah. He was in and out all night, but he completely woke up this morning and immediately started bitching at me for not taking care of myself."

"Well, you haven't," I pointed out.

"Doin' it now," she replied, scooting around me into the bathroom. "I'm going to take a shower and get this nasty hospital smell out of my hair, and then I'm going to sleep for a few hours."

"Sounds like a good plan," I said, hanging my towel up. "You need me to do anything?"

"No, baby," she said, blowing me a kiss over her shoulder. "But I'm gonna sleep in your bed, if that's alright? I don't like sleeping in our bed without Cody."

"Of course."

I backed out of the room as she pulled the band out of her hair, letting it fall in soft blonde waves down her back.

If Mom was home and Dad was awake, it was probably time for me to make my way back to the hospital.

Forty-five minutes later, I was striding into my dad's hospital room.

He was sitting up and grinning about something my Uncle Grease was saying when I got my first good look at him. The tubes and wires were still connected to his body, but the difference from when I'd seen him the night before was startling. He looked like my strong, capable dad again, even with the lines of strain around his eyes.

"Lilybug," he called out when his eyes met mine. "Baby girl, you didn't have to come home."

"Thanks," I replied dryly, making my way into the room. "I feel so welcomed, so loved."

Dragon and Grease stepped back from the bed as they chuckled, giving me room to kiss my dad hello.

"You know I'm always happy to see you," Dad chided as he kissed my cheek with chapped lips. "But you're in the middle of the semester."

"You'll be happy to know that I've already left messages for my professors telling them I had a family emergency."

"What, did you tell them I was dyin'?"

"Close to it," I joked. "I even cried a little."

"Thatta girl," Uncle Grease praised.

"We're gonna head out," Dragon said, reaching forward to flick my dad's foot. "Give you some time with your girl."

"Thanks, man," Dad said with a small nod.

"You need anythin', just let us know."

"I will. Have Brenna and Callie check in on Farrah, would ya? She was keepin' it together, but I don't wanna come home to find out she's got a tattoo on her face or some shit."

"Will do," Grease said as they left the room. Then it was just me and my dad, smiling at each other until his face fell.

"You know what happened?" he asked as I sat down in the chair next to his bed.

"Yeah. Rose told me when we got here. How you feeling?"

"I'm fine." He grew quiet for a minute, staring at the wall in front of him. "Survived, yeah? Can't ask for much more than that."

"You know it wasn't your fault."

"Don't make it any easier that she was ridin' with me because she wanted to get home safe to her boy, and she never made it there."

"Boy?" I asked softly, swallowing hard. I'd never asked and no one had ever volunteered any information about Leo's child. Even my nephews were old enough to know that Uncle Leo wasn't brought up to Aunt Lily under any circumstances.

"Yeah," my dad said, watching me closely. "Leo's got a little boy named Gray."

"Funny name."

"Yeah, Ashley liked it and somehow she got Leo on board."

"Cool," I whispered, staring at anything so that I didn't have to meet his eyes.

"You're gonna have to see him," my dad said gently. "With all this shit goin' on, you're not gonna be able to avoid it, and it'd be shitty if you did."

"I already saw him," I replied with a small shrug. "He was standing outside the hospital when I left last night."

"How'd that go?"

"Fine, I guess." I leaned back in the chair and finally met my dad's blue eyes. "He didn't say much, just walked me to the truck and followed me home."

"Makin' sure you got home safe."

"Yeah."

"I was proud of ya for the way you handled things, you know," he said, his mouth tipping up on one side. "You didn't wallow in shit, just made plans and went through with them."

"Ran away, you mean."

"Got yourself out of a situation you weren't ready for."

"Same thing."

"But I hope you're not holdin' grudges. Life takes some crazy fuckin' turns sometimes. No one's fault."

"I'm not holding a grudge," I protested, picking at a loose string on my jeans.

"You loved him," my dad said easily. "Everyone could see it. But beyond that, you two were friends."

"Yeah."

"He's gonna need a friend, Lilybug."

"He's got plenty of friends."

"You think he's gonna talk to Tommy or Will? I fuckin' doubt it. He loves them like brothers, but there's just some shit you don't share with your brothers."

"Well, Cecilia might be coming up," I said. "Maybe she can be the shoulder he leans on."

"That's shitty, Lily," Dad said sternly, making my head jerk up. "And it ain't you, so knock it off."

"I know." I shook my head in defeat. "But I don't think he wants to see me, Dad. We were friends, yeah, but I left him."

"He always knew you would," Dad said seriously. "Just didn't anticipate the way you'd do it."

"That doesn't make it any better."

"You'd be surprised at what a man can forgive when it comes to the woman he loves."

"He doesn't love me."

"Baby girl, if he doesn't love you then I don't know what the fuck love's supposed to be."

"If I see him, I'll make sure he knows that there are no hard feelings, okay?" I said, trying to make him stop talking. "But he has a lot bigger shit on his plate than catching up with a girl he hasn't seen in two and a half years."

"Good," Dad said. "Cause I need you to stop by the clubhouse today and ask him to come see me."

I opened my mouth to refuse him, but when I saw the way his eyes had darkened, I shut it again. I wasn't sure what my dad had to say to Leo, and it wasn't any of my business, but I had a feeling that a meeting between the two of them was probably necessary.

"Are you—" my words cut off as I tried to figure out exactly what I wanted to say. "Were you good friends with Ashley?"

Dad smiled and snickered before freezing in pain, then shook his head. "You think your mom would let me be friends with a pretty, blonde, twenty year old?" he joked tightly. "No, we weren't friends. Liked her, though. Liked the way she was with Leo, givin' him a say in shit from the very beginning. Liked how she treated their boy. Liked that she made sure the club was a big part of Gray's life like it was for you kids. She was a good girl. Loyal. Sweet. Didn't deserve to die before her kid hit fuckin' preschool."

"I'm sorry, Dad."

"Saw her, kiddo," he said softly. "Tried to get to her before the ambulance got there." He grimaced and shook his head sharply. "Nothin' I could do. At least she was gone quick. None of that lingerin', in pain shit. Just bam, gone."

I nodded and reached out, laying my hand on his good arm.

"She wasn't scared."

"Nah," he said. "She wasn't."

We sat there in silence for a long time after that, until finally my dad spoke up, his voice tight with emotion.

"That motherfucker is lucky he was dead before he made contact, 'cause I woulda killed him."

★ ★ ★

My mom showed up a few hours later, carrying a bag of my dad's stuff, her hair perfectly curled and her makeup flawless.

"Damn it, Ladybug," my dad bitched against her mouth as she leaned down to kiss him on the lips. "I told you to get some fuckin' sleep."

"Don't like sleeping without you," she replied, completely unperturbed. "So I packed you some stuff and had Callie bring me back."

"I told you to sleep," he said again, his voice growing more agitated.

"And that's my cue to leave," I interrupted before I had to watch war erupt in that tiny hospital room.

"You go do that thing I asked," Dad said, turning his head toward me. "Yeah?"

"Yeah, I'll stop on my way home. What's Charlie doing today?" I asked my mom. "Should I go pick her up?"

"Not sure if she'll want to leave Cam's unless she's comin' up here, but I know she wants to see you."

"Okay, I'll stop by there."

I said my goodbyes and left the hospital room just as my dad started in again about my mom not getting any sleep.

There were only a couple people still in the waiting room. I liked to think of them as the skeleton crew, and I waved to them as I climbed onto the empty elevator just as the doors were closing. Now that my dad was awake and on the mend, there would only be two or three people standing guard and providing support until he left the hospital. They'd change throughout the day and over night, with everyone taking a turn.

I felt kind of bad that I hadn't said hi to Rocky and my cousin Tommy as I'd raced onto the elevator, but I just didn't have the patience for small talk when I knew that I had to go find Leo. He hadn't seemed happy to see me outside the hospital the night before, and I was dreading the reaction I'd get when I actually sought him out. Did he hate me?

If I was in his shoes, I'd probably hate me. The way I'd left and never spoken to him again made me cringe. If he'd ever wondered about my maturity level when he'd finally given up other women and set his sights on me exclusively, he must have figured it out when I'd acted like a spoiled brat, pouting for months before finally moving away.

His son had been born before I'd left, and I hadn't made one attempt to find out anything about him. I'd known when the baby was born, but I'd refused to even acknowledge his birth. For me, they'd no longer mattered.

Except they had. They'd mattered too much. And in my eighteen-year-old mind, his child had been the ruination of any relationship I'd dreamed of with Leo. Looking back, I knew how absolutely ridiculous that had been, to blame a child for the end of a relationship I'd walked away from willingly.

I drove to the clubhouse in silence, not even turning on any music to drown out the white noise of the rain. I'd actually kind of missed the sound of Oregon rain. It didn't sound or smell the same anywhere else.

Rain didn't make everything look clean and sparkly the way it did in Oregon, like it was washing away all the extras and leaving only fresh trees and sky.

I waved to the prospects on the gate, and thankfully one of them recognized me so I didn't have to roll down my window before they were letting me onto the property. There were cars parked all over and the garage bays were open, leaving space for Harley after Harley to park inside. I hadn't really expected so many people to be there, but I guess I should have, since it was a Saturday afternoon.

I parked and ran inside before I lost my nerve, then got caught up in a wave of greetings as I pulled off my hood and glanced around the room. It was like a damn family reunion that I wasn't prepared for. Women stood up and hugged me as I made my way across the room, telling me how much they'd missed me and how glad they were that I was home.

By home, I knew they meant the clubhouse that I'd refused to enter in nearly three years.

When I finally made my way to the end of the bar, I stopped on my own and gave the old man sitting there a shy smile.

"You're a sight for sore eyes, lass," Poet said quietly, his eyes soft on my face. "Looks like that school's been treatin' you well."

"It has."

"But now you're home, where ya belong."

"For a little while," I replied.

"We'll see," he said, tilting his head just slightly to the side. "I'm bettin' ya aren't here to see me."

I shook my head and glanced past him at the archway that led to the bedrooms. "Is Leo around?"

"He is, and he isn't," Poet said enigmatically. "Been in his room since last night, not answering when anyone knocks. Might open up for you, though."

"Probably not," I sighed. "I have to try anyway."

"Good luck to ya," he said, patting me on the forearm.

I moved past him and made my way to Leo's room, remembering exactly which one it was. Room assignments rarely changed unless there was a new president. I still remembered when my Grandpa Slider had Dragon's old room, the best room. I'd spent hours in there with my Grandma Vera, painting nails and watching old black and white movies where people broke into song for no apparent reason.

I knocked quietly on Leo's door, then a little louder when he didn't answer. After a full minute of silence, I knocked again. I wasn't sure if hearing my voice would make him open the door or if it was more likely to keep him sequestered inside, so I didn't say a word. Dropping my forehead against the wood, I knocked one more time and made the decision to walk away if he still didn't open it.

Just as I picked my head up and started to turn, I heard the deadbolt click, and then there he was. My eyes took in all the changes that I'd paid no attention to in the dark the night before. His hair was longer than I'd ever seen it, longer than mine. His face was scruffy with a few days' worth of beard, and there were lines at the sides of his eyes that I'd either never noticed or never cared about before that moment. He looked older. Harder. Less like the boy I'd worshipped, and more like a man that I didn't know.

"What?" he asked quietly, his voice hoarse.

"Hi," I said dumbly. I cleared my throat. "Hey."

"Lily," he said, his hands gripping the doorframe on each side. He looked like he was barely holding himself up. "Did you need something?"

"How are you doing?" I asked, cringing at my words. "I mean, shit. I'm sure you're pretty shitty."

"Yeah."

"I mean, are you okay?"

"Hangin' in," he replied.

"I j-just—" I stuttered, trying to find the words that would take us out from under this suffocating blanket of awkwardness and onto some kind of solid ground. "I just wanted to check in. Make sure you didn't need anything, or—"

"Don't need anythin', thanks." He moved to close the door, and I panicked.

It was the only explanation for the way I threw myself toward him, the way my arms wrapped around his waist in a stranglehold before I even realized what I was doing. His skin felt smooth, like it had all those years ago, but that was the only familiar thing about the hug I was forcing on him. His arms didn't circle me like they would have before. His heart didn't beat in a steady rhythm that would make mine calm.

"I'm so sorry," I said, following through with the hug even though I was pretty sure he just wanted me to get off of him. "I'm so sorry, Leo."

"Thanks," he said gruffly, his hands landing on my shoulders.

He didn't push me away, but his intent was clear.

"I—anything you need, okay?" I said as I stepped back. I lifted my face toward his, but couldn't meet his eyes. "I'm here for the week, and if I can help, or—"

"Thanks," he said again, this time a clear dismissal.

"Right." I backed away, my face on fire. I'd shuffled uncomfortably all the way to the hallway before I remembered what the hell I was actually doing there.

I finally met his eyes again, because there was no way that I couldn't.

"My dad asked me to tell you to come see him," I said softly, my stomach clenching as I watched his emotionless face wince. "Maybe you don't want to see him. Or maybe you're mad at him. But he really wants to see you."

"I'm not mad at him," he said with a huff. "Christ."

"Okay," I whispered, suddenly anxious to get the hell away.

"Okay," he replied. Then for the second time in my entire life, Leo closed a door in my face.

## Chapter 18

# LEO

I WAS ON my way to the hospital to see Casper and my hands were sweating. I wasn't nervous. There wasn't anything to be nervous about. But, hell, I wanted a drink.

After I saw Casper, I was going to pick up Gray, and I knew without a doubt that I was going to deal with drama from Ashley's mom, Kathy. Drama that was going to freak Gray out and make me want to throw the woman through a wall. When I'd texted her earlier in the day, she'd gotten back to me an hour later with some shit about how Gray could spend another night at her house. After, I'd told her I'd be there in a few hours to pick him up. While she hadn't come out and actually said it, I knew that Gray wasn't going to be ready to leave when I got there and she was going to argue that shit for a hot minute before she gave up and let me take him. I wasn't looking forward to it.

I also wasn't looking forward to whatever talk Casper wanted to have with me. I didn't know if he was going to rip me a new one or apologize, but neither of those options sounded appealing when I couldn't even get my head straight about what had happened. I knew Ashley was gone intellectually, but it still didn't feel that way. We went days without talking sometimes, that wasn't anything new. If one of us had Gray, and nothing important was happening, we didn't feel the need to chat. Sure, I'd get picture messages and shit every couple of days if I hadn't seen him in a while, but that was pretty much the extent of it. Knowing that Gray was with his grandma made it even harder to feel

Ashley's absence. There wasn't any need for her to contact me.

I wiped my hands on my jeans as I climbed out of the Suburban and lit up a cigarette as I walked toward the hospital's entrance, giving me a few more minutes to stall. I needed to quit fucking smoking. I needed to quit doing a lot of stupid shit now that I was Gray's only parent. Only parent—what a mindfuck. Never in a million years had I thought that I'd be doing that shit on my own. From the first second I'd known about him, I'd had a partner to depend on. Someone I could call in the middle of the night when he had a fever from teething and I didn't know what the fuck to do. Someone to bitch to when he took a permanent marker to the walls in my apartment.

Now it was just me.

I crushed the finished cigarette under the toe of my boot and threw the butt in the trash as I walked inside the hospital and headed toward the elevators. I needed to get this shit done so I could go get my boy. I'd never before needed the feeling of his little body pressed up against mine so badly, the reassurance that he was okay, even though everything around us was fucking spinning.

I asked the nurse on his floor which room Casper was in, and less than a minute later, I was standing in the doorway, feeling like a kid that had just been called to the principal's office.

"Leo," Farrah said, getting to her feet so she could hug me. "How you doin', kid?"

"Alright."

"Liar." She smacked my chest, but gave me a small smile. "You need any help, just let me know. This one's been getting on my nerves, so I don't mind leaving him."

"You're full of shit," Casper said dryly, lifting his chin at me.

"How you doin'?" I asked after I'd cleared my throat. The guy had IVs and tubes coming out from all angles under his blankets, and his skin was pale as hell.

"Pissin' in a bag, but they've got me on the good shit, so there's that," he answered.

"I'm gonna go get some coffee," Farrah said, passing me. "I'll be back later."

"Why don't you go home and take a fuckin' nap instead?" Casper called as she pulled the door closed behind her without responding.

Then it was just me and him, and I had no idea what to say.

"How you really doin'?" he asked as I stepped further into the room.

"Who the fuck knows?" I replied honestly, leaning against the wall.

"Not hittin' yet?"

"Not really. Gotta pick Gray up in a bit, figure it'll be worse then."

"Probably right," he said quietly, looking down at his lap.

"I—"

"So—"

We both spoke at the same time, so I snapped my mouth shut, gesturing at him to go first.

"I'm so fuckin' sorry, son," Casper said gruffly, shaking his head. "He came outta nowhere, and there was nothin' I could do. They took my blood when they picked me up, it's got no alcohol in it, you'll see."

"Didn't think that," I said quickly, raising my hand to try and stop his words.

"I thought I was doin' the right thing—takin' her home—I thought I'd get her outta there before you two said somethin' you'd regret."

"Shouldn't have been fightin' anyway," I replied, my stomach twisting at the memory. "It was about stupid shit that wouldn't have even come up if we hadn't been drinkin'."

"It happens," Casper said gently. "Can't tell you the amount of times me and Farrah have gone at it about the smallest shit you can imagine because we were toasted. That's life, kid. You fight and you make up, and you do the best you can."

I nodded, my throat tight.

"She wasn't in any pain," he said softly, his words like a knife in my chest. I put my hand over my face to block it out, but I could still hear him. "It was over in a second and she didn't have any idea. I swear to ya. She was gone before the car stopped spinnin'."

A sob worked up my throat, but I held it back with sheer will. Nodding so that he knew I'd heard him, I slid to my ass, my knees almost smacking my chin as I landed.

"Not sure how I'm gonna explain it to Gray," I whispered, scrubbing my hands over my face. "Not sure how I'm gonna do any of it."

"Small blessing," Casper replied. "He's so young that this is gonna be a blip on his radar."

"Not sure if that's a blessing."

"It is, son. I promise you that. Hate the fact that he's not gonna know her, hate it. But Christ, it would be so much worse for him if he was any older. The same for you, but worse for him."

I nodded my understanding, even though I couldn't imagine how any of it could be any worse. My son was going to grow up without a mother. There was no way to see that as any kind of blessing.

"When they're little," Casper continued as I let my head fall forward between my knees. "You worry that they'll fall. Constantly watch them to make sure they're not puttin' shit in their mouth or touchin' somethin' that could hurt 'em. Once they're older, though, it get's harder. You gotta worry about other kinds of wounds, the kind that don't leave marks, but stick around a lot longer."

"Kid's fucked with me as a parent," I mumbled.

"Nah, you'll do alright. Every dad thinks that shit, probably every mom, too. No one thinks they're gonna do everything right, and if someone told ya otherwise, they were lyin'. We're all just makin' shit up on the fly, takin' it as it comes and regrettin' half the shit we do."

"You sure she didn't know—" I started to ask again, my mind unable to move past the thought of Ashley scared out of her mind and wondering what the fuck had just happened.

"I'm sure, bud," Casper said, his voice echoing a little as he laid his head back to stare at the ceiling. "She was pretty much passed out by the time we went through the gate. By the time that guy hit us, she was completely asleep. Didn't even see the headlights of his truck."

"You were pretty fucked up, though," I argued. "After, I mean."

"Didn't lose consciousness until I was on my way to the hospital," Casper reassured me, his words coming out choked. "I was awake for all of it, and she wasn't. Not for a second. She fell asleep and she didn't wake up."

"Okay," I said, letting that information seep into my pores. "Okay."

"If there was somethin' I coulda done," he said, his voice almost a whisper. "Swear to Christ, Leo, if I coulda helped her, I woulda. But she was already gone."

"Thanks," I said, nodding absently as I lifted my head.

"Didn't want you thinkin' about that shit, worryin' what it was like for her."

"I was."

"I know, son. I'd have been doin' the same damn thing." He cleared his throat. "That's why I sent Lily to get ya. Wanted to talk to you man-to-man before any more time passed."

"Nice move," I said sarcastically, meeting his eyes. "Sending Lil to me."

"Knew she'd get you here."

"Oh, yeah?"

"Ya haven't been able to tell her no since she was knee high to a grasshopper. Didn't see that changin' just cause you hadn't seen her in a while."

"Asshole," I muttered, only half serious.

"Also figured you'd be glad to see a friendly face."

"Lots of friendly faces around the clubhouse," I shot back.

"None that look like my Lily," he said just as quickly.

"Don't start steppin' in shit that's none of your business," I warned, pushing myself to my feet.

"I'd think you'd realize by now that it doesn't matter how old your kids are, they'll always be your business."

"I appreciate the talk," I said, ignoring his words. "More than ya know."

"Of course," he said.

"You want me to send Farrah back in here?"

"If you see her."

"Hell," I said, scoffing. "You know she's right outside the damn door."

"No doubt," Casper said with a tired smile. "Can't seem to escape the woman."

"Like you'd ever want to," I replied.

As soon as I opened the door, I found Farrah standing across the hall, sipping a coffee as she played a game on her phone. She'd gone where she'd said she was planning to, but I was willing to bet she'd been back in less than five minutes. Like most of the old timers in the club, Farrah and Casper's relationship was an abnormally close one. You didn't see one of them without the other very often.

"He's all yours," I said as I gestured to the door behind me.

"Thanks, hun," she replied, shoving her phone into her pocket. "And thanks for coming to see him. He's been worryin' about it all day."

"Of course."

"I know he sent Lily," she said slowly, watching my face for a reaction. "Since you showed up, I'll assume that you didn't boot her ass out the second you saw her."

"I didn't," I verified.

"Good." She took a deep breath, then gave me a sad smile. "Sometimes shit doesn't work out, you know? And I know there's a lot of hurt on both sides… but try to be kind, alright? My girl was young, and immature, and maybe didn't handle shit the way she should've. But times like these, you're gonna need your friends. And Lily could be one of the best ones you'll ever have."

"I hear you," I replied.

Without another word, she strode toward Casper's room and disappeared inside.

Jesus Christ, what a mess. From the impression I'd gotten, both of Lily's parents were giving me the all clear to… what? Get with her? Start up our friendship again?

I couldn't even wrap my mind around starting shit up with Lily again. The thought of sinking into her and getting lost for a few days held a fuck of a lot of appeal, but that wasn't going to happen. Not only did I have to bury the mother of my child, but I also had to somehow completely uproot my two-year-old son's life and get him used to living with me fulltime. I didn't have the time or the stomach to navigate the minefield that was Lily Butler.

Twenty minutes after I left the hospital, I pulled up to pick up Gray, and had to take deep breaths as I saw Ash's mom peek out the front window and then shut off the lights, trying to pretend that they weren't there. I was exhausted and frustrated and I didn't have the patience to deal with Kathy, no matter how torn up she was about losing Ashley. I tried so goddamn hard to turn my sympathy for her into understanding, but as I knocked on the door over and over with no answer, I finally snapped.

"Kathy, you don't want me kickin' in the door, you'll bring my son out here now," I called, watching the front window. Nothing moved, but faintly I could hear Gray calling for me. He must have heard my voice.

I knocked one more time, and when she still didn't open up, I stepped back, ready to knock the flimsy lock out of the doorframe.

"Oh, Leo," Kathy said, opening the door with a look of fake surprise on her face. "I thought we'd agreed that I was keepin' Gray for another night."

"No, *we* didn't," I replied simply, walking toward her so she had no choice but to move back into the house. I looked around, barely managing to hide my disgust at the musty smell of her house. I'd been there a couple times before, but once Ash had seen the look on my face, she hadn't invited me again.

I trusted Kathy would take good care of Gray when he visited, and I'd never had a problem with him going to her house, but I fucking hated the place. The woman never opened a window or let any fresh air in, and it left the house with a stink that she couldn't hide with the scented shit she stashed on every counter and shelf.

"Gray?" I called.

Within seconds, my son was galloping down the hallway, the thumb in his mouth not hiding the wide grin he was giving me.

"How's my boy?" I asked as I lifted him into the air. "You have fun at Granny's?"

He babbled something I could barely understand about dogs and TV around his thumb, then laid his head on my shoulder with a sigh. He was tired. Kathy probably hadn't given him a nap, and there was no place in her house that he felt comfortable putting himself to bed.

"I really think he should stay here again tonight," Kathy said as I strode toward the door. I looked at her incredulously as she stepped in front of me like she was going to block me from leaving. "Then you can go do what you do. It was Ash's night tonight, anyway."

"Ash isn't here," I ground out, angry that she was bringing any of this up in front of Gray. "And she isn't going to be here."

"Mama?" Gray asked, his little fingers playing with the sleeve of my t-shirt.

"I just think—"

"I know what you think, Kathy," I said, trying to keep my voice from showing my frustration. "But you won't win. You wanna see Gray? I'm cool with that. You let me know when you're up for a visit, and I'll do my best to make sure you get it."

"I'm his only family left."

"No," I said firmly, trying like hell to keep my temper. "He's got a whole other family that loves him."

"So you're just going to cut me out?" she hissed, her voice wobbling.

"I never said that, and I never would."

Gray's fingers tightened in my shirt and started twisting it from side to side, and that's when I knew I needed to get the fuck out of there. I pushed past Kathy's small, wiry frame, and ignored the way her nails dug into my bicep as I stepped onto the porch. I'd almost made it to the steps when I came to a stop, unable to go any further.

Turning around, I met Kathy's eyes. "You're always welcome to see Gray," I said gently, feeling sorry for the old bat as I watched tears run down her face. "And if you need anythin', you just let me know, alright?"

She glared at me, but finally nodded before she spun around and closed the door.

We'd barely made it out of Kathy's neighborhood before Gray was passed out in the back seat. Usually I'd take him back to my apartment and put him to bed if he fell asleep in the car, but I couldn't stand the thought of sitting there alone in the quiet until he woke up. I needed some noise, something to distract me from the knowledge that as soon as he woke up, Gray was going to start asking about his mama. He always did that. If he woke up with Ashley, he asked about me, and if he woke up with me he asked about Ash.

I wasn't even sure how to handle it. He was too young to understand any explanation. Telling him that he wouldn't see his mom again wouldn't have any effect, because there was just no way that his little brain could process that kind of information. I had a feeling that for the next few months, I'd spend most of my time with him explaining that it was Dad's day, not Mom's, until he finally quit asking.

Imagining the confusion I'd see on his face made me nauseous.

The clubhouse was pretty busy when we got there, and I was glad. Even if I laid down with Gray for his nap, I'd still be able to hear people moving around and music playing outside my room. With all the noise, he'd probably wake up before he was ready, but there were enough people around to keep his attention occupied and any fits to a minimum.

Gray didn't stir as I unbuckled his tiny, sweaty body from his car seat. My boy always slept hot. From the time he was about three months old, we hadn't been able to put him in those thick pajamas with the snaps because he'd sweat his way through them in an hour and then we'd have a soaking wet, screaming baby to deal with. Even if he was in shorts and a t-shirt, after just a few minutes of sleep, the hair around his temples and the back of his neck was damp.

I nodded to people as I carried Gray into the main room, but I didn't even make it to the back hallway before I was stopped by a gentle hand on my arm.

"Hi, baby," my mom said softly, laying her hand on Gray's back. "How's he doing?"

"He's alright," I assured her, shifting Gray a little as he started to slide sideways. "Doesn't really have any clue what's goin' on."

"Probably a good thing," she said, echoing Casper's words from earlier. "How are *you* doing?"

"I'm fine," I said.

"No, you're not."

"I'm good as I can be."

"That's a bit more accurate," she said. "Did you go up and see Casper?"

"Yeah." I nodded. "Went and saw him before I picked up Gray."

"That's good. I know he was anxious to talk to you."

"Yeah, he sent Lily to find me."

"Is that right?" my mom asked, and I knew from one look at her face that she'd already known Casper was going to send Lily to me.

"You, too?" I asked in irritation. "What the fuck are you all tryin' to do?"

"What?" she asked in confusion.

"Don't talk to your mother like that," my dad ordered, coming up behind me.

"You realize the mother of my child just fuckin' died, right?" I looked between the two of them in disbelief.

"What kind of question is that?" my dad asked, anger making his voice quieter than before.

"You're sendin' Lily around, tryin' to what, exactly?"

My dad watched me in disbelief, then scoffed. "Givin' you the chance to make up with a girl who you were close with before she went to college, during a time when you're goin' through what you're goin' through, ain't some sort of sinister plot."

"The mother of my child just fuckin' died on the side of the road," I reiterated through clenched teeth.

"The mother of your child," my dad agreed, glancing at Gray. "Right. Not your wife, not your girlfriend. Know you two were close, know you're hurtin', but don't make the loss somethin' it ain't."

"Jesus Christ," I muttered.

"How about I take Gray for a while?" my mom offered, trying to diffuse the situation. "I was going to lay down for a while anyway, it's been a long couple of days."

I thought about it for a second, relishing the feeling of Gray's little hot puffs of breath on the side of my neck, before I relented and handed him over. He'd probably sleep better in my pop's room since it was further away from the main room than mine was. Plus, my mom did look tired. She looked like she was ready to drop.

"Come on, baby," my dad said gently.

"I can make it to the room on my own," my mom pointed out.

"Just as easy for me to walk ya."

Mom shook her head in amusement, then met my eyes over Grey's messy dark hair. "I know what it's like to try and come back after you've pushed everyone away," she said softly. "It's harder than you could ever imagine, son. Cut Lily a little slack, huh?"

I watched them walk away then turned toward the bar. That's when I saw Lily watching me, her face filled with emotion. She didn't look away even after she knew I saw her, and for a second, I was frozen in place.

Then a yell from behind the bar stole both of our attention, and that's when I saw Rose, flipping and spinning liquor bottles like she was auditioning for a talent show. She had a huge grin on her face as her brothers egged her on, and I couldn't help but move closer as she slung drinks like a pro.

"You guys barely have anything back here," she complained as she grabbed a dusty bottle from the shelf. "It's a disgrace."

"Sorry we don't like your fruity-tooty drinks, little sister," Will said, rolling his eyes.

"You'd like them if you tried them," she argued. "I don't even have ingredients for a Long Island Iced Tea! What is wrong with you people?"

"Tequila, whiskey, and beer," Tommy grunted like a caveman.

"Don't forget vodka," Rose said, holding up a bottle of flavored stuff.

"That shit's for the women," Will said.

"Weren't you the one mixing that shit with orange juice at Tommy's place two weeks ago?" I asked, stepping up beside Lily.

"That was one time!"

"Sure it was," Lily said with mock seriousness, joining in on the joke. "Do you prefer the orange flavored vodka or the tangerine? I've noticed that they're similar, but not exactly the same."

"Fuck you both," Will said, pointing back and forth between the two of us.

"When did you take up drinking?" I asked quietly, barely glancing at the woman beside me.

"College," she replied with a shrug, her shoulder brushing my arm.

"She's gotta keep me company while I work," Rose cut in, sliding a drink in front of Lily. "Otherwise, I'd never see her."

"That's not true," Lily protested. "We share a fucking bedroom."

"I see that dirty mouth hasn't changed any," I said as Rose slid a shot glass full of amber liquid toward me.

"Some things never change," she murmured, taking her shot.

I gave her a slight nod of acknowledgement, but the statement shook me more than I would have ever admitted. I quickly threw back the shot Rose had given me, some sort of mixture of booze that I couldn't put my finger on but went down smooth, then turned and walked away. I wasn't at the clubhouse to catch up with Lily.

I sure as fuck wasn't going to try and re-start old shit when I wasn't even sure what my life was going to look like now. Ashley and I had a pretty even split with Gray, even though we'd never made it official. Things changed from week to week, depending on who worked when and if I was going to be out of town, but it always evened out to Gray spending half his time with me and half his time with his mother.

I had no idea what I was going to do now. I'd never had to find a daycare for Gray, or worried about where he'd stay if I was out of town.

Ash had worked as a waitress around my schedule at the garage so that we didn't have to pay for childcare. Now, hell, I had no idea how I was going to make it work. I sure as fuck wasn't going to leave my boy with strangers.

"Hey, man," Grease called as I tried to move past his table. "How you doin'?"

"I'm alright," I said for the millionth time that day.

"Good." He glanced past me at the bar and grimaced. "How the hell am I old enough to have grown kids?"

"And grandkids," I pointed out, making him scowl.

"The grandkids are a gift, it's my own offspring I gotta worry about."

"Seems like they're doin' okay." I glanced behind me to find Rose high-fiving Lily across the bar top.

"Boys are easy, man," Grease said with a shake of his head. "It's the girls you gotta worry about. You send them off to college with their cousin, hopin' that some of that drive'll rub off on 'em, and they come back knowing how to tend bar."

"Good skill to have," I murmured.

"I'll remind you of that when you have a little girl."

"Don't see that happenin'," I said, moving away from his table.

"Hell, son, that's what we all say."

I just shook my head as I headed to one of the couches against the wall in the back. I'd left a book stuffed behind it earlier in the week, and now seemed like the perfect time to block out the world for a while. As I stretched out on my back on the fringe of the crowd, I couldn't help but glance at the bar again. Lily was laughing at something her cousin had done, her head tipped back and her mouth wide open with glee.

It was a beautiful sight. I still remembered when she was in high school and had such a tough time dealing with all the shit that was being thrown at her. Losing her sight so young and then suddenly getting it back had thrown her, and I hadn't blamed her. Everything she'd known over those blind years, even down to the way she'd interacted with other kids her age, had changed in an instant. I should have known back then that starting anything with her, no matter how platonic, wasn't smart. She'd been adjusting to a world she no longer recognized, and if I was completely honest, I never believed she would have stuck with me. Gray just made the decision easier for her.

## Chapter 19

# LILY

Before I knew it, my week at home was almost over. I'd spent most of my time watching the lectures I was missing—thank God for the internet—and trying to keep up with my schoolwork between ferrying Charlie around and visiting my dad. They'd sent him home on day five, which seemed way too early to me, but what did I know? He could barely hobble around, so we'd set him up with a bed in the living room, and since the minute he'd gotten home, he'd been making everyone's life miserable.

I wasn't surprised when my Uncle Grease showed up to keep him company and my mom ushered me quickly out of the house, flipping off the front door as soon as it closed behind us.

"I love your father," she said seriously as we moved toward his truck. "But if I had to stay there one more second, I was going to smother him in his sleep."

I laughed and agreed. He'd been bitching non-stop about anything and everything. He wasn't comfortable. He was bored. Why the hell was the house so cold? Why was it so hot? He was hungry. He was thirsty. He had to piss. He could walk to the bathroom on his own, goddamnit.

I'd been able to close myself in my room for most of it under the pretense of studying, but my mom hadn't felt comfortable leaving him alone. I had a feeling she'd called Aunt Callie and that's why Uncle Grease had shown up before my mom completely lost her shit.

Hopefully, he'd be able to snap my dad out of the pissy mood he'd been in.

"Where are we going?" I asked, adjusting the beanie I'd thrown over my hair in our rush out the door.

"Callie's. She's having the girls over for lunch."

"What girls?" I was in sweatpants and a paint-splattered hoodie of my mom's, but I wasn't really worried about it. I'd known all of my mom's friends since birth, so it wasn't as if they hadn't seen me in my pajamas.

"Brenna, Amy, Molly, Hawk, Trix, and Rose. I'm not sure who else."

"So pretty much everyone."

"Yeah," Mom said with a smile. "We usually don't have the time, but for some reason, none of them were working today."

"Sweet. I need to talk to Rose, anyway."

"Getting ready to head back, huh?" Mom asked.

I nodded. My professors had been cool about me taking the week off as long as I got my assignments in, but I was pretty sure their lenience would disappear if I tried to stay longer.

I was being pulled in two opposite directions. I'd done well in New Haven. I'd found the place where I fit, and I'd become content there. But the thought of flying back across the country made me nauseous.

During the week, I'd been able to hang with my cousins and their spouses. I'd watched Charlie play basketball and had driven her to school. I'd hung with my nephews and kicked their ass on the old school Nintendo. I'd helped my mom with shit around the house and I'd been able to take some of the load off her shoulders with my dad.

If I was completely honest with myself, I felt happy for the first time in years. I don't know if I'd just been too young when I left, or if I'd changed, but I was coming to realize that I was a homebody. I liked hanging with my family and spending time at the clubhouse. I liked knowing everyone and feeling comfortable even in my pajamas.

"Your sister's coming home tonight," my mom said as we pulled into Aunt Callie's packed driveway.

"What?" I turned to look at her, my mouth hanging open.

"Yeah." She shrugged. "She called this morning and said that she was getting in at nine tonight and asked if someone could pick her up."

"Not it!" I practically yelled, startling her.

"Don't be an ass," she chided.

"I am *not* picking her up," I said shaking my head. "I'm an adult now, and you can't make me."

"Oh, you think?"

"*Mom*," I whined.

"Lucky for you, Cam said he'd go grab her."

"Good. He can do it."

"She's changed, you know," Mom said as we got out of the car. "A lot."

"I literally haven't talked to her in years except when she calls on Christmas morning," I pointed out. "She hasn't changed that much."

"Well, it's not like you act like you even want to talk to her," she called over her shoulder as I followed her to the house.

"She freaking left!"

"And what exactly did you do, two and a half years ago?" she asked, raising one eyebrow. My mouth snapped shut as she swung open the front door without knocking and walked inside.

It was different, I told myself as I followed her into my aunt's kitchen. Cecilia had taken off and hadn't come home. I'd come home. I'd made sure to talk to Charlie and my parents and Cam at least once a week. I hadn't cut them out of my life the way she had. I hadn't made my parents wonder how I was doing because my phone calls were so vague that it bordered on insulting. I'd—

My thoughts all flew out the window as I saw all the women standing in the kitchen, their hands flying around as they gestured and laughed and talked. Hawk was making some sort of lewd gesture that made Molly blush and slap her, and Trix was laughing so hard that she was bent at the waist, bracing herself with one hand on the counter. Old Amy's eyes were watering as she laughed at Molly's reaction, and the bracelets on her arms jingled as she patted her back consolingly.

Brenna and my Aunt Callie were looking at something I couldn't see beyond the counter. Then Brenna bent over, and when she came up, it was like the entire world stopped.

I couldn't see or hear anything but him. I couldn't breathe, or speak, or move.

He was tiny, but I'd already known that. I'd seen Leo holding him in the club, and he'd looked even smaller then, but he'd been asleep. When I'd seen him before, I hadn't known how his little hands moved, patting and gripping Brenna's t-shirt as she talked to him. I hadn't seen how long his eyelashes were, or how they framed dark brown eyes exactly like his dad's. I hadn't been able to tell that his hair was long, sweeping his shoulders in soft curls, or the way he impatiently brushed it out of his eyes so that he could watch Brenna worshipfully.

I hadn't really seen him before.

And now I was.

I had never believed in love at first sight. It was silly. Love, real love, was knowing someone and understanding them. Or at least that's what I'd thought.

Now, I knew it was real, because looking at that tiny face, with the bowed lips and the dark brown eyes and the high cheekbones, I fell wholly and irrevocably in love with a child I'd never spoken a word to. In an instant, I was fully in his thrall, willing to do anything to keep him safe and happy.

"Who that?" he asked shyly, pointing at me.

I took a step forward, then stopped as I saw his hand clench on

Brenna's sleeve.

"That's Lily," Brenna said, smiling. "That's Charlie's older sister."

"Charlie?"

"She's at school, baby. Maybe we'll see her later."

He continued to stare at me, his eyes wide and thoughtful, then lost interest and laid his head on Brenna's shoulder, popping his thumb in his mouth.

And the world started to spin again.

"Cute, huh?" Rose said groggily, coming up behind me in pajamas, her hair a rat's nest and her breath something out of a horror movie.

"How are you just waking up?" I asked as she pushed around me to get to the coffee pot.

"She's still on Connecticut time," Hawk said dryly.

"Right," I said. "Which means it's almost four o'clock."

"I'm a night owl," Rose muttered, making a shooing motion at me behind her back.

"Or a vampire," Molly said. "Ugh, don't talk until you've brushed your teeth."

"So much hostility." Rose shook her head as she reached for the creamer sitting on the counter.

We migrated toward the living room once everyone had their lunch and drinks, and I somehow ended up on the floor in front of a couch, squished between my mom's legs and Aunt Callie's.

"It's so nice having a day off from the hospital," Molly said, taking a bite of her food. "We've been short staffed for a month."

"Oh, that sucks," Hawk replied.

I watched as Brenna put Gray down on the floor and fed him tiny bites of her sandwich. He was like a baby bird. He'd take a bite, walk away a few steps to pick up something on the coffee table, then set it back down and go back to Brenna when he was ready for another bite.

The conversation flowed around me, with everyone talking about kids and husbands and work, but I ignored most of it as I watched Gray. He wasn't all Leo, the way I'd originally thought. I could see parts of his mom in there, too. When he tipped his head back and I saw his face in profile, and when he smiled, that was all Ashley. Leo's genes were dominant, though, and there wasn't any mistaking them for anything but father and son.

"Is there going to be a service?" Amy asked, catching my attention. "I kept waiting to hear, we didn't want to miss it."

"No," Brenna said quietly, her mouth tightening. "Her mother had her cremated without saying a word to Leo, and she said she's not having a memorial or anything."

"Daddy," Gray said, nodding.

"Figures," Hawk mumbled.

"She doesn't owe him anything," Trix said reluctantly. She glanced at me and quickly away. "They weren't together. But it would've been nice to know what her plans were before she made them. At least for the little you-know-who."

We all glanced at Gray, who was taking the rarely used coasters out of their little holder and then putting them back in one-by-one.

"We could still have something small at the club," Aunt Callie said.

"I'll talk to my son," Brenna replied. "But I'm not sure he'd want that. He's pretty overwhelmed as it is."

"I can imagine," my mom said, finally joining the conversation. "None of this can be easy for him."

"He doesn't talk to me," Brenna admitted.

Conversation came to a standstill as Gray wandered toward me and handed me a coaster, a shy smile on his face.

"Thank you," I said with a smile.

"Elcome."

Then he walked away and the conversation resumed.

The next time he brought me a coaster, the chatter stayed constant, but I knew without looking up that everyone was watching us.

He brought me all of the coasters, then came back for each, one-by-one, as he put them away again. That happened over and over, and each time he said a few more words to me. I couldn't understand most of it, but I nodded my head seriously and replied anyway, and that seemed to appease him.

Lunch was over and everyone had settled in to drink coffee and chat when Gray plopped down, straddling my lap, and stuck his thumb in his mouth. His head was resting right over my heart, and without hesitation I reclined a little and put my arm around him so that he'd be more comfortable. It only took a few minutes before he'd fallen asleep.

"He likes you," Brenna said quietly.

"New boobs," Trix joked. "He's already had a go at sleeping on all of ours."

"Not true," Rose argued, waving her hand. "I haven't held him."

"That's probably because you're not… nurturing," Hawk said with a laugh.

"I am, too! I'm very nurturing. Tell them, Lily."

"She's very nurturing," I said dryly.

"See?" Rose said with a huff. "It's not surprising that Gray went to her. If he's anything like his dad, he's already half in love with her."

"*Rose*," I hissed, glaring.

"Oh, come on," Rose said in annoyance. "We all know it's true. No use pretending. We're all friends here."

"Right," I said through clenched teeth. "Actually, I need to talk to you. We need to figure out when we're flying back to Connecticut."

"Damn, the week's over already?" she said, her shoulders slumping. "That went quick."

I nodded. "You don't have to go when I do," I said. "If you can get more time off, you should."

"No way," she replied stubbornly. "Where you go, I go, Jack."

"Oh, come on," I said, lowering my voice as Gray shifted on my lap. "Seriously, stay if you want to. I have to get back to class, but you don't."

"Not happening."

Before our conversation could turn into a full-blown argument, Molly and Hawk stood up. "We gotta head home," Molly said. "Reb gets out of school soon."

"And she's my ride," Hawk said, pointing her thumb at Molly. "Thanks for having us over, Callie."

"Anytime," Aunt Callie said, getting to her feet to hug them. "Bring Rebel over for dinner this week. I just got some dinosaur-shaped chicken nuggets."

Soon, it was only Brenna, Aunt Callie, and my mom left in the living room with me and Gray. I carefully stood and walked to an empty couch, fully intending to lay Gray down on it, but at the last minute, I changed my mind. Instead, I laid down on my back, keeping him snug against my chest. Almost instantly, my eyes felt heavy. The kid was like a furnace, and between the lunch I'd just had, the heat, and barely getting enough rest for the last week, I could feel sleep pulling me under.

"I'll just have Leo pick Gray up here, if that's okay with you," I heard Brenna say as I drifted. "He'll be done in an hour anyway, and if I try to move the baby right now, he'll wake up and be a terror for the rest of the night."

"Fine with me," Aunt Callie replied. "I'm just going to clean up this mess and hang out at home for the rest of the day."

"You need help?" my mom asked as their voices grew further away.

"Not unless you're using me as an excuse to not go home. If that's the case, I need a lot of help. Tons. I can't do this without you."

"You *are* looking pretty overwhelmed."

I heard the front door open and close, and then I was out.

I WOKE UP later to quiet voices.

"Thanks for keepin' him, Callie."

"He passed out on her lap and she was right behind him," Aunt Callie murmured. "So I just left them where they were."

"They've been sleepin' since my mom left?"

"They haven't even shifted. I don't know how she stayed asleep in that sweatshirt with Gray sweating all over her."

"Musta been tired."

"I was," I replied groggily, opening my eyes to find Leo standing above me. "Still am, actually."

"I can tell," he muttered with a laugh.

"What?" I shifted a little on the couch and realized that the beanie I'd been wearing had somehow come off and my hair was creating a tangled halo around my head. "Shit."

"Daddy!" Gray said, his voice scratchy. He sat up and nearly fell off the couch before I could catch him.

"Whoa, Turbo," Leo said, lifting him off me. "You have a good nap?"

"Lily," Gray said, pointing at me. I glanced down and snorted at the wet spots on my sweatshirt. He'd not only drooled all the way through it, making the fabric stick to my collarbone, but had also wet through his diaper, leaving a huge wet spot on my stomach.

"Careful," I said, pushing myself up. "Someone needs his diaper changed."

"Aw, man," Leo said, flipping Gray until he was dangling under one of his arms. "You're all wet, son."

"Wet," Gray said.

"My mom leave a bag?" Leo asked Callie.

They moved away from me to get the diaper bag and I quickly

smoothed my hair and pulled my hat back on. I didn't have anything but a bra under the sweatshirt, so that was a lost cause unless I asked Rose for something… and I didn't want to do that. I was worried that Leo would leave if I went upstairs.

"Can you give me a ride home?" I asked, shuffling up behind him as he knelt on the floor changing Gray's clothes.

"Thought you were a driver now," he replied without looking at me.

"I am," I said. "But I rode with my mom and it looks like she left without me."

He was silent for so long that I started to fidget.

"It's fine," I said finally. "I can just ask Aunt Callie."

Just as I started to turn and walk away, his voice stopped me.

"I'll give you a ride," he said gruffly. "Give me a minute to get him dressed."

It didn't take long before I was riding in the front seat of his SUV, my arms wrapped around myself to keep warm. Those wet spots on my sweatshirt had grown cold and clammy once we'd gone outside.

"Don't—" He stopped, scratched at his scruffy face and then spoke again. "Don't go messin' with my son, alright?"

"What?" I asked in confusion, glancing back at where Gray was kicking his feet.

"You're leavin'," Leo said. "He's got enough a'that right now. So just keep your distance."

"What?" I said again, quieter.

"You got another life, yeah? I get it and I got over that shit a long ass time ago. But he won't understand that."

"Leo," I said, shaking my head. "I wasn't trying to—"

"You're never tryin' to do anything, Lily," Leo said, impatience threading through his voice. "But you've made it real easy to leave everyone behind, and my son's two. He doesn't understand that shit yet."

"You think I'd do anything to hurt him?"

"I think you look out for Lily first, and anyone else has gotta just deal."

"But you got over that shit a long ass time ago, huh?"

"Fuck, woman," he snapped, his voice growing louder. "This is my kid we're talkin' about. Not fuckin' ancient history."

"It doesn't sound like that to me."

"Daddy?" Gray called.

"It's all good, son," Leo replied through clenched teeth.

Without another word, he took two left turns in the wrong direction and pulled into an empty parking lot and threw the rig into park. "Out," he ordered.

I was just mad enough to unbuckle my seat belt and climb out of my seat, but caught myself from slamming the door behind me. I was fully expecting him to leave my ass stranded, but as I rounded the hood of the SUV, he met me there.

"There's no reason for you to have any relationship with my kid," he yelled, the veins in his neck bulging.

I took a step back, startled at the volume of his voice, but it didn't take me long before I was yelling back.

"I have every reason."

"The fuck you do. That kid just lost his mom, you get that? He's got no idea that his life is completely changed, and you're playing house with him at Callie's like you ain't about to leave again for God knows how long!"

"I hung out with him for a couple of hours," I screamed, throwing my hands up in the air. "And you're being an asshole! What, did you expect me to treat him like crap? Ignore him when he wanted to play?"

"Seemed likely, considering the way you acted when you found out about him."

"That was never about him, and you know that. For fuck's sake, Leo. The man I was in love with was having a kid with someone else."

"In love with?" Leo laughed derisively. "You don't know what the fuck that is."

"And *you* do? You just let me go. I made you leave, but you never fucking came back. You didn't even try to change my mind."

"That was because I love you, you stupid bitch," he screamed, making my head jerk back in surprise. "You think I was gonna hold you back? You honestly think I would've begged you to stay? For what? So you could go to some shitty community college or worse, get a fucking job and play house with me?"

"Who are you mad at?" I asked, shaking my head. "Me or yourself?"

"All of it," he yelled, bringing his hand down hard on the hood of his truck.

"Leo, don't," I gasped, reaching for his hand.

The minute I was close enough for him to grab, his hand was fisted in the front of my sweatshirt and he was dragging me against the front of his body.

"How the fuck did I get here?" he asked, his forehead dropping to rest against mine. "How the fuck did I get here, Dandelion?"

His body shook with a silent sob, and I reached for his face, framing it with my hands. It was no longer about me and him. It was no longer about our history or past hurts. No. Now it was about us, the us that we'd always been before. The two people that could let their guards down for one another. And Leo's guard was down. All of his "Alrights" and "Doing fines" over the past week had led to that moment in the deserted parking lot in the pouring down rain, and I was terrified that I wouldn't be able to do for him what he'd done for me all those years.

"It's going to be okay," I whispered, rubbing my thumbs down his cheeks, both scarred and perfect.

"She's gone," he said, shuddering. "What the fuck am I going to do?"

"You're going to keep doing what you've always done," I replied, smoothing back his long hair. "And you're going to tell Gray a lot of stories about his mama."

"What am I gonna say when he asks if I loved her? What am I gonna say if he asks about any of it?"

"You did love her," I murmured, the words feeling oddly light on my tongue. "She gave you Gray, of course you loved her."

"She shouldn't have been in that car," he ground out. "We were fightin' and she shouldn't have been in that car."

"No," I shook my head gently, my fingers tightening in his hair. "Don't do that. Don't try to make it something it's not."

"If she woulda stayed at the club—"

"Then it could have happened on her way home the next day, or the day after that. You don't know, Leo. You have no idea what would have happened."

"I do," he ground out. "She woulda picked Gray up at her mom's and everything woulda been like it was before."

His eyes closed in pain, and there was nothing else I could say. How did you explain a freak accident to someone that had just lost their partner? Leo may not have been in a romantic relationship with Ashley, but they'd been partners in raising their son. They'd been a team, and now he was alone. Surrounded by people who loved him, but alone all the same. I couldn't make that better for him.

"Now is probably when I tell you something that fixes it all," I whispered, tears making my voice tight as I repeated what my dad had said to me years ago. "But I can't. Life's not fair. We've all learned that at one point or another. You just have to push through it."

Leo nodded and his hand slowly lost its grip on my sweatshirt.

"Gray's probably losin' his shit," he said quietly, taking a step back so that my hands slid off the sides of his face. He turned without another word and rounded the car to open Gray's door.

My clothes were soaked through when I climbed back into the Suburban, and I shivered as Leo talked to a surprisingly calm Gray in the back seat. His voice was calm and level, and even after he'd climbed into the driver's seat and put the car in reverse there was no sign of the meltdown he'd had just moments before.

As he drove me home in silence, it was as if our conversation in the rain had never happened. The only evidence left was our wet clothes and my runny nose. By the time he stopped in my parents' driveway, I was dreading the moment I got out of the car.

"I'll see ya around, yeah?" he asked, staring out the windshield.

"Yeah," I confirmed, my voice hoarse. "Sure."

If I'd thought that something had changed between us, or that maybe some of the ice had broken, I'd been completely wrong.

I climbed out of the Suburban, but I couldn't make myself walk away. Not yet.

"Thank you," I said finally, my hand so tight on the door handle that my knuckles were white. "Thank you for letting me go."

"I'll always do what's best for you, Dandelion," he replied instantly, still refusing to look at me. "Don't you know that yet?"

As soon as I closed the door he started backing up, and within seconds was driving back down my parents' driveway, leaving me there in the rain.

"Lily," Charlie yelled from the front porch as I stood there staring at his retreating taillights. "Ceecee's coming tonight!"

"Fucking wonderful," I muttered, closing my eyes in defeat.

## Chapter 20

# LEO

"Party tonight," Tommy told me as I climbed out of the Buick I was working on. "Cecilia's home."

"Say what?" I asked in surprise, almost hitting my head on the doorframe. "Since when?"

"Got in last night," he replied. "Came home to see her pop, I guess."

" 'Bout damn time," I muttered.

"Yeah, no shit. Can't imagine how that's playin' out."

"I won't be there tonight," I said, popping the hood of the Buick.

"Bullshit."

"I've got Gray—"

"He can stay at our house," Cam cut in. "Your sister's havin' someone stay with the boys, they can keep Gray, too."

"Who?"

"No idea," Cam replied. "But anyone who keeps our kids is gonna be someone who'd keep Gray." He laughed. "Fishin' in the same pool, man."

"Yeah, alright," I said with a shrug.

As I started work on the Buick, I thought about the girl I used to know. I was curious to see Cecilia after all this time. I hadn't heard a word from her since she'd gone to California, and a part of me wondered if she was the same girl who'd left. I didn't know how anyone could be gone that long and not change quite a bit, but if there was anyone who could do it, it would be her.

I wondered how Lily was dealing with Cecilia showing up. They'd always had such a weird fucking relationship. Lily had idolized her sister, and Cecilia had been so damn jealous of Lily that it was hard to understand the fascination. Sure, Cecila could be sweet. I knew that firsthand. But she could also be a viper with little or no provocation. You just never knew with her. God, I hoped she'd mellowed while she'd been gone, at least for Lily's sake.

After Cecilia took off, it seemed like Lily's blinders when it came to her sister disappeared, but I didn't know what their relationship was like anymore. Maybe they'd kept in touch and gotten closer over the years.

I grunted. It didn't seem possible that anyone could get close to Cecilia. It had always amazed me how two kids from the same parents could turn out so differently. I couldn't imagine Cecilia treating Gray with the same reverence and tenderness that Lily had. That shit had turned me inside out. Half of me had wanted to beat my chest and yell *mine* and the other half had wanted to jerk him out of her sleeping arms and tell her to stay the fuck away from him. Because I knew how Lily's tenderness felt and I also knew how fucking bad it stung when it was snatched away.

I caught my hand on a piece of metal and cursed. I needed to get my head straight before I fucked up and did any real damage. Shifting my attention to the work in front of me, I deliberately forgot about the Butler sisters.

I forgot about them, that is, until a few hours later when Lily dropped down beside me on the picnic bench where I was eating my lunch.

"My sister's back," she said, slapping her hands down on the table.
"I heard."
"Did you also hear that they're having a party in her honor?"
"Heard somethin' about that, too."

"I'm not going," she said mulishly, reminding me of when she was a kid. "This is fucking prodigal son bullshit."

"They're just happy to see her—"

"You know my dad can't even go, right?" she asked, ignoring me. "He's stuck in bed and they're having a party for Cecilia. Like, awesome Ceecee, you came home when your dad was in a major car accident and could've died. Good job. Have a party."

"You're workin' yourself up over nothin'," I pointed out, trying to calm her ranting. "You know the boys'll use any excuse to have a party."

"I bet *you're* super stoked she's here," she said, her voice almost a hiss. "Bet you can't wait to catch up. Or have you guys been talking all this time? Once I left, just started all of it back up again?"

She shoved to her feet before I could answer and stormed inside the clubhouse, pissing me off. That, what she'd done right there? That was Cecilia bullshit. Making accusations and then running away before a person could say anything back. Jesus, that shit got under my skin.

I followed her inside, leaving my food sitting on the bench, and as soon as I got to the bar, Poet pointed over his shoulder with a thumb to tell me where she'd gone.

"Nope," I growled as she started into her dad's room. I grabbed her around the waist and threw her over my shoulder.

As soon as we hit my room, she was pinching me with the knuckles of her first two fingers, making bruises I was sure would be the size of quarters on my back.

"Knock it off," I barked, tossing her onto the bed. "You're acting like a brat."

"I hate that she's here," she replied. Her words were filled with venom, but her eyes told another story completely as she pushed herself to her feet.

"She's your sister, Dandelion."

"She's—" Lily shook her head in defeat. "How can everyone just forget that she took off?"

"Same way they did with you, I'd imagine," I said gently. I didn't want to hurt her feelings, but if she was expecting her sister to get some kind of cold shoulder from the club, she'd be waiting a long time. I had a lot of issues with how shit with Cecilia had gone down when we were kids, and I didn't particularly want anything to do with her, but to the rest of the club, she was just another kid home visiting. She hadn't done anything to earn their contempt.

"It wasn't the same," she said, her eyes filling with tears. "Why do people keep saying that?"

"Guess it depends on who you ask."

"I went to college."

"And Cecilia went to California and got a job."

"I—" Her voice faded and her eyes filled with tears. "She left me. She left and she didn't even come back when I started to see again."

"I've never been able to understand your sister, baby," I said softly, reaching for her. "And I doubt you ever will, either."

"She's acting like everything is fine," Lily whispered against my chest. "And I just want to scream at her that it's not."

"So why don't you?"

"Because," she said, shaking her head. "You haven't screamed at me."

Her hand found its way under the back of my t-shirt, and I closed my eyes at the feeling her fingers on my bare skin. Without thought, my arms tightened around her back and one hand found the hair at the base of her neck.

"I did scream at you," I reminded her, dropping my head so that my lips were brushing her ear.

"That wasn't even about me," she said with a shudder. "That was everything boiling over at once."

"You think I want to scream at you for leaving?"

"I'd want to if I was you."

"Hell," I murmured, my hand tightening in her hair. "I'm so fuckin' proud of you, Dandelion. Any anger I had about you leavin' was gone when your dad came in wavin' that first report card around like a flag."

"I would've stayed," she whispered. "I would've stayed if you'd asked me to."

"Don't say that," I groaned, finally losing any restraint I had when it came to her.

Both of us moved at the same time, but the kiss I'd been planning on giving her, full of frustration and need, never happened. Instead, our lips barely brushed. It was the first time I'd had my mouth on hers in so long that I couldn't help but savor it.

"I should've been here with you," she said against my mouth.

I shook my head gently and pressed my mouth more firmly against hers to shut her up. My hands were shaking as I traced her body from shoulders to thighs and back up again. She was bigger than when she'd left. Her breasts were bigger, her ass was bigger, her waist was bigger, her thighs were bigger. It wasn't something most people would have noticed, it wasn't a huge difference, but I knew. I'd held her before. Had carried her and grabbed her ass and had felt her pressed up against me. The experience had been something that I'd never been able to forget, and I could feel the differences between then and now.

For some reason, those changes in her body turned me on even more. It was like physical proof of all the ways we had changed since that first time I'd kissed her. She wasn't a kid anymore. She'd been on her own and had experiences outside the bubble she'd grown up in. I knew she'd met far more interesting people than me, smarter, richer, well-traveled and yet, she was in *my* arms. Her tongue was in *my* mouth, and her nails were digging into *my* lower back.

She'd left and she'd come back to me, something I'd never thought would happen.

"You're fuckin' beautiful," I murmured, my voice almost surprised. "Shit, I—"

"I'm the same as I've always been," she said distractedly as she pushed my cut off my shoulders.

"You're not," I argued, helping her. I pulled my t-shirt off and closed my eyes at the feeling of her hands on my chest.

For the past week, my mind had been racing non-stop. I hadn't been able to escape it even after I'd closed my eyes at night. But right then, feeling her soft fingers tracing my chest and belly, everything else disappeared and my mind was finally silent.

"You're the same," she said, leaning forward to press her lips against my sternum. "You're exactly how I remembered you."

"I'm not," I argued, my hands shoving her coat off her shoulders and immediately finding the bottom of her shirt so I could pull it over her head.

"You love me?" she asked, meeting my eyes as she stood there in her jeans and bra.

"Impossible for me to stop," I replied honestly.

"Then you're the same," she said with a shrug.

After that, we didn't talk much. I stripped her slowly, discovering every inch that I'd never seen before, her belly button, the underside of her breasts and the nipples that pointed faintly upward, her hipbones and the short thatch of hair in between. I traced the curve where her ass cheeks met the backs of her thighs with my tongue and pressed my thumbs into the dimples at her lower back.

While I was marveling at all the places that I'd never before touched, she was doing her own exploring. Her hands drifted over my chest and arms, ran along the waistband of my jeans and then slowly peeled them off, gripped me through my boxers, then ran down the backs of my thighs and in between them.

Every movement was unhurried. There wasn't a second of awkwardness or fumbling, not even when we had to pause to kick off our shoes. Instead, we just took shit as it came, unable to stop and unwilling to rush.

By the time I had her spread out below me and was rolling the condom down my cock, it felt like I had just run a mile, but still had the energy to run a marathon.

"It feels like I've been waiting forever," she said, making me shudder as she used one finger to trace down the inside of my hip.

"You waited?" I asked, my throat tight as I met her eyes.

She winced and barely shook her head. "I'm not a virgin," she said, filling me with relief and jealousy that I'd never in a million years admit. "But it wasn't like this."

"I don't want to know," I murmured, coming down on top of her so that our mouths were level.

"It was only once," she said, running her nose along the side of mine.

"I don't want to know," I repeated.

"It—" her breath came out in a rush as I slid inside.

She was snug and warm and wet and so goddamn perfect.

"Leo," she said, her eyes wet. "Finally."

I kissed her face as I started to move, breathing her in.

It didn't take long before both of us were pushing for more. I lifted one of her legs over my shoulder as her nails dug into the back of my neck. Her hand ran between us and explored where we were connected as I worshiped her nipples, biting and sucking and leaving marks on her breasts that would be there for days. It was almost a fight, the way we went at each other once the thrill of exploration had turned into a craving for connection. Both of us struggled to get closer, to feel more and squeeze out every ounce of pleasure we could get.

She came with a whimper, her teeth clenched as she shuddered and as soon as her body went boneless, I had both of her knees on my shoulders. It didn't take me long to follow her over the edge, and when I did, it was better than any high I'd ever had.

Less than ten minutes later reality intruded and my quieted mind started to spin again. All it took were a few words from her.

"I'm going to transfer to a school out here," she whispered, snuggling closer against my chest as my stomach sank. "I can go to U of O. It's a good school."

"No," I blurted, unable to keep my mouth shut. "No, you're not."

"What do you mean, I'm not?" she asked, her entire body stiffening.

"You go to Yale," I said, staring down at the top of her head. "You're goin' to a fuckin' crazy good school. You're not ruinin' that."

"I wouldn't be 'ruining' anything," she said, lifting up to look at me.

"Your life's out there. You've got a couple more years—"

"So, what was this?" she asked, pulling away until our bodies were no longer touching. "A one-off? Letting off some steam?"

"Does it gotta mean you completely change your life?" I asked, sitting up so she was no longer hovering above me. "Your life ain't here with me."

"It could be," she snapped, crawling off the bed.

"I've got a kid, Lily," I reminded her. "I go to work and I take care of my boy. That's my life. That the life you want?"

"I want a life with you," she ground out.

"What, you're just gonna come back here and play house with me?"

"Why do you keep using that phrase, 'playing house'? It's fucking insulting. I'm saying I want to live out here and go to school near my family and you, and that's a bad thing?"

"You think you're gonna stick with school when you're makin' a life with me? Be able to keep up with all that work when you've got a two year old that's askin' for milk and a story and his blanket and for you to play with him?"

"A lot of people do it," she yelled, throwing her arms up in annoyance. "Even people at Yale."

"You know that Ashley had a good job when she got pregnant with Gray?" I asked, sliding to the edge of the bed so I could pull my jeans on. "Gray got sick a few times when he was baby and she had to take off work, so they fired her. Went from being the manager in an office to waitin' tables at a fuckin' restaurant at the mall."

"What does that have to do with me?" she asked, angrily pulling on her clothes.

"Priorities fuckin' shift," I said. My head was starting to pound. "I'm not gonna be the reason that you don't finish school."

"I will finish," she replied stubbornly.

"I know you will," I said, throwing on my t-shirt and cut. "Cause you're staying in fuckin' Connecticut and going to fuckin' Yale."

I shook my head and turned to leave, but I couldn't make myself do it. Turning around, I found her standing there with her arms wrapped around her waist, her eyes filled with tears.

"You're so much better than me," I said quietly, reaching out to cup her face in my hand. I leaned forward and kissed her gently. "It's only a couple more years, alright?"

Then I left before the look in her eyes could make me change my mind.

## Chapter 21

# LILY

I WAS LIVID. Even after refusing to meet Leo's eyes as I got into my dad's truck, and leaving the clubhouse in a spray of gravel, I still couldn't get my temper under control.

I understood where Leo was coming from and I loved him for it, I really did. He was trying to protect me, the way he'd done for as long as I could remember. But he'd forgotten one simple fact as he'd tried to make my decisions for me back in his room.

I was no longer a child.

He may be older than me, but I'd been making my own decisions for a while now. I wasn't a scared, seventeen-year-old kid who ran when things got hard. I also wasn't a pushover.

My phone rang as I parked in front of my parents' house.

"Hello?" I barked, annoyed that anyone was interrupting my internal tirade.

"Wow, you sound chipper," my sister-in-law replied, laughing. "Bad time?"

"No," I said shortly, then felt instantly like shit. "Sorry, I got into it with your brother today, and I'm still pissed."

"Oh no, what did he do?"

"It's nothing," I replied, unwilling to discuss any of it with Trix. She was Leo's sister and she was married to my brother, and I'd realized early on that it wouldn't be fair of me to complain about Leo to her. "What's up?"

"I was just wondering if you were going to the party tonight?"

"No," I replied instantly.

Trix laughed. "Don't feel like celebrating Cecilia?"

"I'd rather break my own arm," I replied dryly.

"That's imaginative," she said in surprise. "I was just calling to see if you weren't going, if you could watch the boys tonight? I'm not sure how late we'll be home, but you could just crash at our place if you wanted."

"Sure," I said as I climbed out of the truck.

As I walked inside, Trix filled me in on the details of when she needed me, and I was paying close attention, so I didn't realize how quiet the house was until I'd gotten off the phone. I retraced my steps back to the entryway and found my dad reading in his bed in the living room.

"Hey, how'd you get left here alone?" I asked, grinning when he snarled at me.

"Ceecee took your mom and Charlie to get their nails done," he replied.

"What's she driving? I had the truck."

"Rented a car," he said easily.

"Well, isn't she fancy?" I mumbled under my breath.

My dad made an annoyed sound in his throat, and I immediately regretted saying a word. I usually tried to keep my thoughts to myself when it came to Cecilia. My parents loved us all equally, and they hated when one of us said anything bad about the other. As far as they were concerned, family loyalty trumped everything. I agreed with them, to a point. I wouldn't bitch about Ceecee to anyone, but I kind of hated that I couldn't even say a word against her to my own parents. Nonetheless, I knew better, and if I hadn't still been pissed about Leo, I would've kept my mouth shut.

I made a face of apology and sat down gingerly at the foot of his bed. "Why did you drop out of Yale?"

"You thinkin' of droppin' out?" he asked, dropping his book into his lap. I almost rolled my eyes when I saw a very famous theoretical physicist on the back cover.

"No," I said, meeting his eyes. "But maybe transferring?"

"Is that a question?"

"I don't know," I mumbled.

"You wanna transfer schools, I'm not gonna talk you out of it," he said, surprising me.

"What? You practically bullied me into going to Yale."

"Nah," he argued with a wave of his hand. "Did I want you to go? Hell, yeah. Wanted you to see what was out there. Spread your wings a little. There's a lot more in this life than the Aces' clubhouse, Lilybug."

"I just don't know if I want to be anywhere else."

"I can understand that," he said with a nod. "To answer your question, I dropped out because my family needed me."

"Because of Aunt Callie?" I asked, getting more comfortable on the bed.

"Yeah, your Aunt Callie. Also, your great gram. She was gettin' older, and every time I came home to visit, I'd notice her slowin' down more and more. Scared the hell outta me." He chuckled. "Also hated that place with the fuckin' trust fund babies and chicks that cared more about their hair than what they were studyin'."

"And you ended up with a woman who won't leave the house without full makeup," I joked.

"Far more to your ma than her looks," he said with a soft smile.

"True," I said with my own smile.

"Leo got anythin' to do with this decision?" he asked, his face growing serious.

"Yes," I replied honestly. "But it's not only him. I want to be home. I miss seeing everyone and going to Charlie's basketball games and hanging out at the parties that I'm finally old enough to drink at—"

"Not quite old enough," he mumbled.

"He doesn't want me to stay," I said with a grimace. "He says that I'll end up dropping out of school."

"That your plan?"

"No. I want to finish college. I'm not sure what I want to do yet, but I want to have that degree."

"Then that's what you'll do," my dad said simply. "I've never seen you give up on anythin' you set your mind to, kiddo. That ain't your style."

"You really won't be mad if I come home?"

"Not a bit," he said immediately. "You do what's best for you, Lily. I'll support ya."

"Thanks, Daddio," I said softly, giving his foot a squeeze.

I was still sitting on the end of his bed when my mom and sisters came in the door, laughing.

"I like the black," Charlie said, looking at her nails instead of where she was walking. "They make me look fierce."

"You do look pretty fierce," Cecilia replied with a smile. She glanced up at me and my dad and her smile disappeared.

"I'm gonna go take a shower," I said, glancing back at my dad. "I told Trix I'd keep the boys tonight."

I left the room and detoured to the kitchen to grab a glass of water before I headed upstairs. For some reason, I figured that Cecilia would avoid me since I'd been giving her the cold shoulder, but of course, my sister never made things easy.

"Where were you today?" she asked as she sat down at the counter. "You could've come with us."

I don't know what made me say it. Maybe it was a mixture of leftover anger at Leo and frustration that my mom was acting the happiest I'd seen her in years. Maybe it was just that I wanted to aim a well-placed arrow at Cecilia for once instead of the other way around, but whatever it was, it had my mouth opening and the words spilling out before I could stop them.

"I was busy fucking Leo."

"Jesus Christ, Lily," my mom said in frustration as she stepped into the kitchen.

I didn't even look up. I was too busy staring at my sister's emotionless face.

"Well, I hope it was good," she said finally, turning away.

"Much better than a manicure," I said smugly as I walked out of the kitchen.

It wasn't until I hit the stairs that my stomach churned with disgust. I'd used something between me and Leo, something that was significant and special, to make a dig at my older sister. A dig that hadn't even seemed to hit the mark.

I grabbed some clothes and hopped in the shower, still castigating myself about what I'd said. It wasn't anyone's business that I'd slept with Leo, and somehow I'd made it into something it wasn't. Something that looked a lot like revenge, when in reality, it hadn't had a single thing to do with Cecilia.

I was washing my hair when her voice piped up beyond the shower curtain.

"I know you're still mad at me."

"Goddamnit, Ceecee," I yelled as shampoo got into my eyes and nose. "I locked the fucking door!"

"That lock is easy to jimmy. Don't you remember when you were little and accidentally locked yourself in when I was babysitting? I thought you were going to have a heart attack, and you just kept telling me to slide fruit snacks under the door so you wouldn't starve."

"And of course, you didn't," I snapped.

"Nope, I unlocked the door instead and got you some ice cream, if I remember correctly."

"What do you want?" I asked, wiping the last of the shampoo from my face. "Spit it out and then get out."

"Why are you still so mad, Lily? Jesus. It's been years."

"Exactly," I ground out. "We haven't seen you in years and suddenly you're back and renting cars and taking Mom to get her nails done, and I'm supposed to... what? Welcome you with open arms?"

"That's the general idea," she said dryly.

"No. Fuck you. You left me. You left and you didn't even come back when I needed you."

"When you got your sight back?" she asked curiously. "Is that when you needed me? Because I thought about it. I even asked Mom if I should."

"Right," I replied derisively.

"She told me to stay where I was. Said that you were having a hard time and she didn't want anything making you more upset. I think she was afraid that something was going to trigger you and make you lose your sight again."

"That's bullshit," I muttered.

"Swear to God, Lil. We decided that it was probably better if I just stayed away."

"It's been years since that happened."

"Yeah, and Mom and Dad have been to San Diego twice to see me."

"You shouldn't have left," I said, shaking my head even though I knew she couldn't see me.

"I had to, kid," she replied with a sigh.

"What, because you and the 'rents got in a fight? Jesus, dramatic much?"

Cecilia laughed, but there was no humor in it.

"That night, before I'd come home, I'd had sex with a guy I didn't know outside the bar I was partying at. He wasn't the first. He wasn't even the fifth. But that guy," she paused. "He was rough. Mean. And I just kept thinking, 'this was a bad idea, what the fuck am I doing?' So when I stumbled home and Mom and Dad were yelling and pretty much telling me how horrible I was—"

"You ran away," I said.

"No, I got away," she clarified. "I had to. I was spiraling, Lil. For whatever reason, I just couldn't seem to get my shit together here."

"And you got it together in San Diego."

"Yeah. It took a while. Honestly, when Mom told me not to come home when you got your sight back, I was a little relieved. I mean, I would've come. Absolutely. But I was still on shaky ground back then, and I was terrified that if I came back, I'd fall back into everything I'd left behind."

We were silent for a long time.

"Okay," I said finally.

"Okay?"

"Okay, I'll forgive you."

"Um, thanks," she said drolly.

"But can you please go so that I can get out of here? The water's getting cold."

"Oh, please," she said, but I could hear her moving. "It's not like I haven't seen you naked before."

You haven't seen these hickies on my boobs, I thought, staring down at my chest.

I heard the door open.

"Hey, Ceecee?" I called. "I'm glad you got your shit together."

"Me, too," she called back.

★ ★ ★

"I HOPE YOU don't care that Gray's here, too," Trix said as I followed her into the game room. "Cam kind of volunteered you when he was talking to my brother earlier."

"No worries," I replied, watching Gray climb all over Curtis, who was sitting on a bean bag playing a video game. "He knows I'm watching Gray?"

"Not sure," she said with a rueful smile. "I didn't mention it."

I laughed.

"Hey, Aunt Lily," Draco said, hugging me around the waist as he made his way to his own bean bag. "Mom got us pizza for dinner."

"Sweet! I brought candy, too."

"Score," Curtis said distractedly, leaning around Gray so he could see the TV screen. "Did you get the good stuff?"

"Do I ever bring anything else?"

"Nope," Draco chimed in, lifting his fist in the air and bringing it down quickly in a completely dorky move that I'd seen my brother do a million times.

"We'll be home late," Trix said. "The boys can stay up as long as you want, and Gray will probably find a cozy spot and crash when he's tired."

"They'll be fine," I said, smiling when Gray finally lifted his head and caught sight of me. "And I'll try not to burn down the house."

"Thanks," she replied. "Because I'm pretty sure we couldn't afford to replace it."

"Lily," Gray said, scrambling off Curtis' lap.

I didn't even notice when Trix left the room.

## Chapter 22

# LEO

They hadn't scrimped on Cecilia's party. After I'd dropped Gray off with my sister and got in a quick shower and a shave, I walked to my room with the sounds of loud voices and music ringing in my ears. It hadn't taken the boys long to get the party going, and I laughed as I heard a woman screeching in annoyance.

Because the party was for one of the grown kids, there wouldn't be any side-pieces hanging around, but that didn't mean that things would be any less wild than usual. There would still be girlfriends dancing on tables. Hell, sometimes it was wives. I'd seen Farrah shaking her ass on the pool table more than once. When we had a family party, things stayed pretty mellow for the most part, but when the littles were gone, the adults felt free to let loose. There weren't any little ones there tonight.

As soon as I was dressed, I headed out to the main room to grab a beer. My gramps was already at his place at the end of the bar, and Grams was standing between his knees, fixing his beard. She was always fussing with him, trying to make him look a little more presentable, but beyond the button down shirt he was wearing, it was a lost cause. The old man looked like exactly what he was, an old biker that could still throw them back with the boys but had a hard time standing for long periods of time.

"Beer," I ordered, tapping the tabletop. The prospects were serving for the night, probably because one of the old timers that I didn't have much use for had been banging our usual bartender on the side.

"Hey, baby," my mom said, coming up beside me, her face flushed. "You got a sitter for Gray?"

"He's at Trix's with the boys," I affirmed with a nod. "Havin' fun?"

"Yeah," she laughed. "I've been dancing with the girls. It's nice, you know? Ignoring everything else for a while?"

"Yep." I agreed. All of us needed a night when we could forget the last week. I was pretty sure it wasn't going to happen for me tonight, but I'd had a few hours earlier in the day when everything outside my room had disappeared.

"I swear," my mom said. "Some of the shit Hawk does isn't normal."

"Half the shit Hawk does isn't normal," I said with a chuckle.

"She was bent in half and shaking her ass. I thought Tommy was going to come unglued."

"Sounds about right."

"I'll see you later," Mom said, glancing behind her. She stole my beer off the bar top and walked away before I even realized what was happening.

"The fuck?" I said in amusement, watching her go.

"Beer!" a voice called from behind me. It was one I recognized, but hadn't heard in years.

"Ceecee Butler," I said, turning around. "How you been?"

"Good," she replied with a huge smile and a nod. Looking at her face, I knew she was telling the truth. Gone was the spoiled girl who felt like the world was out to get her, and in her place was a woman that seemed genuinely happy.

"Glad to hear that," I said with a grin.

"How about you?" she said. "I was sorry to hear about Ashley."

"Thanks." I nodded to the prospect that handed me a new beer. "Tryin' to figure out where I go from here."

"With Lily," she said nonchalantly, turning to lean her back against the bar.

"Say again?"

"You're with Lily, right?"

Immediately, my hackles rose. Five minutes of normal interaction didn't erase years of manipulation, and I wasn't quite sure what she was getting at. "Your sister's livin' in Connecticut," I replied.

"Yeah," she grinned. "My dad must've lost his shit when she agreed to go there."

"He was pretty proud."

"I don't doubt it. I was surprised when she left. I didn't think she'd ever leave Eugene."

"Why's that?" I asked, taking a sip of my beer.

"Because she loves it here. She loves the rain and the trees and hanging out with family. It just never seemed like she'd be happy so far away."

"She seems to be doin' alright," I muttered. I was over the conversation already, and regretting the fact that I'd even said hello.

"You think so?" she mused. "I think she's probably counting the days until she's home for good."

"Doubt it," I argued.

"Nah, she's not like me," Cecilia said.

"You think?" I shot back.

"I guess I deserved that," Cecilia replied ruefully. "I used to be so jealous of her."

"That's fucked."

"Oh, I know." She laughed uncomfortably. "It just seemed like everything came easy for her."

"She was blind," I said flatly.

"You loved her," she said calmly.

I opened my mouth to tell her to fuck off, but before I could say a word, she shook her head.

"I know it wasn't like that," she said, raising her hands in surrender. "You've never been a creep. But, you did care about her. I wanted that type of devotion, you know?"

"To get it, you gotta give it," I murmured, glancing sideways at her.

"Yeah," Cecilia said softly. "I'm learning that."

"Daughter, you're slacking," Farrah yelled, walking our way. "I told your dad he could have one beer, and you're over here drinking it while he's over there bitching."

"Casper's here?" I asked in surprise.

"Yeah, the pain in my ass wouldn't stay home. He's over there on one of the couches, holding court and wishing he was home in bed—not that he'd ever admit it."

Farrah grabbed a couple more drinks and then towed Cecilia across the room, leaving me mostly alone at the bar. There weren't as many people at the party as there usually were, so I could see pretty much everyone around the room. I spotted the boys at the pool tables, so I headed that way. Hopefully if I was surrounded by people, I could pretend like I was having a good time, when in reality, I was wishing I was at my apartment with my boy, watching car shows on cable.

★ ★ ★

A FEW BEERS later, I was feeling good. I'd gotten just enough of a buzz to relax into my surroundings, but not enough of one to make anything fuzzy. I'd been playing pool with the boys for hours, taking turns and watching the women make bets on their men. Hawk had already lost at least a hundred dollars because Tommy was on the far side of drunk, but I had no idea who was actually winning. As the games had gone on, the bets got smaller and smaller as the women realized that all of the guys were pretty evenly matched and there was no way to guess who would win.

Rose had started betting on me, which I appreciated, until she whispered that she was betting with my money.

"Thought you were makin' bank bartendin'," I said, throwing my arm around her shoulders.

"Please," she scoffed. "Those college boys don't tip for shit if they're not trying to impress you. Spoiled assholes. As soon as I made it clear I wouldn't be serving anything but drinks, they stopped trying to impress me."

"That's bullshit," I said, grabbing my beer off a table.

"I still make enough for rent," she said with a shrug. "If we gotta eat ramen for a while, I can hang. Plus, Lily gives me her dining card all the damn time and we look enough alike that no one ever says anything."

"Mmm, cafeteria food," I said jokingly.

"Hey, don't knock it," she said, saluting me with her glass. "I'm getting fully cooked meals that I don't have to clean up."

"Fair enough," I conceded.

"Still," she said, watching her brother play. "It's been fun, but I think we're both ready to come home."

"She's still got two years left."

"I doubt we'll be there that long," she replied. Then her attention was diverted. "Tommy, you suck!"

I was just chalking my cue to start the next game when all hell broke loose.

"Fire!" someone yelled from the front door. "Fire!"

"What the fuck?" I heard my dad bellow as he ran toward the door.

Every person in the room ran for the exits, and I had a sinking feeling in my gut as I realized that if this was some sort of attack, we'd be fucked. I pushed through the crowd trying to make my way outside, but was getting nowhere until Cam shoved his way past me. Following in his considerable wake, I made it outside before almost everyone else.

And then I looked around in confusion. I couldn't see a fire. The building was fine. The garage bays were open and untouched. The grass and trees were so fucking saturated that we couldn't get a fire going there if we tried.

"The house," Cam said, running toward the edge of the building where my dad had broken out into a sprint. "Our fuckin' house!"

Everything became white noise as I ran as hard as I could toward the property where Cam and Trix's house sat. It wasn't actually on Aces' property, the old president who'd lived there before made sure of that, but the properties butted up against each other. The two buildings were in walking distance from each other, but I couldn't believe how long it took me to get across the field that separated them.

The house was lit up like a fucking Roman candle.

And my son was inside.

"Call the fuckin' fire department," Grease screamed as he ran beside me. I didn't know who he was talking to, but I didn't bother to reply. There were people coming up behind us. I could hear them, but I didn't give a shit who it was. One of them could call. I wasn't stopping.

The thing people don't really mention about a house fire is that they're loud. Really fucking loud. You hear all about the smoke and the flames and the heat, but no one ever really tells you how loud that shit is. It's practically deafening.

"Not again," Cam said, as I caught up with his broad frame. "Fuck, not again." He ran for the front door.

I followed him, my lungs screaming as I got closer and closer to the closed front door, but before I could make it there, I was being tackled from behind.

## CHAPTER 23

# LILY

I COULDN'T SEE.

I couldn't see and I was in the middle of a room.

What room was I in?

I scooted forward, ignoring the throb in my cheek as I swept my hands back and forth in front of me. After what felt like forever, my hand brushed up against something hard. I wrapped my hand around it.

It was a chair. A kitchen chair. One that Trix had been so happy to refinish after she'd found the set at a garage sale the year before.

I was in the kitchen.

I continued reaching forward and ran into a wall. No, it wasn't a wall. It was a counter. I started to get to my feet, but dropped back down when my lungs started burning. No. No standing.

Lifting my arms above my head, I felt for the edge. I was at the corner.

The corner of the counter in the kitchen.

I knew where I was. Closing my eyes against the smoke, I clenched my hands together in front of me and urged my breathing to slow. It was getting hard to find any air, and I had to be careful with what little I had.

Pushing myself to my hands and knees, I moved away from the counter, counting. I knew my way around this house. I knew that it took thirteen steps from the counter to the hallway. Another seven steps forward and one step to the left and I'd be in the office. From the door of the office to the panic room was another five steps along the wall.

My steps were off. I realized that as soon as I'd reached thirteen and couldn't feel the corner of the wall. Dropping my head against the floor in defeat I re-traced where I'd been in my memory. I needed to move. I needed to get going. The boys knew not to come out until someone came to get them. They were just sitting there. Waiting for me while the house burned down around us. I had to *move*.

My steps were shorter, I finally realized. Shuffling along the floor wasn't the same as walking and I just hadn't gone far enough. God, I was tired. No, no I wasn't. I was *fine*. I had to keep moving.

I pushed myself back up and kept going. A few more shuffles and I reached for where the wall should be. Still nothing. A few more. There. There it was.

I coughed and gagged as I dragged myself down the hallway, my movements feeling sluggish and slow. Seven steps. Add a few more. There was the doorframe. It was the first door on the left. I'd found it.

I reached up and felt for the door handle. It was cool.

I shuddered in relief. Oh, thank God.

Pushing it open, I hurried inside as fast as I could and slammed the door behind me.

The room was less smoky than the hallway had been, but something must have been wrong with the power, because the light switch didn't turn on any lights. It was pitch black in the room, and even though the air was a little bit less smoky, I still couldn't see anything.

Pulling myself to my feet using a bookshelf by the door, I laid my hand on the wall and took five steps forward. Bingo.

My hands fumbled as I ripped the picture off the wall hiding the keypad that would open the panic room.

Oh shit. Oh, fuck. No.

I couldn't remember the code.

*I couldn't remember the goddamn code.*

Tears ran down my face from frustration and panic as I searched my memory. I'd known it. It hadn't changed since Trix and Cam had moved in. It was a date. A date or a number or a song that I should have remembered.

Think.

Think.

I *knew* it. I had to.

I just had to block everything out. This was just like that time when I'd gotten lost outside the clubhouse. I hadn't been able to remember what direction I'd walked off in, and I'd had to sit down and retrace my steps in my mind. This was the same.

I sat down on the floor and made myself ignore the way that more smoke seemed to be seeping under the doorframe.

Cam had told me the code. He'd brought me into the room and he'd taken the photo down. Then he'd put my hand on the keypad. What had he said?

*"Up, down, left, left, right, down, up, little sister. Feel that? Now say it back to me."*

Scrambling to my feet, I lifted my hand to chest level and felt for the keypad.

"Up, down, left, left, right, down, up," I sang to myself the way I'd done the first time.

A green light flickered and the door came open with a click, making me sob.

"Aunt Lily?" Draco called, his words broken with coughing.

"I'm here," I said, my voice barely audible. "I'm here, guys."

"What's happening?" Curtis asked, his little hands finding mine in the dark.

"The house is on fire," I said quickly. "Come here."

I felt four little hands grasping at my arms and almost fell to my knees in relief.

"Where's Gray?" I asked, gripping their hands.

"He was right here," Curtis said. "Gray?"

"Gray?"

A large boom shook the house and my breath stalled in my throat.

"Go to the window," I barked, pushing them out of the panic room. "Don't go to the door, just go to the window behind your dad's desk. Go. Push out the screen and jump out."

"But where's Gray?" Draco said tearfully. "Gray?"

"I'll get Gray," I said, still shoving at them. "Go now."

"We can't just leave you," Curtis snapped. "Gray? Come here, buddy!"

"Curtis," I yelled, shoving him hard. "I said to fucking go!"

I heard the sound of pain he made, but I ignored it as I dropped to my knees.

"I can't see," Draco said. "Aunt Lily, I can't see the window."

"That's because the curtains are closed," I yelled, trying to sound reassuring and failing over the sounds of crashing coming from other parts of the house. "Four steps forward, guys, okay? Then you'll feel the desk. Go around it and you'll find the window."

"Aunt Lily," Curtis cried, his voice warbling.

"I'm right behind you. I swear. Go."

It took a few seconds, but as soon as I saw moonlight coming in the window, I knew they'd found it. A rush of air whooshed in as they slid it open, but I was no longer paying attention. I was crawling inside the panic room on my hands and knees, searching for a tiny boy that was probably curled up somewhere, scared out of his mind.

I heard the screen screeching as they shoved it out the window just as I found Gray sitting under the small table in the corner of the room.

"Gray, come here, baby," I said, sliding my hands up his legs and torso until I could feel his little armpits. I pulled him out from under the table and held him tight to my chest as I got to my feet, staggering under the slight weight of him.

"Lily's got you," I said, keeping my face next to his as I bent at the waist. Smoke had filled the room in the short time since I'd closed the door, and I kept my eyes shut tight as I pressed Gray's face against my neck. "Almost there," I rasped, opening my eyes just long enough to watch Draco's shape disappear out the window.

"I've got you."

The house shifted and I tripped, almost falling to my knees as I took those short steps to the desk. Every inch forward seemed like it took an eternity.

"Lily," I heard just in front of me as I finally felt a very faint brushing of cool air against my face. "Come on, baby girl."

Two more steps and my stomach hit the window ledge.

"Gray," I rasped, pushing him toward the person I couldn't see.

I opened my eyes as my cousin Will took Gray from my arms. "I've got him. I've got him," he reassured me as he pulled Gray away. The baby's little hands had been holding my t-shirt so tight that Will had to forcefully yank him back.

"Lily," he called, scratching at my arms as he tried to keep his hold on me.

As soon as he'd handed Gray off to the person behind him, he reached inside the window and dragged my tired body out.

I don't remember the next few minutes.

I know that the fire department got there. They quickly took over and placed masks on each of our faces, and within a few minutes, had us loaded into ambulances.

I saw my mom running toward me.

I saw my brother falling to his knees between the boys, who were sitting in the grass, holding hands.

I saw Leo, holding Gray, but staring at me, terrified.

Then, from above me, a familiar face smiled reassuringly as they got me onto a stretcher.

"Hey, stranger," he said. "How you doing?"

"Brent," I rasped, reaching for his arm. "The baby?"

"You're pregnant?" he asked, glancing at his partner.

I shook my head and waved my hand toward Gray. "The baby."

"Oh," he said, nodding his understanding. "He's going to be just fine."

"Him before me," I ordered, shaking my head in protest as they started to load me into the back of the ambulance. "No. Him before me."

I sat up and started tearing at my mask, frustrated that he obviously couldn't understand me. I met Leo's eyes across the grass, pulling at the shit they'd used to strap me down.

"Dandelion, don't," Leo shouted, taking a few steps forward.

I grunted when Brent's long fingers gripped my wrist and pulled it gently away from my restraints. He slid the oxygen mask back on my face before speaking.

"He's okay," Brent said sternly as my mom climbed into the ambulance with us. "You have to go first, okay? He's getting checked out, but you're *my* responsibility and we have to go now."

"You're okay, baby," my mom said, her hand coming to rest comfortingly on my shoulder as the ambulance doors closed. "Everyone's okay."

I closed my eyes and passed out.

## Chapter 24

# LEO

IN A DAZE, I rode with my boy to the hospital to get checked out.

It took them a few hours, but the doctors finally decided that beyond a little smoke inhalation, he was perfectly fine. The paramedics hadn't seemed particularly concerned when they'd driven us to the hospital, which had calmed me a bit, but when they'd advised me to have him checked, I'd jumped on it. He was so little that I had a hard time believing that he was fine.

When I'd seen that smoke coming out of the house, and then the windows upstairs shattering from the heat, I'd nearly vomited. Tommy had been the one to tackle me into the grass, and if he hadn't, I don't know what I would have done. It had taken him and Rocky to hold me down. Will and Grease had held Cam.

I gritted my teeth at the memory as I wrapped Gray's sleeping form in a blanket and readjusted him on my shoulder. I could have killed them for what they'd done, and if there hadn't been two of them, I probably would have.

Watching a house burn when you knew your world was inside was something I wouldn't wish on my worst enemy. There wasn't a word that adequately described the terror I'd felt. It was all-consuming, suffocating, so intense that I'd thought at any moment, it was going to literally kill me.

When someone had yelled across the yard that Lily was inside, my entire body had gone limp with defeat. A part of me had felt relieved for just a sliver of a second. I knew without a shadow of a doubt, that if Lily could get him out, she would. She'd never stop trying to get those boys out of danger. I knew that. But staring at the house, I hadn't understood how they could still be alive.

I wouldn't have survived it if they were gone.

Will and Grease climbed off of Cam as Trix reached him. She could hold him back better than any two men, without question.

Then, like a fucking miracle, we'd seen the screen on a window downstairs bowing before it popped out of a window. Curtis fell out first, landing on his ass. Seconds later, Draco came tumbling out behind him.

The guys climbed off me as I stared. I was paralyzed as I watched Will and Cam running toward the window. They lifted the boys off the ground and listened to them for just a second before sending them running from the house.

Sirens wailed behind us as I scrambled to my feet. Will and Grease were still staring at the window.

And then, there they were. From my vantage point, all I could see were Lily's arms, but I could see Gray's entire body. He looked fine. He looked scared, but fine. Will pulled Gray from Lily and I'd wanted to scream. Get them both, goddamnit, what are you doing? But nothing came out.

I made it to Grease and my baby boy just as Will pulled Lily out the window. She was limp.

I swallowed down the lump in my throat as I walked down the halls of the hospital. My mom texted me Lily's room number an hour ago, and as soon as they'd given the all clear, I'd headed in that direction. I needed to see her. To feel her. To kiss her face and make sure she was okay.

"And then, the door popped open," Curtis said from the foot of Lily's bed as I reached the open door to her room. "And we were kind of worried that it was the Russian dudes."

"But it wasn't," Draco interrupted. "It was Aunt Lily, and she was all, 'Go out the window'."

"Well, first she asked where Gray was."

"Yeah, and then when we couldn't find him, she said to go out the window, but it was so dark that I couldn't see anything."

"Yeah, and I didn't want to leave her behind, so she pushed me *really* hard."

"And she was all, take this many steps forward and then use the desk to guide you," Draco said. "Did you know she could do that? She found us *in the dark*."

"So we counted our steps to the desk and she went to go get Gray."

"And then we jumped out the window."

"We didn't want to leave them," Curtis said, looking guiltily at his dad. "She made us."

"You did the right thing," Cam said gruffly, nodding his approval. "We knew just where to get your aunt and cousin because you guys came out that window. If she hadn't made it out, we knew just where to look."

"She was really brave," Draco said, his chin wobbling.

"You were pretty brave, too," I said, walking fully into the room. "You guys stayed with Gray in the safe room?"

"Yeah," Curtis said, giving his brother time to bring his emotions under control. "We played games and stuff."

"Good job," I said, kissing his head and then Draco's. "Thank you."

I smiled, and finally lifted my eyes to Lily's.

Her lips were trembling as she tried to smile, and her cheek was swollen and purple.

"Hey, Dandelion," I said, moving to the head of her bed. "How you doin', pretty girl?"

"Like I just inhaled a fuck-ton of smoke," she replied, her voice broken and raspy.

"You're not supposed to be talking," Cecilia reminded her from her place near the window. "You're supposed to let your throat heal."

"I love you," Lily said, ignoring her sister. "Is he okay?"

Her eyes moved to Gray, and my eyes watered as I laid his sleeping form in between her side and her arm.

"He's okay," I said, leaning down to press my lips against hers. "Thank you."

I kissed her again. "Oh, God, *thank you*."

"Time to go boys," Cam said from behind me, lifting his sons off the bed.

"Where are we gonna sleep?"

"Gramps' and Nana's," Trix said, helping to usher them out of the room. "You can sleep in Uncle Leo's old room."

"But there's only one bed," Curtis complained.

"Oh, good. You guys can cuddle," Cecilia said as she shut the door behind them.

"God, Lily," I whispered as the room around us grew quiet. "I thought you were gone. I thought both of you were gone."

I buried my face in her neck, hardly able to smell her beyond the scent of smoke.

"I wouldn't let that happen," she rasped, her IV covered hand rising up to smooth my hair back. "I'd never leave you like that."

"If anyone else had been watching the boys," I ground out, shuddering.

We both knew the answer to that. If anyone else had been watching the boys, there was no way they could have found them in the smoke. After Lily had been taken away in the ambulance, I'd heard a couple of the firefighters talking about it. They had no idea how she'd managed to make her way from the kitchen to the office. Most people would have been too disoriented in the smoke to get themselves out the front door. It would have been impossible for them to find the boys inside a locked room.

"You're sure he's okay?" she asked again, shifting a little so that Gray was pressed more firmly against her.

"He got an all-clear from the doctors," I said, kissing her forehead. "He's just tired and freaked out."

She nodded and then laid her head back on the pillow, her face filled with exhaustion. "Don't leave, okay?"

"I'm not goin' anywhere." Sitting down at Gray's feet, I rested my hand on her hip as she rolled to the side and curled around us, her knees resting against my back.

I stayed that way for a long time after she'd fallen asleep.

★ ★ ★

"WHAT'S THE WORD?" my dad asked after slamming his gavel angrily on the table.

It was a few days after the fire and we were in church, trying to figure out what the fuck was going on. Once Lily had been able to describe what had gone down in the house, every man with connections had been on the phone and taking meetings. We'd been searching non-stop for the last two days and I was losing patience with how little we knew. It just took one connection to get to the truth, but we had to sift through hundreds to find that one.

"Sokolov," Gramps said, pushing his way into the room with a small scrap of paper in his hand.

"You got news?" Casper asked, shifting uncomfortably in his chair. I didn't know how the guy was doing it, but he'd been at the club every day since the fire, pouring over shit we knew and shit we didn't, trying to figure out what had happened. He must have been swallowing massive amounts of painkillers.

"Two boys, Sokolov, flew into Eugene from Russia, one week ago.

Talked to a friend at a bar near the airport four days ago."

"The fuck?" Will asked in confusion. "We didn't even kill that fat fuck! What the hell do they want?"

"Don't know, but they were askin' about the club," Gramps replied. "Contact at the bar said they were askin' him questions and didn't give him the option of keepin' his mouth shut." He paused and cleared his throat. "Our guy says he gave them Cam's name, because he was sure that was one place they couldn't get to."

"Jesus Christ," Tommy muttered, tossing the pack of cigarettes in his hand across the room.

"He tried to warn us," Gramps said quietly. "But the number he had was one of Casper's burners. I'm thinkin' probably the one that was lost in the accident."

"The perfect goddamn storm," Grease muttered, shaking his head. "You got a place we can find these fucks?"

Cam and I were on our feet before Gramps could finish rattling off the address of the cheap motel.

"Take Will," my dad said, not bothering to argue with us. "He'll make sure you don't act like fuck-nuts."

It didn't take long to get to the motel, which was a pretty standard throwback from the sixties. All the doorways faced one direction and it was only two stories.

From the minute we stepped off our bikes, each one of us was on high alert. No way that the Sokolov boys hadn't heard us coming, but there was no way to know if they would run, or try and make a stand OK-Corral style. It could go either way if they were feeling froggy, and since they'd already burned down my sister's house and punched my woman in the face, I was betting they were feeling pretty damn froggy.

"Boris and Hank," Will called, his lips twitching at the nickname we'd come up with, since none of us knew how the fuck to say the guy's name. "You in there, boys?"

Oddly, the door opened wide, and there stood a big guy with a scowl on his face.

"What you want?" he asked in heavily accented English.

Cam grinned and punched the big guy, knocking him flat on his ass. We stepped around him and into the room before the littler guy could pull his weapon.

"I'd keep your hands visible," Will said, pointing his gun at the little one. "I don't take chances and my woman would be pissed if I got shot."

"Who are you?" little guy demanded as he stood from the bed.

"Pretty sure you're the one who's been lookin' for us," Cam grunted. "Who the fuck are you?"

Little guy's expression filled with understanding before rage took over his features.

"You killed my father," he spat, his words almost impossible to understand. "Like a dog in his bed."

"I've never killed a dog in its bed," I said under my breath.

"Who the fuck would do that?" Cam replied.

"My father was Karl Sokolov," the guy said proudly, lifting his chin.

"Not sure you should go around boastin' that shit," Will said as he turned his head toward the man waking up from his stupor. "Just stay down, idiot," he warned.

"You burned down my motherfuckin' house," Cam said, done with the conversation. "With my fucking sister and kids inside it."

"You poison my father, yes? Like a woman," the guy barked.

"Nobody fuckin' poisoned your dad," I replied. "I mean, I woulda killed his ass, but I fuckin' didn't. He was dead when I got there."

"You lie," the little guy said, but his face didn't look so sure anymore. "We have autopsy done in Russia. Say, poison."

"Why the fuck would I lie?" I asked.

Just as the final word left my mouth, I saw the big one reach for something on the floor next to him, and less than a second later, I was raising my arm and pulling the trigger. The hand holding the gun he'd been trying to pull fell to his side and he slumped backward, the hole in his forehead not even bleeding.

"Son of a—" Two more gunshots split the room and I looked over to see the small guy hit the wall with a thud and slide all the way to the floor.

"Idiot went for his piece the minute you shot his brother," Will said in annoyance.

"We're gonna need a cleaner," Cam mumbled, shoving his gun back in the holster he wore in the back of his jeans. " 'Cause I'm not doin' it."

"Me, either," I mumbled, stepping over the dead big guy as I left the room. "You think anyone heard anything?"

"Nah," Will said, putting his phone to his ear. "Even if they did, no one would say anything."

As soon as Will had the clean up settled, we got back on our bikes and took off. On the way home, each of us wiped down our weapons and threw them in separate parts of the river. Getting a new weapon was nothing, but trying to convince the police that ballistics from your gun didn't match the hole in a dead man was a bit harder to manage.

Something the Russian fuck had said nagged at me as I pulled into the forecourt and turned off my bike. What had he said? That they'd had an autopsy done on Sokolov and he'd died by poison. Had the guy had enemies besides us? There was something that I wasn't piecing together, and it was driving me fucking nuts.

Then, before I'd even stepped into the building, I figured it out.

I fucking knew, and I was livid.

"Why the fuck didn't you tell me?" I growled as he answered the phone. "Motherfuckers burned down Trix's house and almost killed Lily and the boys because I had no goddamn idea what you'd done."

"I don't know what you're talking about," my Uncle Nix said easily. "But I'm at work, so I'm going to have to call you back."

"I don't care how old you are," I said. "I'm gonna beat the shit outta you when I see you."

"I love you, too," he said. "Give all the boys a kiss from me and tell them I'll be down this weekend."

"You fucking douche," I hissed as he hung up on me.

"That your uncle?" Gramps asked as he stood in the doorway.

"You fucking know?" I asked, stalking toward him.

"I pieced it together once you'd left and gave him a call. He didn't deny it."

"Son of a bitch," I grumbled. "Why the hell would he do that?"

"Because he's your uncle," he said simply, turning to go back into the club. "He'd rather the mess was on his own hands."

I followed him inside, cursing under my breath. It had been bad enough that the man had been dead from natural causes before I'd gotten there. Knowing that my uncle had somehow poisoned his ass made that shit a million times more humiliating. I couldn't even describe how livid I was that he'd created an enemy we hadn't known about and they'd almost killed my family.

I pulled my cut off as I walked into my room, then paused when I found Lily sitting at the end of my bed.

"What're you doing here?" I asked, reaching out to run my fingers through her hair. "You should be in bed."

"I'm done with that," she said simply, getting to her feet. "I'm glad you're back."

"Me, too," I murmured, leaning forward to kiss her gently. "You wanna take a nap with me?"

"Can't," she said with a shrug, her face stiff. "I have to catch a plane."

"What?" I asked, unable to stop from blurting out the word.

"Now?"

"Yeah." She took a deep breath. "I need to get back before all of my professors fail me. I can only use family emergencies so many times before they start to get suspicious."

"That's bullshit," I said, shaking my head. "You're barely better."

"I'm good enough to fly," she said gently. This time it was her leaning forward to kiss me. "I don't want to do the whole goodbye thing, okay?"

"Have your doctors cleared you?" I asked, unable to comprehend that she was leaving, just like that.

"Yes," she replied. "I'm not doing the long goodbye," she repeated. "I'll see you soon, okay? I love you. I'll call you when I get home."

She left me standing there with my heart thundering and my stomach rolling like I was going to heave all over the floor.

We'd spent the last few days together. I'd held her while she slept and I'd cooked her and Gray dinner while they laid in bed watching cartoons. She hadn't said anything about flying back to Connecticut. She hadn't said anything about going back to Yale at all.

I strode out of my room and across the common area as fast as I could without running. I wasn't sure what I was going to do, but I had to do something. She couldn't just take off. That wasn't how it worked.

Her dad's truck was just pulling out of the gate as I hit the forecourt, and I stopped moving when I realized that she was actually gone.

That's when I began to debate shit in my head. I was acting on emotion. That wasn't how I was supposed to do things. I'd *told* her to go back to Yale. I'd told her that was what I wanted for her. Just because we'd lived through something big didn't change that. I was being a pussy because I wasn't ready for her to leave, but I knew that's what was best for her.

She deserved to go to that school. She deserved to have those doors opened for her. She deserved the world. And just because I'd forgotten for a moment that she belonged somewhere else didn't mean that I had the right to drag her back home.

I spun toward the garage and found Cam staring at me.

"Did Lily leave?" he asked, wiping his hands on a rag.

"Yeah." The word came out choked and I cleared my throat to disguise it.

"She'll be back." He turned and walked back into the garage.

# CHAPTER 25

# LILY

IT HAD BEEN three weeks of talking with professors, and packing, and long conversations with the admissions people in Oregon, but I was finally home.

Well, sort of.

I was actually standing in the middle of Leo's kitchen with my bare ass hanging out of the back of my apron as I waited for him to get home. I'd been standing there for almost an hour, and even though I'd figured out my sultry pose and couldn't wait to see his face when he saw me, my legs were starting to get tired from standing in one position so long and I kind of had to pee.

I cocked my head toward the door as I finally heard his key in the lock, then turned toward the stove so that the first thing he'd see when he came in the door was my bare backside only covered with some apron strings.

"I'm tellin' ya, that F250 is fuckin' toast—"

I spun around with my eyes almost popping out of my head at the same time Leo saw me and froze, except for the arm that he used to shove whoever was behind him away from the door.

"Leave," he ordered, taking a step forward and slamming the door shut behind him.

"Honey, I'm home," I said with an embarrassed snicker. "That was not how I planned for that to go."

"What're you doin' here?" he asked, striding toward me.

"I'm back for good," I replied, a smug smile on my mouth. "I transferred to the University of Oregon and I start next term."

"No, you didn't," he argued as he reached me.

"Yep." I stood quietly as his hands slid around my hips and came to rest on my ass. "And there's not a fucking thing you can do about it."

"We're discussing this," he said seriously, his hands starting to wander. "Once I can focus."

Then he threw me over his shoulder and strode toward the bedroom as I laughed.

# Acknowledgements

Readers and bloggers: Thank you for always being so excited to read my stories. Without you guys, my life would look entirely different. I'm so thankful for your support.

Mom and Dad: Thank you for all of your help… especially that day when Dad took the girls ALL DAY so that I could finish this story.

Girlies: I love you. I know you get frustrated and annoyed… and I also know you proudly tell everyone at school what your mom does for a living. You can't fool me. I hope you find a career that you love as much as I love this one.

Sister: Thanks for listening to my venting and cheering me on, like always.

Missy and Joey: My oldest and dearest friends. Thanks for being so proud of me and making sure I know it. It means more than you know. Here's to 25 more years of friendship, I'm pretty sure we'll be making dirty jokes in our retirement home.

Donna: Thank you. Again. Because I'm always going to thank you. Every. Time.

Lola: I gave you a very vague idea of what I wanted on this cover and you came back to me with perfection. I wasn't surprised.

Nikki: You're the best sounding board I've ever had, and I don't just mean as an editor. You push me and smack sense into me and make me better in all ways. I love you and you're stuck with me.

Toni: Peas and Carrots. I'm so proud of you, dude.

Heidi: I never would have finished this book without you cheering me on. Again.

Amber and Melissa: Best betas ever. Thanks for reading in a hurry… again.

Marisa: Thanks for having my back, like always.

Clint: Why on earth did it take us twenty years to figure this out? I love you.

www.ingramcontent.com/pod-product-compliance
Ingram Content Group UK Ltd.
Pitfield, Milton Keynes, MK11 3LW, UK
UKHW031430161224
3699UKWH00056B/2180